The Moonstone Major

Moonstone Landing Series
Book 3

by
Meara Platt

ARE YOU SIGNED UP FOR DRAGONBLADE'S BLOG?

You'll get the latest news and information on exclusive giveaways, exclusive excerpts, coming releases, sales, free books, cover reveals and more.

Check out our complete list of authors, too!

No spam, no junk. That's a promise!

Sign Up Here

www.dragonbladepublishing.com

Dearest Reader;

Thank you for your support of a small press. At Dragonblade Publishing, we strive to bring you the highest quality Historical Romance from some of the best authors in the business. Without your support, there is no 'us', so we sincerely hope you adore these stories and find some new favorite authors along the way.

Happy Reading!

CEO, Dragonblade Publishing

Additional Dragonblade books by
Author Meara Platt

The Moonstone Landing Series
Moonstone Landing (novella)
Moonstone Angel (novella)
The Moonstone Duke
The Moonstone Marquess
The Moonstone Major

The Book of Love Series
The Look of Love
The Touch of Love
The Taste of Love
The Song of Love
The Scent of Love
The Kiss of Love
The Chance of Love
The Gift of Love
The Heart of Love
The Hope of Love (novella)
The Promise of Love
The Wonder of Love
The Journey of Love
The Dream of Love (novella)
The Treasure of Love
The Dance of Love
The Miracle of Love
The Remembrance of Love (novella)

Dark Gardens Series
Garden of Shadows
Garden of Light
Garden of Dragons

Garden of Destiny
Garden of Angels

The Farthingale Series
If You Wished For Me (A Novella)

The Lyon's Den Series
Kiss of the Lyon
The Lyon's Surprise
Lyon in the Rough

Pirates of Britannia Series
Pearls of Fire

De Wolfe Pack: The Series
Nobody's Angel
Kiss an Angel
Bhrodi's Angel

Also from Meara Platt
Aislin
All I Want for Christmas

Chapter One

Moonstone Landing
Cornwall, England
July 1821

"LOOK OUT!" A deep male voice shouted as Lady Chloe Killigrew stood frozen in Moonstone Landing's busy high street, a yellow phaeton drawn by a pair of matched grays careening recklessly toward her. She had just emerged from Mrs. Halsey's tearoom, her arms laden with packages, and the last thing she expected to do on this beautiful summer's day was die.

Several people screamed.

Perhaps she was one of them, for facing imminent death had stolen the wits from her and put her in a fright. To her horror, she could not move her legs, no matter how wildly her instincts urged her to run.

She closed her eyes and was about to accept her fate when someone knocked her out of the path of those horses. The carriage careened harmlessly past her in a noisy clatter toward the harbor. A hot summer wind brushed against her cheeks, and she felt a jolt of pain as she landed awkwardly, partly atop her savior and partly hitting the muddy ground.

She sucked in a deep breath of relief, laughing as the scent of this morning's rain and the less pleasant scent of lathered horseflesh permeated the air.

"Chloe, thank goodness," her rescuer said in a gruff, resonant whisper, his strong, magnificent arms closing around her as their bodies sank into the mud. She was too relieved to care her gown was ruined.

Was she addled?

Could it be?

Fionn Brennan.

There was no mistaking the owner of that gloriously hard body or the muscles rippling beneath her as he attempted to shift them to a less awkward position. "Are you all right?"

How could she be anything but perfect while crushed in his embrace?

"I…I…think so, Major Brennan." Never mind that she was partially sprawled atop him in scandalous fashion and struggling to regain her breath. While he had taken the brunt of their fall, they had both hit the ground quite hard.

She tried to slide off him, half tumbling and half rolling onto the oozing earth beneath her body as a dozen spectators hurried forward, some gawking and others offering assistance.

"Stand back, please," Fionn ordered them, slowly sitting up. "Give Lady Chloe some room to breathe."

He then put a hand lightly on her shoulder and ordered her not to get up just yet. "I heard you cry out in pain. Let me check you for broken bones. I'll be as gentle as possible, but I must…I must run my hands over your…ah, over you."

"Yes, I understand."

Was this really happening?

This gorgeous man was about to touch her everywhere?

Her gown had ridden up her legs.

He calmly and ever so subtly tugged it down, grazing her leg with his fingers as he did so, and shooting tingles through her with the accidental touch.

Those hands.

She sank back on the muddy ground and moaned.

"Blast, did I hurt you just now?" His gaze was one of concern.

"You? No. You saved me." Lying flat on her back as she was, Chloe could feel the ground rumble against her ears and recognized that vibration as the sound of pounding hooves now fading into the distance. Those frightened carriage horses must not have been calmed and remained on a mad gallop toward the harbor.

She hoped the fool of a driver would get a good soaking when the carriage tipped and spilled him into the water.

He certainly deserved it.

"Those beasts missed trampling you by a hairsbreadth, Lady Chloe," someone in the crowd called out.

She could not make out who had spoken, for everyone was now chattering at her and Major Brennan, tossing them a thousand questions as he continued to gently poke and prod her.

Right, those broken bones.

It was almost worth suffering a mild break to gain his attention.

"Give the lady room," he said, once again motioning the onlookers to back away. It was missed by no one that he still had his hands on her.

Oh, that deep, resonant voice shot tingles through her.

His eyes were a gorgeous silvery gray, and they overlooked little in their sharp assessment. His hat must have fallen off, for the dark waves of his hair blew lightly in the breeze. One curl fell over the brow of his handsome face.

She wanted to reach up and brush it back.

How could she when half the town was gathered around them and still gawking?

"We've drawn quite an audience," he murmured, casting her a reassuring smile.

She tingled again.

A numbing warmth flowed through her like a gentle tide.

Perhaps she was just dazed and bones were indeed broken, but she did not think so. Fionn Brennan, with his silver eyes and brooding soul, always had this effect on her.

He finished running his hands up her spine and ruled her fit to sit up.

His lips lightly brushed against her cheek as he helped her. "Feeling better now?"

"I will be in a moment. I am quite a bit shaken. It was a narrow escape."

"Of course. You might have been killed. I had better carry you off the roadway." He did not give her the chance to protest.

Not that she ever would.

The crowd cheered as he swept her in his arms and rose with a breathtaking air of command.

It was all she could do not to cheer aloud as well.

Every lady in town knew exactly what she was thinking, for they were all of one mind when it came to the major.

He was exceedingly handsome, and they all wanted him.

Of course, she was a lady and could only desire him in her dreams. "And what of you, Major Brennan?" she asked, holding on to his broad shoulders. "Did I not hurt you as I fell?"

He had damaged his leg some time ago, perhaps during the war or shortly before it, and still walked with a slight limp. She wasn't merely asking the question to be polite. The weakened bones of his leg might easily have snapped and left him in agonizing pain.

He gave a soft, rumbling laugh. "No, I am built rather sturdily."

Well, that was an understatement. He had the body of a Greek god.

He cast her a soft smile that had her tingling again. "Lady Chloe, do you not understand the nature of men? Even if your weight had crushed me and I now ached like blazes, I would never admit it. Especially not to you."

"That makes absolutely no sense." She laughed, then winced as pain shot through her ribs. "Ow."

He frowned and quickly carried her into Mrs. Halsey's tea

shop. "What did that pain feel like? Sharp? Or a general ache?"

"General," she replied, certain she had not broken a rib.

He strode to a quiet corner of the shop, mumbled an apology to Mrs. Halsey for tracking mud into her pristine tearoom, and then eased Chloe onto one of the ornate wrought-iron chairs. "Tell me if it hurts when I press down."

He splayed his hands along her sides to explore lightly.

She stared into his magnificent eyes, feeling nothing but heaven in the gentleness of his touch. They were seated beside one of the shop's large windows, and sunlight streamed through it to surround Major Brennan in a halo of light. Not that any female in Moonstone Landing needed a reminder he resembled Apollo, the Greek god of the sun. "Oh, yes. Right there. I'm sure it is nothing but an insignificant bruise that will disappear in a day. Ow!"

He turned to the crowd that had followed him in. "Has anyone gone for the doctor?"

One of the locals stepped forward, a young man Chloe recognized from the local bank. "He's out at the Harbison farm, Major Brennan. I doubt he'll be back for another hour or two."

"Blast," Fionn muttered. "I see. Thank you, Mr. Garfield."

He now turned to Chloe. "Do you feel up to leaving for home?"

She cast him a wry smile. "My ribs are bruised and I think my hip might be, too. I feel my ankle swelling. But yes, I can make it home on my own."

"On your own? Don't be daft. I'll escort you. Your ankle is now swelling. That was my fault. I think I hit it with my knee as I was trying to avoid falling atop you."

"It is nothing," she assured him, wiping a little mud off her gown and realizing his uniform had to be soaked through and stained as well. "Nor are you to blame for our damaged clothes. I'll have yours repaired and cleaned, since all of this is my fault."

The major shook his head. "Nonsense. If anyone is to pay, it is the owner of the phaeton." His eyes glittered and he smiled again. "I wonder if he's ended up in the harbor by now. A good dunking would serve him right."

Chloe laughed and then winced again.

"You are more seriously hurt than you have let on," he muttered, giving her cheek a light caress.

Too bad he never meant the gesture to be romantic.

Other men found her pretty and exceedingly charming. Why couldn't he?

She suddenly recalled her reason for coming into town. "Oh, my packages!"

She pointed to the center of the high street, where they now lay strewn about and squashed beyond repair. The boxes of cakes had gone flying the moment Major Brennan grabbed her to knock her out of the way.

She supposed it was better to have them, and not herself, crushed beneath the phaeton wheels. That could have been her in the street, lying there lifeless and with her bones ground to dust.

It was too awful to contemplate.

He followed her gaze to the center of the street. "Those are easily replaced. You are not."

So could her gown be replaced, she decided as mud continued to ooze through the fabric into her undergarments.

"Don't fret, Lady Chloe," said the town constable, Malcolm Angel, striding through the crowd to reach their side. "We'll clean up that mess, but your well-being is more important." He cast a glance at the major.

"I'll stay with Lady Chloe," the major assured him. "Do whatever you must. There isn't much we can tell you other than the phaeton was careening toward her."

"Lord save us from those London nobs and their fancy carriages," Constable Angel muttered. He motioned to several bystanders to follow him back onto the street and help him gather up the damaged packages to hold as evidence.

"Let me look at your ankle in the meanwhile," Major Brennan said, kneeling beside her and carefully removing her walking boot.

Heavens be praised.

More touching?

Why did she not think of almost getting killed by a runaway team of horses before? She had dreamed of this moment... Well, not quite like this. Trampling and death were not what she had envisioned.

But why quibble about how or why his big, rough hands were all over her?

Her heart thumped like a war drum as he ran them from thigh to ankle, his touch slow and methodical. Several *eeps* escaped her lips, and it had nothing to do with pain.

He cast her a melting smile. "The good news is nothing seems to be broken."

"Just sprained?"

He nodded. "I think so. Can you stand? Do it carefully. There may be a light fracture that I have not detected. Just be careful when I help you up."

He rose and wrapped an arm around her waist to assist her.

Dear heaven.

She felt the light ripple of his muscles as he drew her closer to lean against the rock wall of his body. "Try gently putting your weight on that foot. Don't worry, I have you. I won't let you fall."

She caught Mrs. Halsey grinning at her from behind him.

Did everyone know she was wildly in love with the major? Why was he the only one too dense to notice?

Or perhaps he had noticed and been purposely avoiding her this entire month, ever since his return to Moonstone Landing. She had first met Fionn Brennan three years ago when he was a young lieutenant scouting potential locations for a new army hospital. He was now commanding officer of the local army fort and had the added duty of overseeing construction of the new military hospital about to be built here.

Finding a location for the new hospital had brought him to

their quiet village several times over the past three years. With each visit, Chloe had fallen more deeply in love with him. This feeling was quite unbearable now that she knew it would never be reciprocated.

She did not understand what had suddenly happened to interfere with their easy friendship. They used to enjoy each other's company, but now their every encounter seemed strained.

Even now, she could see the turmoil in his eyes.

They had gone from referring to each other by their given names, Fionn and Chloe, to the more formal address one was required to use among acquaintances when in polite company.

She glanced at this magnificent man with eyes the color of silver crystals.

He was looking away, as though he could hardly stand to look at her.

Why did he not like her in any romantic way?

She was considered a catch.

What did he not like about her?

Chapter Two

"CAN YOU STAND on that leg at all?" Fionn asked Lady Chloe, aching to keep her in his arms and knowing it was the worst thing possible.

Blessed saints, he ached every moment he was apart from her...and ached worse whenever they were together.

"No, Major Brennan. Please, help me sit back down. It truly hurts."

He could see the strain on her lovely face and the clearly etched pain reflected in her eyes. He helped her back into her chair, maintaining a supportive arm around her as he said, "Mrs. Halsey, will you please fetch Lady Chloe a cup of tea? She doesn't look well at all."

"I'm sure I will be fine in a moment." She cast him a sweet smile of assurance that did nothing to stem his worry. "But what about you? Are you certain you were not hurt?"

"Not a scratch." Fionn had grown up on the streets of London, hardened by the daily desperation of staying alive. Because of this, joining the army to fight Napoleon had not been much of a hardship for him. Nor was he very much troubled by the leg wound that had never properly healed. He was left with a limp hardly worthy of notice.

Growing up wretchedly poor and now permanently lame was not nearly as intolerable as seeing Lady Chloe Killigrew again and knowing he could never have her. She was an heiress, the elegant daughter of an earl, and would be courted by the loftiest men in the land.

Who was he to merit her?

He might have tried to compromise her were he the sort without scruples. But he was no fortune-hunting knave.

He may have been born in filth, but he had his pride. Indeed, this was all he had. He did not even know his real name or if he had ever been given one.

How could someone like him ever be a suitable prospect for this beautiful earl's daughter?

He remained beside Lady Chloe, an arm still wrapped around her while she looked as though she was about to faint.

She had to be in terrible pain.

He moved another chair closer and very carefully lifted her swollen foot onto it. "Keep it there for now. Having it elevated will help ease the discomfort."

She emitted a breathy sigh. "Thank you."

Mrs. Halsey's tea shop was still crowded with onlookers, most of whom were wringing their hands in worry. Lady Chloe and her sisters, Henley and Phoebe, were beloved in this village, and no one ever wanted to see them come to harm.

He stared at her in dismay. "Do not think to put your elegant boot back on. Just sit quietly while I gather your things, and then I'll escort you home."

She cast him another charming smile.

He was little more than a street rat, but even lowborn wastrels like him knew true beauty when they saw it. If he were one to believe in angels, then Lady Chloe was surely one of their best sent to Moonstone Landing to watch over his wretched soul.

Fionn shook out of the thought, for he was not a churchgoing man. However, if the Good Lord found him worthy to hold Lady Chloe in his arms and keep her there for the next hour while he helped her home, who was he to argue about it?

He'd started to rise in order to leave her side and fetch a

carriage when she suddenly turned ashen and moaned. "Major Brennan…wait… Oh, dear."

Her head fell against his shoulder.

"Lady Chloe!"

"I…I…" The pain was obviously making her dizzy, and she was struggling not to faint. Poor thing.

Where was Mrs. Halsey with her tea?

He stroked Chloe's hair and held her against him so she would not tumble out of her chair. "Try taking small breaths. Gently, now. Not too deep or you'll hurt your ribs."

She managed a few, inhaling lightly and wincing each time. Then she began to laugh softly against his neck, her lips lightly brushing his skin. "You are better than smelling salts. What is your scent? It is quite nice."

He chuckled, relieved she seemed to be reviving. "Now I know you must be addled. We both landed in a puddle of mud and our clothes reek of stale water."

"But you don't, although perhaps I do."

"No, you are lavender and roses, Lady Chloe," he said in a whisper, not wanting the crowd to overhear.

"Hardly, but thank you." She breathed him in again. "Do I detect a hint of bay spices? It blends nicely with the warmth of your skin."

She sat up with a groan, appearing to have survived her fainting bout as the color returned to her cheeks. "Major Brennan, how can I ever repay you for saving my life?"

The comment startled him, for he hadn't thought twice before rescuing her from those panicked horses. "None required. Your safety is all the reward I need." He gave her cheek another light caress. "Do not try to get up. You are still too wobbly on your feet."

"All right. But I must say, you are quite modest for a savior."

He wanted to tell her that he would protect her always, but how could he make such an admission without giving away what was in his heart? "All in the line of duty, Lady Chloe."

She clutched the sides of her chair and stared down at her foot. "I am trying very hard to hold myself together, but I fear I will come undone in another moment. I was a heartbeat away from dying until you came along. I will never forget this...or you."

They stared intently at each other, as though sharing a special moment. He supposed it was a common enough thing for a rescuer and the person rescued to feel something pass between them. One might call it a forever connection deep in their souls.

He certainly felt this way about her.

In truth, he'd felt a connection to Chloe long before this incident. He often passed through Moonstone Landing while on assignment with the army and regularly encountered Chloe and her family.

Then, a month ago, he'd found himself promoted to the rank of major and put in command of Fort Arundel, the local army outpost here in this charming seacoast village. Chloe had come with her family and the village leaders to greet him on the day he arrived. The world and everyone in it had melted away in the precise moment he saw Chloe walking toward him, all grown up now and beautiful beyond belief.

He'd lost his heart to her in that moment, and the realization struck him like a hammer blow to the head.

He was still reeling from it a month later.

Mrs. Halsey returned and set a cup of tea on the table beside them. "I've put a little honey in it. Drink up, lamb. You need the fortification."

Chloe's hand trembled slightly as she put the cup to her lips. "Mrs. Halsey, I'll need to replace all those damaged cakes."

"Of course—let me pack up some fresh ones for you right away." Mrs. Halsey lumbered off behind the tea shop's display counter to attend to the task.

Fionn watched her for a moment before returning his attention to Chloe. "How did you come into the village?"

"I took the wagon from Moonstone Cottage."

"Why did you not avail yourself of one of the Duke of Malvern's rigs? Or those of the Marquess of Burness?"

"There was no need to disturb either brother-in-law for something so trivial as a ride into town. I've often taken the wagon into Moonstone Landing on my own."

"Where is it now? I did not see it outside."

"I left it at Mr. Bedwell's mercantile. His clerks were loading it with supplies while I ran to Mrs. Halsey's to pick up a few cakes for this afternoon's tea party. You should join us."

Before he could reply, Constable Angel, accompanied by several of the earlier bystanders, tramped back into the tearoom with Chloe's reticule and parasol in hand as well as Fionn's hat. "Major Brennan, have you completed your assessment? How badly is Lady Chloe hurt?"

"A bad ankle sprain and a few bruised ribs. She will be sore for several days, but I expect her to make a full recovery. Tragedy has been averted. However, I think you may have a phaeton and its unfortunate driver to fish out of the water."

The constable laughed and handed him their belongings. "My men are attending to the phaeton as we speak. In truth, I had better head down there to supervise its safe removal. Hopefully, the dolt driving it has not broken his neck. Shall I send up my nephew to assist you?"

Fionn set Chloe's reticule and busted parasol on the table beside them. "No, I have it all under control. Lady Chloe will be fine in my care."

After exchanging a few more polite words, the constable nodded and waved the crowd away. "Everyone go on about your business. The lady is not a circus attraction."

Fionn raked a hand through his hair once they were alone again. "Blasted idiot... Not you, Lady Chloe. I mean the driver of the phaeton. I am going to beat the stuffing out of that pompous fool. I warned him not to race his carriage in town."

"Who do you mean?"

"Lord Claymore. He and his party are staying at the Kestrel

Inn. That shiny racing carriage is his latest toy, and he's been showing it off to his friends for the past two days. It will serve him right if he takes a dunk in the harbor along with that fine conveyance."

He was going to place a hand against her cheek once more, but stopped himself and turned to Mrs. Halsey. "See that Lady Chloe behaves while I collect her wagon."

"Yes, of course." He noticed her winking at Chloe as he strode out.

What was that about?

"Behave myself, indeed," he heard Chloe mutter into her cup of tea. "He is wonderful, isn't he, Mrs. Halsey?"

"Yes, lamb."

He pretended not to hear the remark.

This spark between him and Chloe was extremely dangerous and something never to be ignited.

As he strode to Mr. Bedwell's mercantile, he noted a few remaining packages still squashed on the street. The townspeople had gathered most of them, but none were salvageable, including these that were too ground into the earth to bother retrieving.

That could have been her, squashed and broken.

Thank goodness he had been there to prevent it.

He continued to the mercantile and drove her wagon around the corner to the tea shop. Chloe smiled at him when he strode in. "I did not mention it earlier, but my invitation for you to join us is because the Marquess of Burness's nieces have arrived for the summer, and we are going to celebrate with a welcome party. This is why I was here, to pick up cakes for our little celebration. Do you remember Ella and Imogen?"

He nodded. "Of course. Nor will I ever forget the summer I met you all. No one ever treated me more kindly than your family."

"I hope you accept. You really must."

He tensed. "No, Lady Chloe. I couldn't."

"Why not? Everyone will be happy to see you. We are

friends, are we not?"

His silence in response to the casual remark obviously hurt her, but he dared not encourage anything more than a casual acquaintance between them.

She emitted a ragged sigh. "May I impose on you a little longer? Will you help me carry the replacement cakes to my wagon?"

"Of course. I won't leave you to do any of your errands yourself. Do you have any others remaining to be done?"

"No, I only needed to pick up these cakes. Mrs. Halsey has just finished wrapping them up."

He took a moment to load them into the wagon then returned for her. He lifted her into his arms and set her on the passenger side of the driver's bench. "I'll take you to Westgate Hall. But I cannot stay for your celebration. We fell into a puddle, if you will recall. I am fine, but my uniform is caked with mud. I'll walk back into town after I drop you off. It isn't far, and I'll need a little time to cool down or else I will do Lord Claymore physical harm."

"My gown is muddied, too. But as for your uniform, Melrose will see to its cleaning while you allow us the pleasure of your company. You are about the same size as my brother-in-law. I'm sure he will give you the loan of clean clothes while yours are tended. As for Lord Claymore, he is a viscount, is he not? You will only get yourself in trouble if you hit him."

"I know." He grinned as he climbed onto the wagon beside her. "But I still want to hit him."

Chloe laughed. "Me too. I know these London dandies are good for the economy of Moonstone Landing, but if only they weren't so arrogant or dismissive of common courtesy while on holiday here."

"There is no patroness here to keep them in line."

"Unlike London or Bath," she muttered.

He quirked a dark eyebrow. "Is that dissatisfaction I sense? Are you not eager to make your London debut?"

"I dread it. I would much rather remain here, where I know I am loved and respected."

"Lady Chloe, you will take London by storm. You'll be the *ton*'s brightest diamond."

"I would much rather be considered Moonstone Landing's diamond. Truly, why would I wish to put myself in the company of boors like the viscount?"

"Well, you certainly cannot wish to be in my boorish company." He gave the reins a flick to move the horses along. "Your ankle does not look good. It has swollen to the size of a melon. You had better stay off it for at least two or three days. Constable Angel left word for the doctor to pay you a call when he returns to town."

"But—"

"Lady Chloe, do not be stubborn about this. Put your leg up, and you are to give the ankle a good soak once I get you home."

"Moonstone Cottage is my home. I am only at Westgate Hall until I come of age and can move back in there on my own. Sorry, I suppose I sounded quite petulant just now. Are the rumors true?"

"What rumors?"

"I hear you have taken a lease on Moonstone Cottage for yourself and are planning on moving in this week."

He nodded. "This week or next. Yes, that's the plan."

"Since I am not permitted to live there yet, I can think of no one better than you to occupy it. I'm glad you've taken it for the year. But why did you do it? To remove yourself from the hospital construction while it is underway?"

"The fort and the hospital construction site are going to be a mess for the entire year. I thought it easier to be able to work in peace and quiet whenever necessary. Not just for me, but on occasion for my officer staff. At some point, we will also have to shuffle patients around, and Moonstone Cottage will be a perfect place to house them temporarily."

"Why did you not tell me you had let our cottage?"

He shrugged. "I assumed the Marquess of Burness would tell you. He is married to your sister, after all. And you are living with them, are you not?"

"Yes, Phoebe would not have it any other way. But...do you think so little of me that you would not bother to write to me and tell me yourself? Did you get any of the letters I sent you?"

"I did receive them," he said with a nod. "And I thank you for your kindness in thinking of me. It was rude of me not to respond. The truth of the matter is that I had no idea what to say to you. All I did was work. I thought you would find my news exceedingly dull."

Her lovely eyes rounded in surprise. "I wouldn't ever."

"Lady Chloe, I—"

"And do stop calling me Lady Chloe. Why are you suddenly so formal around me? I have always been simply Chloe to you, and you have always been Fionn to me unless we are in company."

He sighed. "That was fine before. But you are now of marriageable age and above my station. We should not be so familiar with each other even when alone."

"Fionn, I will hit you if you say that again."

"Ha! Ungrateful chit. Did I not just save your life?" He laughed, a deep, rumbling chuckle. Perhaps he was being too hard on her, and quite unfairly. It was not her fault he was struggling with these impossibly strong feelings for her.

But the true danger was in the fear she might reciprocate them.

He was no brash coxcomb, but he knew he was nice looking and women fancied him. Finding one to warm his bed had never been a chore.

However, it was different with Chloe. She was not some passing infatuation or casual dalliance.

That she might reciprocate his feelings elated him and also filled him with dread, for their affection for each other could never lead anywhere.

"Yes, you saved my life. But Fionn, this is exactly the reason why we shall always remain close friends. Why are you frowning? Don't you want us to remain friends? Or do you have a special lady who might not like us to be so familiar with each other?" She yelped as the wagon hit a rut that rattled through the footboards.

Fionn immediately put his arm around her. "Sorry. The road is a little uneven."

She waited a moment for him to answer her question. "Well?"

He arched a dark eyebrow. "Well, what?"

"Have you a lady you care for?"

"That is none of your business, Chloe."

"On the contrary, it is completely my business, because I... Friends ought to care about each other. Have you ever thought of marrying?"

"No."

Blessed saints.

This was worse than he realized.

Was she suggesting *she* wanted to marry him?

And now it was important for her to know whether she had competition? Hah! If only she realized how desperately he adored her. How could there ever be anyone else for him?

"Well, if you do not see fit to confide in me, then I shall keep all my secrets from you and never tell you if I am being courted by anyone."

He chuckled. "I know you are not."

She frowned at him. "What makes you so certain?"

"Because you would have told me."

She tipped her chin into the air. "No longer. From this moment forward, I shall keep everything to myself."

"I doubt it. You never keep anything from me. Most of your letters to me were pages long."

"And yet you never saw fit to respond to any of them." She was hurt by this, and it clearly showed on her lovely face. "I did not mean to pester you. I thought you would enjoy knowing all that was going on in Moonstone Landing."

He took her hand and gave it a light squeeze. "Pay no attention to me. I'm just a surly oaf. I did enjoy your letters. I've saved every one of them."

"You have?"

"And read them often."

"You do?"

He nodded. "I am an orphan," he said with a light groan, knowing it was a mistake to share any of his thoughts or dreams with this girl he liked too much already. "Never knew my parents. Nor do I know whether I have any siblings. You are the closest thing I have to family. I appreciated all your letters. You have no idea how much I looked forward to receiving those massive tomes."

She laughed. "Massive? Tomes? They weren't that long."

"Yes, they were. Three or four pages each. I did not think that much went on in Moonstone Landing. However, I liked your keeping me abreast of the news."

"So you don't have a lady friend?"

He sighed and shook his head. "Chloe, there is no one special. All right? How can there ever be? I am a mere army major. What have I to offer a genteel lady?"

"But you must have saved enough of your wages to let Moonstone Cottage from us. You've paid your lease in full in advance. How did you manage it?"

"A ridiculous splurge on my part. It has taken up most of my inheritance. I was left a small sum when my benefactor died. Not enough to support a wife and children. I'll be back in the barracks when the year is out. But there's something special about your cottage. I know you and your sisters love it. I am drawn to it as well. I cannot explain why. Only that living there was something I had to do."

"I know what you mean. I've been longing to move back in. But neither Cain nor Cormac," she said, referring to her sisters' husbands, "will allow it. They say I am too young to live there on my own."

"You will be married by next year. Your sister, Henley, married the Duke of Malvern, and Phoebe married the Marquess of Burness. You can aim just as high for yourself."

She frowned at him.

If he hadn't just saved her life, she might have punched him.

Well, she was not a violent girl, but his remark had obviously angered her.

"My sisters married for love. Hen did not care about Cain's title. Nor did Phoebe care about Cormac's title."

"I know they made love matches, but the outcome might have been quite different had the Duke of Malvern been a mere blacksmith instead. Same for the Marquess of Burness. Wealth and title are factors in their appeal. I know your sisters are not greedy and sincerely care for their spouses. Still, you cannot deny that a title and fortune count for something."

"Perhaps for most women, but I am considered an heiress. I do not need a man with a fortune when I have a significant one of my own."

"Do not go around talking about it. You will attract the wrong sort of man."

"I don't ever talk about it. Only to you."

"Why me?"

"Because I trust you. Do not bother to scold me and tell me that my trust is misplaced. You saved my life today. You put your own at risk to save mine."

He shrugged it off and said no more because he was in too much of a roil over her already.

"By the way, I will not be offended if you take a moment to remove your soaked jacket. It cannot be comfortable for you to keep it on while driving the wagon."

"We're almost at Westgate Hall. I'll hand it over to Melrose when we get there."

She inhaled lightly. "Then you'll stay for Ella and Imogen's welcome party?"

He gave a curt nod.

Staying close to Chloe was the worst thing he could possibly do, but his heart needed this additional time with her.

He wished it were not so.

"Thank you, Fionn. It is good to have you back with us in Moonstone Landing. Will you be angry if I tell you that I missed you?"

He smiled at her. "I won't mind."

"Good, then consider yourself told. Did you miss me at all?"

Chapter Three

HAD HE MISSED Chloe?

Only every second out of every day.

"Major Brennan, what happened?" Cormac, the Marquess of Burness, called out to him as they drew up in the wagon. Concern etched his face, and he now hurried down the steps of his manor house when he noticed Chloe's injured ankle.

Fionn quickly told him about the runaway phaeton.

"Dear heaven, Chloe! You might have been killed."

"But I came out of it with just a sprained ankle," she assured her brother-in-law.

"And bruised ribs," Fionn added with a grumble, for he did not want her making light of what had happened. "Wrap your arms around my neck while I lift you in my arms. Do not be so foolish as to claim you can walk on your own."

"Fine. You needn't be an ogre about it." She sighed. "I owe Major Brennan an enormous debt of gratitude that I can never adequately repay."

"I've told you. You owe me nothing."

"Stop being so valiant. I find it quite irritating, you know." She laughed lightly and immediately winced. "Ow."

His heart tightened, for her every wince or gasp reminded him of just how closely she had come to being killed. "Stop cracking jokes. You'll only strain your injured ribs worse."

"You needn't bark orders at me. I am not one of the soldiers under your command."

He tried not to smile, but couldn't help it. "I should hope not. I am not in the habit of carrying them in my arms."

"Follow me, Fionn." The marquess shook his head. "Blessed saints, we had better get her comfortably settled before her sisters see her." He led the way, making no attempt to take her, since he had lost an arm shortly after the battle at Waterloo and could not possibly handle the task of carrying her inside.

Fionn did not mind at all, for Chloe's body was sweet perfection and he was in no hurry to let her go.

But this was the closest he was ever going to allow himself to get to her.

After today, he would never touch Chloe again.

"Melrose will show you the way upstairs to Chloe's room. Let me get Phoebe. She's with my brother and his family. They've just arrived for their annual visit and are having refreshments on the terrace. You will stay and join us, of course."

Chloe shot Fionn a grin. "See, I am not the only one who wants you here."

He sighed.

"You both look a mess. My wife will help Chloe, but you'll need the mud stains brushed out of your uniform. I can loan you some clean clothes to wear while my staff attends to your garments."

Chloe's grin turned even smugger. "I told you my brother-in-law would offer."

"My valet, Gunyon, is a marvel. He will attend to you. But Chloe, what are we to do with you? Your ankle looks very bad."

"It is," Fionn agreed, for he had learned a little about medical treatment while on the battlefield. "It needs to be soaked in cold water or have ice put on it, if you have any. Then it must be firmly bound and Chloe's foot elevated. She needs to keep off it as much as possible, at least for the next three or four days."

He met Chloe's stubborn gaze. "Don't scowl at me. You

know I am right. You need to remain in bed, and that's an end to it."

"And miss seeing Ella and Imogen?"

"They are here for the entire month," the marquess said. "You will have plenty of time to enjoy my nieces. Listen to Fionn—he knows what he is talking about. I'll send one of the footmen into town to summon the doctor."

Chloe shook her head. "Constable Angel took care of that. I'm sure Dr. Hewitt will stop in once he is through at the Harbison farm."

"Ah, good. In the meantime, stop putting up a fuss when it is obvious you are hurt." He next turned to his butler, who was also fretting over her condition. "Melrose, lead the major upstairs. I'll send Lady Burness up right after you. Then show him into one of the unoccupied guest chambers so he can wash up and change into clean clothes. Gunyon will see to whatever else he needs."

"Very good, my lord."

Fionn followed Melrose, his entire body in a tight coil as he entered Chloe's bedchamber and set her down on the little chair beside her vanity. The room was not quite as large as he expected, although he had not really had any idea what to expect. There was no denying its elegance.

The drapes, her counterpane, and the bed's canopy were of a cheerful yellow silk, and the exquisite floral rug picked up the light hues of the room. The wallpaper had small flowers on it, yellow roses with green leaves and stems.

The furniture was also light in color, the same delicate shade of ivory as the wallpaper. All in all, the room had a breezy feel about it, perhaps enhanced by the windows being open and a gentle wind blowing in the scent of roses from the garden and a salty tang from the sea air.

His life and Chloe's could not have been more different. She had grown up amid this splendor.

He had spent most of his childhood sleeping in a box in a London alleyway. If not for the kindness of Viscount Brennan, a man who had rescued him off the streets and taken him home instead of turning him over to the authorities for vagrancy, he would have ended up imprisoned.

He shook out of the thought and returned his attention to Chloe. Her clothes were muddied. For this reason, he had not set her down on the bed.

Mother in heaven.

The thought of Chloe in bed.

With him.

He ached to hold her, run his fingers through her vibrant curls that were a magnificent blend of fiery colors, sometimes a flame-tinged, dark gold and sometimes more a dark amber-honey. It depended on how the sun struck her hair.

She also had the loveliest eyes that always seemed to sparkle like the deepest green emeralds.

At times, he felt as though they sparkled just for him.

He dared not allow himself to think so. Courting Chloe was out of the question and something that would never be. Indeed, it was the last thing he ever wished to happen. It would be disastrous if she were to fall in love with him, for he would never propose to her.

How could such a marriage ever work?

He drew over another small chair, grabbed a decorative pillow from her elegantly decorated window seat, placed it on the small chair, and very carefully propped her foot on it. "Keep it elevated."

Chloe's sister, Phoebe, soon hurried in, along with her maid.

Fionn gave her quick instructions regarding Chloe's ankle sprain and then allowed himself to be bustled off to another of the elegant rooms in Westgate Hall.

Melrose spoke to the Burness housekeeper, Mrs. Norman, who in turn ordered one of her maids to bring up fresh water, soaps, drying cloths, and light refreshments for him. Then Melrose and the marquess's valet, Gunyon, fussed over him, assisting him out of his uniform. While Melrose took his attire downstairs to freshen, Gunyon brought in several garments for him to try on. "I am certain these will fit you, Major Brennan."

"Thank you, but none of this attention is necessary." He had never in his life worn clothes so fine or had anyone pamper him in this fashion, even in the years when he was with Viscount Brennan.

Yet this was how Chloe was used to being treated.

To their credit, she and her sisters did not behave as spoiled princesses. In truth, they were remarkably kind and did not shirk hard work. Their husbands were honorable men and quite valiant. Both of them had faced deprivation and hardships on the battlefield. The marquess had lost an arm for it. But even they had now returned to lives of privilege and given their wives every benefit the wife of a duke or marquess could have.

How could he ever offer this to Chloe when he had nothing to his name?

"Thank you, Gunyon," he said when the valet finished assisting him with the cuffs of the shirt and handed him a vest of dark gray silver to put over it. He had also borrowed a pair of black breeches.

Fortunately, the attire for Imogen and Ella's celebration was informal, no jacket or cravat required, since they were to remain only among family. The marquess had not even bothered to don a vest, preferring the comfort of just a casual shirt.

Gunyon was about to hand him back to Melrose to be escorted downstairs when he heard chatter emanating from Chloe's bedchamber. "Am I permitted to look in on her? I want to be certain her ankle is properly bound and left elevated."

Melrose nodded. "Give me a moment."

He fetched Mrs. Norman, who then went to knock at Chloe's open door. "Yes," he heard Phoebe say. "Of course, bring him in."

Phoebe, now a marchioness since marrying the Marquess of Burness several years ago, cast him a warm and generous smile. "My sister is stubbornly refusing to remain in her bedchamber.

She is eager to see my husband's nieces. Would you mind terribly helping her downstairs? We'll make certain to set her up properly and not allow her out of the chair."

He nodded. "Do you mind if I check the binding first? It has to be tied snug. And if you have ice, wrap it in a handkerchief and keep it pressed against her elevated ankle. It will help ease the swelling."

Chloe laughed gently. "I think if you ever tire of being in the army, the hospital you are building for them will gladly take you on as a doctor."

"No, I assure you," he said with a wry smile. "This is about the extent of my medical knowledge."

He took her in his arms again, trying hard to suppress all the feelings he should not be having for this girl, and carried her downstairs.

Blast it.

He was a street rat, grew up in surroundings where it was every man for himself. He had learned to use a knife with expert skill by the time he was seven years old, and did not hesitate to use it a time or two when one of the older street boys attempted to steal his food.

He should not be having any delicate feelings.

In truth, he should not be feeling anything at all.

A lovely breeze blew off the water and onto the terrace as he strode outside with Chloe in his arms. He was pleased to see her family, for he had come to know most of them well on his many sojourns to Moonstone Landing.

The marquess's little nieces, Ella and Imogen, were delightful girls and rushed forward to greet him, almost knocking him over before he had the chance to put Chloe down.

This was why he adored this family. They did not see him for the nobody he was.

Once he had properly settled Chloe, he bowed to each niece in turn. "Lady Ella. Lady Imogen. It is a pleasure to see you again."

They giggled and introduced him to their parents. Their father, Lord Stockwell, was a younger brother to the marquess. His wife, Charlotte, was a shy woman with a gentle smile.

Of course, he knew Chloe's other sister, Henley, and her husband Cain, the Duke of Malvern. They were just as warm in welcoming him.

Nor did they refer to each other with any formality. The marquess was Cormac. The duke was Cain. And Lord Stockwell was merely John. Same for the ladies, merely using their given names. No *Your Grace* or *Lady* used among family.

He had never met people so loving and generous before this. Of course, his benefactor, Viscount Brennan, had been kind to him. A caring mentor who had fed, clothed, and educated him. The viscount had been a good man, but the rest of his family were an odious pack of jackals.

Someone placed a lemonade in his hand, and he somehow wound up seated beside Chloe as they all now settled in to enjoy the cakes they had brought over from Mrs. Halsey's tearoom. He did not mind finding himself beside her, since he had resolved to make himself responsible for her care until the doctor arrived to properly treat her ankle.

"What made you decide to let Moonstone Cottage?" Lord Stockwell asked him.

Fionn truly did not know the reason other than to describe it as a feeling that led him to do it. "Perhaps the cottage ghosts summoned me," he said in jest. "But in truth, it is also an excellent location to hold concerts or other special functions for the recovering soldiers. We may need to move some of them here for a few weeks during the worst of the hospital construction. I have made arrangements with the vicar to accommodate most of the wounded men at the parish church during this time, but I don't think they can handle all of them."

Little Imogen, almost nine years old now, regarded him solemnly. He tried to stifle a grin, for her eyes were almost as big as her head. "Yes, Imogen?"

"I think you look like him."

"Who do you think he looks like?" Chloe asked.

"The ghost captain."

The marquess choked on his chuckling. "Blessed saints, Imogen. Don't jest about a thing like this."

"She isn't," her Ella, now almost eleven, said in all earnestness. "It is in the eyes. There is a resemblance between Captain Arundel and Major Brennan."

Chloe was now gaping at him. "No... Well, yes. Now that you mention it. Perhaps the tiniest bit around the eyes. But not their color. The captain's eyes were blue, while Major Brennan's eyes are silver."

"And his mouth is similar, too," her own sister, Phoebe, added.

Now everyone was staring at him.

He groaned. "The notion is preposterous. Coincidence, nothing more."

To his relief, Dr. Hewitt arrived just then and broke up their conversation. Fionn rose to give the doctor his seat so he could more easily check Chloe's bandages. He watched as the doctor began his examination. After checking her ribs and ankle, he had her raise her hands, turn her neck. Twist her body to the right and to the left.

He peered closely into her eyes and then had her follow his finger with just her eyes without turning her head. "Excellent," he murmured once done.

Fionn breathed a sigh of relief. "Then you don't think she has suffered more than a few bruises and the ankle sprain?"

"That is all. Her ribs are tender, but those will heal with simple bed rest. Lady Chloe ought to be fit to resume her activities in a week's time. You did a fine job, Major Brennan. I could not have provided better treatment for her myself."

Everyone now breathed a sigh of relief, except for Chloe, who did not look pleased. "An entire week?"

"Yes," the doctor said, casting her a stern look. "You are to do exactly as Major Brennan advised. Stay off that foot for at least three days. Minimal exertion and lots of bed rest for a full week for those bruised ribs. I'll come by to see you tomorrow, and I had better not find you hopping about."

He closed his medical bag and rose to leave.

"Might I grab a ride back to town?" Fionn asked.

"Of course, Major Brennan."

Fionn turned to the marquess. "I'll return these garments to you tomorrow, if you don't mind. I had better get back to the fort."

"Come by anytime," Phoebe said. "We shall be staying close to home until Chloe is feeling better. Thank you again for rescuing her."

"Indeed," Chloe's eldest sister, Hen, said with heartfelt warmth. "That was too much of a close call. I think my husband must have a little talk with Lord Claymore."

The duke nodded. "I shall attend to it first thing tomorrow."

The marquess, apparently, was not to be left out. "I'll join you. I may have only one functioning arm, but I can still throw a solid punch. If he dares utter a smart remark, he'll find himself missing a few teeth."

Dr. Hewitt groaned. "Please, I have enough patients to treat without adding that London set to my roster."

Chloe tried to get up. Everyone shouted at her to sit down.

Fionn knelt by her side. "I will stop by to see you tomorrow. Rest your ankle, Lady Chloe. The parish church dance is at the end of the month. You want to be fit for that, don't you?"

Her eyes brightened.

He adored the way they sparkled.

"Will you be attending?"

He shrugged. "Maybe."

"No maybe about it. You must attend and claim a dance from me."

"Isn't it usually the other way around? Am I not supposed to ask you?"

He saw the hurt in her eyes as she said, "Would you have asked me?"

"Probably not." He glanced at his lame leg, using it as an excuse. "I cannot manage the livelier dances for fear this damaged limb will give out from under me."

She cast him a stubborn look, refusing to be deterred. "Then you and I shall hobble together to the strains of a waltz. We can spin about the floor at our own speed, slow enough for us to manage."

Well, he wasn't getting out of that with more feeble excuses. "Very well. Save a waltz for me."

The dance was still weeks away.

Perhaps she would forget him by then.

He left with the doctor and remained quiet until his rig rattled out of the courtyard. "Quite a bit of excitement," the doctor remarked. "I'll stop by the Kestrel Inn next to see how Lord Claymore is faring."

Fionn nodded. "I'll come with you. I want to question him."

"I'm sure Constable Angel has done this already."

"Still, an added warning from me cannot hurt. He and his friends have been recklessly racing about Moonstone Landing. I don't care that they are racing—they just need to do it away from our busier roads. By the way, is everything all right at the Harbison farm?"

"Yes, one of their boys fell out of a tree and broke his arm. It is a clean break, not too bad. He will recover."

"Good."

It was not too long before they reached the inn.

The ostler, a wizened, older man with a leathery face, ran forward to take the doctor's carriage. "Ye're here to see Lord Claymore, I expect. Constable Angel and his men brought him back here a while ago. Soaking wet, he was. And quite angry as he strode into the inn."

"So he was able to walk on his own, Mr. Matchett? Fool lord, he's lucky to be alive," Dr. Hewitt muttered.

"Odd thing, though. I don't think it was his fault those horses went wild. Constable Angel said one of them had a dart stuck in its rump. Some prankster must have shot him with it. The constable is going to investigate. Probably some wayward lad, although no one saw any children around. Who else would have been stupid enough to pull a jest like this? Well, he'll keep asking around and get to the bottom of it."

Fionn and the doctor exchanged glances.

So, this was more than some pampered lord behaving recklessly. Fionn was even more eager to question him now.

"Sounds like the viscount was not hurt at all, or else everyone would have been rushing up to me and dragging me to his bedside," the doctor muttered. "How about I meet you back here in fifteen minutes, Major Brennan? We can walk in to see him together."

"Sounds like a plan." Fionn took a moment to return to his quarters and don a fresh uniform. It would not do to approach Lord Claymore dressed in the marquess's borrowed clothing, even if the shirt was of finest lawn and the vest was silk.

The doctor also returned to his infirmary to clean up.

Thaddius Angel, the inn's new owner, hurried forward to greet them when they strode in together a short while later. "How is Lady Chloe? We are all so worried about her."

"She will be fine," Dr. Hewitt assured him. "But we're here to see Lord Claymore. I gather he took a rather nasty spill into the water."

Thaddius nodded and began to chatter as he led the way to the viscount's quarters. "Good thing he did not break his neck. He seems all right, but you had better examine him. Did you hear what they say happened? One of his horses was struck with a dart. Malicious trick. Could have killed Lord Claymore, Lady Chloe, and other innocent bystanders."

The door happened to be open, providing Fionn with a view of what turned out to be an entire suite comprised of an elegantly furnished parlor with bedchambers and dressing rooms on either side of it. The parlor itself had a seating area and a small dining table, all of it finely furnished with mahogany furniture, blue silk chairs, and damask settees.

A crystal chandelier hung from the ceiling. The wall sconces were of burnished silver. Everything was highly polished and gleaming.

Of course, a viscount would be used to this luxury and expect no less.

Several of the viscount's friends were seated around him, their postures languid and exuding privilege.

"Do come in, Dr. Hewitt," the viscount said with surprising politeness. "And you, Major Brennan. I am entirely in your debt for averting disaster. How is Lady Chloe? I understand she is the sister-in-law of the Marquess of Burness and the Duke of Malvern, two gentlemen I have no wish to make my enemies."

"She has a sprained ankle and a few bruised ribs, but she will recover," the doctor assured him.

Fionn said nothing, still taking the measure of the man.

Since his clothes were obviously dry, it was clear Lord Claymore had been fit enough to change out of his soaked garments. Of course, such men had valets to assist them. Still, the viscount looked hale and no worse for wear after tumbling headlong into the water. His hair was still damp and he had a small bruise on his cheek under his left eye. Other than those few telltale signs, one would never guess he had taken what could have been a deadly spill mere hours ago.

"I will ride over to Westgate Hall tomorrow to deliver my sincerest apologies." He now turned to Fionn, assessing him in return. "You took quite a fall. I noticed you are limping. I—"

"It is an old injury, that's all."

"Ah, then it is not a result of the unfortunate incident?"

"No, my lord. I may have an ache or two come tomorrow, but that is about all. What of you?"

The viscount chuckled with surprising good nature. "The horses came to an abrupt stop at the harbor, fortunately separating from the phaeton at that moment. The phaeton kept rolling straight into the water and took me splashing in along with it. Thankfully, this is where I landed…in the harbor at full tide. Had I hit hard ground, I doubt I would be alive to talk about it now."

"I know you spoke to Constable Angel about what happened, but would you mind if I asked a few questions as well?"

"Not at all, Major Brennan." He turned to his friends, none of whom had been introduced to Fionn or the doctor.

No doubt the slight had been on purpose, but Fionn did not take it as a matter of rudeness on the viscount's part. Rather, he sensed it was his friends who had no desire to be introduced to the Moonstone Landing locals.

The viscount told his friends, two gentlemen and two ladies, all of whom reeked of haughtiness and entitlement, "I shall meet you downstairs for tea in a few minutes."

"Honestly, Claymore. How many times are you to repeat the story? You are becoming as tiresome as these rustics," one of the dandies in his company said. The men were dressed in garish colors, the pair of them resembling peacocks. The two ladies were young and pretty, and dressed quite finely as well.

Too finely for Moonstone Landing, but this was just Fionn's opinion.

As for their looks…they were pretty, but in a cold way. Their eyes held contempt for those they considered beneath their rank, which he supposed was everyone they had met while here.

One of them began to rake her gaze over him.

In the next moment, the other lady did the same.

He understood what those hot, ravenous glances signified. Women had been coming on to him for years. Even innocent Chloe thought him nice looking.

These ladies were obviously of noble bloodstock, but he knew neither of them was a virgin. One could not ignore the knowing way they ogled him.

He expected each would find a moment to proposition him

before he left the inn.

He thought it humorous that he was not deemed fit to be properly introduced in company, but they had no qualms about lying naked with him in their beds.

If this was how the London debutantes behaved, he wanted Chloe to have no part of it. Indeed, women like these two would eat her alive.

As for their potential propositions, were he of a different nature, he would have no issue with a meaningless romp with either of them. But somehow, it felt like a betrayal to Chloe, and he could not see himself ever doing this.

Which was ridiculous, since he did not intend to court Chloe.

His heart did not seem to care.

There was no help for it—he was going to be loyal to Chloe whether he ever courted her or not.

Perhaps this cursed claim she had on his heart would fade once she was settled and happily married to someone of suitable rank. He had no desire to spend his life as a monk, but he feared this would be his fate so long as Chloe remained unattached.

He shook out of his thoughts and took a chair opposite the viscount when he motioned for him to sit down.

The viscount's friends had now sauntered out and grudgingly left them to their privacy.

"Major Brennan, give me a moment while Dr. Hewitt examines me, and then I shall answer all your questions. Would you care for a drink?"

"No thank you, my lord."

Dr. Hewitt finished his inspection quickly, for there appeared to be no injury worse than the small bruise to the viscount's cheek. He closed his medical bag and nodded to each of them. "Good day, gentlemen." He walked out and shut the door behind him.

Fionn now had Lord Claymore's full attention. "My lord, where were you exactly when the horses suddenly spooked?"

"I had just turned onto the high street, not far from the bank.

I noticed you striding across the village green and about to cross the street. Good thing you were there at precisely that moment. I did not see Lady Chloe until it was too late, and then I could not control my team to maneuver around her."

"Did you notice anyone suspicious just before you turned onto the high street? Perhaps someone who looked as though he did not belong."

"Someone with a furtive look in his eyes, you mean?" The viscount shook his head. "I wasn't paying that close attention, and anyway, I would have no idea who did or did not belong in your village. Nor do I know who the troublemakers are. Constable Angel would know this better than I."

"Where were your friends when this incident happened?"

He arched an eyebrow. "You cannot think they were involved. No, I'm sure they were still sleeping. None of them ever stir before noon. Anyway, we stayed up rather late last night. Nothing untoward, I assure you. We were celebrating my birthday. I turned twenty-seven yesterday, hence the lovely phaeton. It was a gift from my mother. She won't be happy to learn it is now destroyed."

Fionn grinned. "Ah, I gather she is formidable and going to give you a hard time about it."

"She will blister me thoroughly," the viscount said with a wry smile. "But I am hoping she will take some pity on me when I tell her how it happened. Some local miscreant thinking to scare the upper-crust invaders from London."

"In truth, this is a quiet village and not the sort of mischief the local boys get into. Not that I would rule it out. But is it possible you have an enemy? Someone you've angered in business, or perhaps in a more personal matter?"

Lord Claymore seemed surprised. "No, certainly not that I am aware."

"What about your friends? Forgive me for asking, but who are the ladies in your company? Are you sure they have not left behind husbands or fathers who are not pleased to learn they are on holiday with you?"

"No, Lady Gemma and Lady Sarah are here with their brother, Lord Hollingsworth. He was the gentleman dressed in blue silk. The other is his cousin, Lord Danson. They were schoolmates of mine at Oxford. Where did you get your education, Major Brennan?"

"Nowhere you would recognize."

Lord Claymore cleared his throat. "Yes, how stupid of me. But you are definitely educated, and your manner is surprisingly refined."

Fionn shrugged. "I pick up things quickly."

"Even so, one does not usually rise to the rank of major on their own merit. Nor does one get schooled in architecture without family backing. I am eager to hear more about this army hospital you are building."

"Perhaps another time, my lord. I will be happy to show you around one afternoon this week. However, I came here today to interrogate you. But it seems I am the one being interrogated."

The viscount laughed. "Sorry, you have piqued my curiosity. I cannot place you in a tidy box, and it puzzles me. I do not like to be puzzled. Nor will Hollingsworth's sisters be pleased when I can give them no information about you. I saw the way they were eyeing you."

"My lord, I have no intention of pursuing either one of them, so you need have no concerns on that score. I know my place, and it is not with either of them. But since we are discussing your friends, have they had any bad encounters recently? Perhaps offended someone here in Moonstone Landing?"

The man grinned. "You disapprove of their loose morals? I will not pretend the young ladies are fresh out of a convent, but they are not so bad."

Fionn arched an eyebrow. "It is not my place to judge."

"Still, you think all my friends are boorish."

"Perhaps you think so as well, since you did not see fit to make introductions. Nor did they wish to be introduced. I gather you dragged them here and they are not enjoying our quieter society."

"Major Brennan, let me ask you a question."

"More interrogation? Go ahead," Fionn said with a nod.

"What brought you to Moonstone Landing?"

He shrugged. "I am an architect for the army. I was tasked with finding a suitable location for the new hospital you claim to be eager to hear more about. That search led me to this part of Cornwall, since the area appeared inadequately served militarily and could do not only with enhancing its medical facilities but also expanding the barracks established here centuries ago. Moonstone Landing itself has a good harbor within easy distance of Plymouth and can easily take on any of the overflow of returning soldiers from that major port."

"So you are here for the duration of the construction?"

Fionn nodded. "To oversee it as well as serve as commanding officer at Fort Arundel. I will stay on until the higher-ups decide to move me elsewhere."

"How well do you know these townspeople?"

"Fairly well, since I have been back and forth here regularly over the course of the last three years. But my promotion to major and placement in charge of the fort is new. I only took over those responsibilities a month ago. This is a nice community, and that sort of malicious mischief rarely takes place. Which leads me back to my earlier question. Are you certain you have not offended anyone who might now have it in for you?"

"Other than our offending every resident in this town?" The viscount shook his head and gave a mirthless chuckle. "I know we have angered them by racing our carriages. But beyond this, I cannot think of anyone who would want to do me or any of my friends harm."

"I'll talk to Constable Angel. He was born and raised here, so he knows these villagers better than anyone. What will you expect him to do if it turns out the culprit is a child?"

The viscount cast him a wry smile. "I am not an ogre, Major

Brennan. I do foolish things even as an adult, such as getting carried away with a new gift and racing it through town. But I was properly admonished for it yesterday and had no intention of defying the warning today. So it would be quite callous of me to hold a child to a higher standard."

"I'm glad you see it this way, my lord." Fionn rose to leave. "Please summon me if you think of something else that might be helpful to this investigation."

"I will." Lord Claymore rose along with him. "Brennan…would you be any relation to Viscount Brennan?"

Fionn regarded him with some surprise. "Did you know him?"

"Not very well. He was a quiet, thoughtful man, and a bit older than myself. Ours was more of a political acquaintance in the halls of Parliament. But I know his nephews and nieces. We travel in the same social circles." Fionn tried to smother his disapproval, but Claymore easily saw through his silence. "You don't like them either, do you?"

"As I've said, it is not my place to judge."

"So? You are related to them?"

"No, my lord." Fionn walked out before the man continued the conversation. Why should any of that lofty lot care who he was? Had Lord Claymore heard Viscount Brennan's odious family disparaging him as a lowborn beggar during one of their elegant dinner parties? Did he now intend to taunt him about it?

That taunt would be the last words out of Lord Claymore's mouth if he dared.

Fionn strode out of the inn, ignoring Claymore's friends, who were now sprawled in their languid poses in the seating area near the entry. As expected, the ladies ogled him and tried to gain his attention, but he merely kept walking down the street to Constable Angel's office, which was just beyond the village green and closer to the harbor.

The residents of Moonstone Landing were not an unruly lot, but as the village expanded, one could not overlook the possibility of thieves, cutpurses, and other unwanted miscreants coming into the area along with the wealthy.

The constable's so-called prison would not hold a hardened criminal. It was comprised of two cells designed to hold drunks or petty thieves. Perhaps Fionn would talk to the Duke of Malvern and Marquess of Burness about expanding the town's prison facilities. He would help with its layout and construction.

He strode into the constabulary office just as Constable Angel was about to walk out. "Glad I caught you," Fionn said. "What do you think happened?"

The man scratched his head. "It wasn't a child's prank. I know all the children here, good and bad. They are all accounted for at the time the dart would have been shot. Same for our usual group of ne'er-do-wells and layabouts. Most were already in their seats imbibing at the Three Lions tavern. No, this smells of an outsider's doing."

"Someone staying at the inn?"

"The Kestrel Inn? Unlikely. It is much too fancy for a common cove to afford. I'll ask around at the local lodging houses and check the nearby woods for sign of a campsite. But don't get me wrong, I haven't ruled out the viscount's friends or other inn guests. Thaddius has promised to write up the list of everyone staying at his inn, although I cannot imagine any of them carrying such a weapon around or ever bothering to get off their vaunted arses to commit this sort of mischief."

Fionn nodded. "They are a lazy lot, aren't they?"

The constable rolled his eyes. "Lazy, insufferable, and generally useless. And they think they are our betters? Ah well. Such is the luck of the draw in life."

"Indeed."

Fionn was glad the constable was going to continue investigating the incident. So was he, but there was something none of them had considered because it seemed too remote a possibility. What if this incident was not about Lord Claymore and his friends?

What if the culprit had meant to harm Chloe?

Chapter Four

T HE FOLLOWING MORNING, as the midday hour approached, Chloe was comfortably ensconced in a shady spot on the terrace with her foot bound, packed in ice, and elevated on a tufted ottoman. She had just taken a sip of her lemonade when Fionn paid her a visit. "Good day," she said, her heart beating a little faster as he strode toward her. "A very hot day, isn't it? The rest of the family is down on the beach, but they should not be gone long."

"Hot as blazes," he muttered in agreement, and settled his large frame in the seat beside hers, inching it closer so that he also sat in full shade. "I might have a swim later to cool down."

She sighed. "I wish I could. That would be lovely, but I am not allowed out of this chair on pain of death."

He chuckled. "It is for your own good. How are you feeling today? Any better? Actually, I'm glad I caught you alone."

"You wanted to be alone with me?" Tingles of excitement ran through her, and her heartbeat quickened further still.

Was he finally realizing she was the only woman who could nourish his lost and wounded soul?

"I need to ask you some questions."

Had he anguished over the possibility of losing her and realized time was fleeting and precious?

Was he going to ask her to marry him?

"About your foot…"

Gad, how could she be so stupid? Yesterday's fall must have left her addled. "What about my foot?"

"I was worried about you, Chloe. Afraid it had gotten worse and you were in pain."

"No, I am feeling much better because of your sound medical advice. How about you? Any aches and pains? Your tumble was just as bad as mine, so do not pretend it wasn't."

He studied her with his soul-piercing eyes and then broke into an appealingly boyish smile. "A few aches, but nothing more. You know I am not going to tell you if anything really hurts."

She laughed. "Why are men such prideful idiots? What if you've suffered a sprain or fracture?"

"Do I look as though I have?" He crossed his heart. "I promise. I haven't."

She eased back. "Good. Care for a lemonade? Or something stronger?"

"Lemonade is fine." He shot her a quelling look when she attempted to rise, for the pitcher was on the table just out of her reach. He easily attended to the task himself and then settled back in the chair beside her. "Chloe, do you mind if I ask you a few personal questions?"

"Personal? Not at all. My life is a dull and completely open book. Not a single juicy secret lurking anywhere. What do you wish to know?"

"Have you had any unpleasant run-ins with anyone recently? Someone angry enough to wish you harm?"

"Me?" She shook her head, the question genuinely surprising her. "No. Is this about the dart they found on Lord Claymore's horse?"

"You heard about that?"

She grinned. "Yes, Constable Angel stopped by last night and told us. Of course, we already knew because one of our grooms happened to be in town on an errand when the news came out and immediately rushed back to report it to Melrose, who then rushed to report it to Cormac, who then told all of us. This all happened shortly after you left us yesterday. We expected you would learn of it the moment you arrived back in town."

"I did. The ostler told me and Dr. Hewitt as soon as we pulled up in his rig."

"The Moonstone Landing gossip brigades are most efficient, don't you think? I suppose this means you refrained from beating the stuffing out of Lord Claymore."

Fionn chuckled. "Yes, he is safe from me for the moment. In truth, he was surprisingly polite when I questioned him. He's going to pay a call on you today."

She shrugged. "He hasn't bothered to come by yet. Perhaps he won't."

"He will. He struck me as a man of his word. As I said, he was unexpectedly polite to me and conveyed sincere concern about you. His friends were insufferable, however. So I am not about to extol his virtues just yet."

"Fionn, why did you ask if I had any enemies? Have you ruled out Lord Claymore being the target of the prank?"

"Not at all. In fact, I expect he was the intended victim. But neither Constable Angel nor I have found a likely culprit. We've ruled out the usual village troublemakers. I know it wasn't any of the men under my command. We've checked all the local lodging houses, and went through the Kestrel Inn's register for likely suspects." He raked a hand through his hair in obvious consternation. "This should have been an easy investigation."

She pursed her lips in thought. "Is it possible you cannot find the person because he never made his presence known in town? Could that dart have been fired from somewhere on the outskirts and then the villain hurried off?"

He nodded. "It seems more and more likely this is exactly what happened. Still, it is a bit of a stretch. Lord Claymore was adamant about not having any enemies. Not that I would take him at his word. Any man in his position would garner the envy of others."

He leaned forward and regarded her in all seriousness. "Any young woman in your position might also find herself envied. Chloe, you will be one of next season's *ton* diamonds. There is no question in my mind. Is it possible others want you out of the way in the hope their daughter will be noticed instead of you?"

"No, it is absurd to think so. Who else from this little patch of England will be having their London come-out? And what makes me so special? There will be at least a dozen debutantes who are stiffer competition. Truly, this incident cannot be about me. But what of you? Is it possible someone wants you out of the way? Perhaps they saw you about to cross the street and intended the runaway phaeton to squash you."

He laughed. "What would be gained by it? I own nothing and have no family."

"Well, you do have family. You just don't know who they are. But what if they know who you are and are afraid you might learn something about your heritage now that you are settling here?"

He groaned. "I am not related to your ghost captain, if this is what you are thinking. Emma and Imogen were just letting their imaginations run wild."

She took a sip of her lemonade while she studied him. "What if they are not wrong? You felt drawn to our cottage. And it was once owned by Captain Arundel."

"Let me put a stop to this right now," he said before gulping down the last of his drink and setting it on the table with obvious annoyance. "Your hero ghost does not strike me as the sort who would ever abandon a child of his."

"What if he did not know of your existence? He was often abroad, sailing around the world and sometimes gone for years. Perhaps he had despicable relatives who harmed your mother and disposed of you. Greedy men like our weasel cousin Willis, the new Earl of Stoke, abound. Well, I suppose our weasel cousin isn't really new anymore, since my father has been gone for many years. But you know how he tried to steal our inheritance. Why is it so far-fetched that someone in your family might have done the same to you?"

He reached over to caress her cheek. "I know you want to believe this romantic story…the long-lost son, finally found again. But it is not so. Someone in Moonstone Landing would have known about it. You know word spreads like a wildfire in this village. Even if I were his son—which I assure you, I am not—he never married my mother. I am still baseborn. This is what I am, and you cannot elevate my standing no matter how strongly you wish it, Chloe."

He must have noticed she was getting upset, so he quickly changed the topic. "Tell me, what have you planned with Ella and Imogen this summer? They've grown so much in the few years since I met them."

She managed a small smile, but remained overset by his words. "I have grown quite a bit as well—haven't you noticed?"

"Every man with breath in him has noticed how lovely you have turned out. The little Killigrew caterpillar has turned into a beautiful butterfly."

She blushed.

In truth, she was not used to being flattered and did not want to hear false words of praise, especially from him. Although being called a caterpillar was hardly gushing praise. Perhaps she was now pretty as a butterfly, but he did not seem to be taken with her at all.

He was concerned for her. Protective of her.

But also…afraid of her?

Dear heaven, he confused her.

She was saved from a response when Melrose appeared. "Lady Chloe, you have a gentleman caller."

Her eyes widened in surprise, and she tried to stifle a giggle, but it came out in an unladylike snort. "A gentleman? Calling on me? Who would… Oh, is it Lord Claymore come with hat in hand to apologize?"

"Yes," the stoic butler said.

She glanced at Fionn, uncertain what to do, since neither Cormac nor Phoebe were here. It was one thing for Fionn to pay a call on her, for the family considered him a friend. But this viscount?

"It is all right, Chloe," he said, reaching for her hand to give it a light squeeze. "I am here and will make certain he behaves."

She nodded. "Show him out here, Melrose."

Fionn rose to bring over another chair and place it on the other side of her.

She cast him a wicked grin. "No, leave it in the sun. I don't want to make him too comfortable."

"He is a viscount. He'll kick me out of my shady spot and leave me to swelter in the sun." He placed the spare chair next to hers, chuckling and obviously amused by her suggestion. She supposed it did not matter, since it meant Fionn would remain beside her, too.

Fionn was already standing to greet the viscount when he strode onto the terrace. "My lord."

"Good to see you again, Major Brennan." Lord Claymore turned to Chloe, studying her as she remained seated in her chair. "And by the unhappy state of your elevated foot, I gather you must be Lady Chloe?"

Chloe held out her hand to him.

He was not a bad-looking man, but she was not quite ready to forgive him for racing his phaeton about the village. "Yes, I would like to say it is a pleasure to meet you, but considering the circumstances…"

"Quite understandable. I hope in time your opinion of me will improve and we shall become good friends. It is important to me, since I am planning on building a house for myself in the area."

"You are?" This obviously surprised Fionn as well, for his lips were pinched and those soul-piercing eyes of his were no longer softly gleaming but hard and angry. Cold, gray steel. She would not like to be on the receiving end of that look.

The viscount nodded, his attention now solely on her. "This village is one of England's hidden gems…as are you, if you will forgive my boldness. I was enchanted by the place the moment I arrived."

"Your friends do not seem nearly as enamored of Moonstone Landing as you are," Fionn intoned.

The viscount shrugged. "They enjoy livelier society and are eager to return to Bath or Brighton."

"As most people would," Chloe said. "We move at a much slower pace here. Our parties and our way of life are far more casual. Your set would call us dull. Have you settled on a property yet?"

"No, I have not started looking. But I have an appointment scheduled with your local land agent for tomorrow. Of course, I hope he has a decent carriage to drive me from place to place, or I shall have to hire a conveyance for the day, since my lovely phaeton is now smashed to pieces."

Chloe covered her mouth with her hand and pretended to cough over her laughter. "Yes, what a shame."

He had the good grace to take full blame for the loss. "I think you are dancing a jig in your head and quietly laughing at my abject misery, Lady Chloe. If it will make you feel any better, I shall have a blistering set-down from my own mother as well when she learns of the incident. Yes, even though I am a grown man and a viscount, that dowager dragon shall never allow me to get too full of myself."

He said it with a gleam of amusement, so she suspected he had a good relationship with his mother. That was a point in his favor. The woman really could not be all that much of a dragon because he spoke of her with obvious affection. Likely, she had a hearty spirit and a sensible head on her shoulders.

That his mother was not a featherbrain was another point in his favor.

But Chloe was not going to rush to judgment. She had only just met this viscount and meant to take her time assessing him.

Still, he was nice looking.

He had dark blond hair and intelligent blue eyes. Also, he appeared to have a sense of humor. But he needed a little more admonishment before she was ready to forgive him. "We look out for each other here in Moonstone Landing. This is why your tearing up our roads was not appreciated."

"I shall endeavor to make amends to the townspeople."

"And will your friends do the same?"

He arched an eyebrow. "They are not children and will do as they wish. In all likelihood, they will leave here by the end of the week."

"And take you along with them?"

"No, Lady Chloe. I will not be following them, since I am serious about my plans to settle here. I hope to stay through the summer."

"Ah, yes. Your house search."

"It is not merely a house search. My reasons are a bit too complicated to discuss here and now, but I hope you understand my plans are now meant to include you."

It took her a moment for the import of his comment to sink in. "Me? What do you want with me beyond apologizing profusely for almost killing me?"

"I should think it is obvious. Yes, a little more groveling may be warranted on my part, but now that I have seen you up close…are you surprised I shall be asking your brothers-in-law for permission to seek a closer acquaintance? Is anyone currently courting you?"

She knocked over the bag of ice on her ankle as she attempted to leap to her feet, and immediately yelped as a blinding pain shot up her leg. "Save yourself the bother of asking for their permission. You may ask me directly, and I shall refuse you. How dare you make such a bold comment?"

Was the man demented? Courtship? They had hardly been in each other's company more than a few minutes.

Fionn's arms immediately went around her as she was about

to topple. "Chloe!"

He was blazing mad, probably at her because she was lambasting the viscount.

Obviously, he was not upset by the viscount's glib remarks, since he wanted nothing to do with her in a romantic way.

This upset her all the more.

"Sit down," Fionn said in a gentler tone.

"Did you hear what he said to me? If you do not let me punch him, then will you?" She curled her hands into fists and glared at the viscount.

"I am not going to hit him, nor are you, so unclench your fists and calm down. Why are you surprised he is infatuated with you? Did I not tell you this would happen once you were introduced into Society?"

"But I am not in London yet."

"Well, it appears London has come to you." But then he rounded on the viscount. "You have no right to jest with Lady Chloe on such a serious matter. She is not here for your amusement. I assure you that if you ever hurt her, you will be answering to me."

The viscount was not quite as big as Fionn, nor was he as muscled, but he was no fragile lily either. "Whom I choose to court is none of your business, Major Brennan."

"It is my business if we are speaking of Lady Chloe. You will find Malvern and Burness equally as adamant about this. Had Burness been present, he would not have been as polite in warning you. Indeed, you would have been picking your teeth off the floor. He may only have one arm, but his punch still packs a wallop."

Lord Claymore held up his hands in a sign of surrender. "Seems the rules of engagement are quite different here than in London. Any other debutante would have had her claws dug into me so fast and deep, I would have bled to death trying to disengage them."

"Lady Chloe does not have claws. She has a good and caring

heart, so you had better tread carefully."

"So be it." He turned to Chloe. "I shall bide my time and allow you to get to know me better before I declare for you again. But make no mistake, my intentions are honorable. You will come to know I do not jest on a matter as important as finding myself a suitable wife."

She glared at him. "You have not started off very well, Lord Claymore. If you wish for my opinion, you have a lot of ground to make up before you are even back to square one in my regard."

He cast her a wry smile. "My mother will like you immensely."

She arched an eyebrow. "Are you sure you want two dragons in your household?"

"Yes, Lady Chloe…especially if one of them is you." He held up his hands again. "Do not blister me for the comment. I know quality when I see it, and I am not going to pretend you are just like all the other eager debutantes hunting for a title when you are obviously someone special."

"All you have seen of me so far is my sprained foot." She glowered at him. "I do not want to hear another word about this from you."

Fortunately, Cormac and Phoebe returned from the beach to relieve her of the chore of entertaining the viscount. He was not a horrible man by any means, but he was unacceptably rash in deciding to court her and far too glib about it.

Besides, how could he be interested in her when she was bordering on rude to him?

He certainly deserved a set-down.

That he was taking it like a gentleman also made her uncomfortable. She did not want him around, even if on paper he seemed an excellent catch.

Perhaps what upset her most was Fionn's taking the viscount's courtship declaration in stride.

Why was he not in a blinding, jealous rage?

Chapter Five

FIONN COULD NOT see straight for the fire blazing behind his eyes.

Lord Claymore intended to court Chloe.

He knew someone would come along to claim this beautiful girl, but he hadn't expected it to happen so soon or that the man would be so clearly a good fit for her. Of course, the viscount had leaped a little too quickly in declaring his intention to court Chloe. But as he'd just said, he had been in search of a wife for several years now. It was not all that shocking the viscount should know what he wanted the moment he spotted Chloe.

Why was Chloe so angry? Claymore was no prideful fool. If anything, he was a wealthy lord who seemed the sort to give her a real love marriage.

As for Fionn, he wanted to rip the man apart with his bare hands.

The thought of someone else touching Chloe.

Holding Chloe.

It was all he could do to keep his heart from tearing to pieces before her very eyes.

"Your family is back and I am needed at the barracks," he said, his body in a hot roil. "You look better, Chloe."

"Must you go?" She took hold of his hand.

He eased out of her grasp. "Yes, you know I have no place

here."

They spoke quietly, having a moment to do so now that the viscount had been introduced to Cormac and Phoebe and was busy conversing with them. Cormac's brother and his wife also came up from the beach with their two girls, and all of them now surrounded the viscount.

But Chloe's attention remained on Fionn. "You *always* have a place with us. Do you think that man will ever hold a candle to you?"

The comment was ridiculous and made him laugh, for it was so like Chloe to think with her heart and never her head.

He truly loved that kind heart of hers. How could he fault the viscount for wanting to marry her?

Did he not wish to do the same?

"Goodbye, Chloe." Oh, how he ached to kiss her, to touch his lips to her soft cheek and have the right to do this every day of his life.

He had to leave before this sweet girl burst into tears over him. When he turned once more to go, she grabbed his hand again. "You owe me a waltz. Do not forget your promise."

"I won't." Did she not understand he lived for every moment he could touch her? "You had better keep that foot rested so you don't look like a frog hopping to a waltz."

"The dance is still a month away. I'll be fine by then."

"Not if you fail to give your injury sufficient time to heal." He glanced at his own lame leg. "I know from experience."

"Join us for supper," Cormac said before he could make it off the terrace.

There was an undertone of command in that request. Fionn knew he had to accept the invitation even though every moment in Chloe's presence would now be torture for him.

Well, when was it not?

He shook his head. "Thank you, Lord Burness. I shall return later."

He strode out before any other requests were made of him.

His leg felt stiff, and he now limped noticeably with every stride. He had taken a hard fall when saving Chloe and now felt the aches deep in his muscle and into his bone.

Although he strode out, he did not immediately return to town. He was curious about what Imogen had said to him the other day. Was his slight resemblance to the Moonstone Cottage ghost significant? After all, he had felt drawn to the sea captain for some reason. Was it possible he did have a connection to the man?

It would explain why he felt compelled to squander his entire bequest on a year's rental.

He rode over to the cottage.

"Major Brennan, we did not expect to see you today," Mr. Hawke, the cottage's groundskeeper, said, running forward to take his horse as he dismounted. "My wife hasn't prepared any meals for—"

"I did not mean to impose, Mr. Hawke. I won't be staying long. Just hold on to Sophocles for me." Fionn handed over the reins of his bay gelding. The horse was standard army issue, bred for strength and durability. Nor did Sophocles actually belong to him. Horse and rider were merely assigned to each other.

In time, he hoped to save enough of his wages to purchase him outright. He had nothing of his own, not a blessed thing.

He walked into the cottage and emitted a long, shattered breath.

It was a beautiful place. He would never earn enough in two lifetimes to afford purchasing it.

The viscount, however, could pay for it out of his pocket change.

Fionn emitted another breath, suddenly finding his situation quite hopeless. He had no family and no assets other than the small inheritance he had just blown on letting this cottage for the year.

How could he ever declare himself to Chloe?

He climbed the stairs and entered the large bedroom that

would be his for the coming year. The portrait of Captain Arundel was hanging where it always had been, on the inner wall. He came to stand before it and stared into the captain's eyes. "Are we related?"

Of course, the portrait did not answer him.

He shook his head and left.

The day was hot, and the stifling breeze now felt damp as he rode back into town. Constable Angel waved to him from across the street and hurried toward him as he was about to enter the fort and climb the steps to his office.

The stone fortification erected sometime in the thirteenth century was situated near the harbor and overlooked it. The massive building was like a rabbit warren, with lots of passageways shooting off in every direction and leading one to the general sleeping quarters, kitchen, larder, offices, map room, dining hall, or armory.

The fortress was ancient but the stone walls kept the place cool at night, which was a blessing in the summer. The enormous hearths to be found in almost every room spread heat throughout the place in winter.

His office was of decent size, as were the meeting room and map room just off it. The officers' quarters were just beyond the map room. His was largest, since he was commanding officer, but even his quarters were still too small for more than one person to comfortably occupy.

He waited for Constable Angel to reach his side. "Anything new to report, Mr. Angel?"

"Yes, Major Brennan. We've found the culprit."

Fionn's heart raced with anticipation. "Who is it?"

"An outsider who claims to know you."

The comment genuinely startled Fionn. "Are you holding him in custody?"

The constable nodded. "Although I'm not sure how long my cell will hold one such as him. He is a cagey weasel and doubtless capable of escaping even the strongest prisons."

A few old friends from Fionn's past came to mind. They had all been an unsavory lot, living off the streets and taking to a life of petty crime to support themselves. But what would a London street urchin be doing here? Why toss a dart at a viscount's horse?

He raked a hand through his hair in consternation.

What profit was there in this sort of mischief? And why would any culprit follow a viscount and his friends all the way from London to here? Merely to pick their pockets as a crowd gathered?

Was this why the culprit shot a dart at the viscount's horse? Cause a commotion and then make his way through a gathering crowd?

It seemed too elaborate a plan and needlessly reckless. And why here? Pickings would be far more profitable anywhere else.

The notion seemed absurd, but many of the street urchins he had come to know were not the brightest and could not see beyond their noses to understand the consequences of their actions. Whatever tactics worked in busy London would not work here.

First of all, the locals would spot the outsider immediately. Second, the locals themselves were not wealthy and knew how to secure their coins inside their clothing. Even the top-lofties who showed off their wealth with careless abandon took care with their coins. In any event, none of them had been on the street or even awake when the incident occurred.

He followed the constable to his office.

"Well, I'll be demmed," the prisoner said, recognizing Fionn instantly. "Ye've done all right for yerself, haven't ye? *Major Brennan.* I could hardly believe m'own ears when I heard 'em call ye that."

Blessed saints.

Were his eyes deceiving him?

"How are you still alive, Ducky? You were always a terrible pickpocket. I was sure they would hang you before you were old enough to grow whiskers," Fionn said, his heart in a roil as his past life now confronted him.

"I survived. But I wouldn't have taken the job had I known ye was the target. We all thought ye was dead in the war. Good to find ye very much alive."

Fionn exchanged a glance with Constable Angel before returning his attention to Ducky. As a boy, the fellow had been a likeable dimwit. Highly unprincipled, and yet always willing to share his ill-gotten gains with Fionn. "Why was I the intended victim? Who would want to be rid of me?"

"Guv, that's what I was suddenly thinking when I realized it was ye that cove had me try to kill. Sorry about the pretty lady. I didn't see her walking across the high street until it was too late. Good thing ye're quick as ever. Then that fancy gent went tumbling into the harbor, and I thought I might have killed him, too."

"Ducky, you're an idiot. Good thing you failed on all counts. But that does not absolve you from your attempted crime."

"Ooh, listen to all 'em fancy words. Ye always was smarter than the lot of us."

"Who paid you to kill me?"

"One of 'em relatives of Viscount Brennan. Not the eldest nephew who took over as the viscount after the old man passed. One of the other younger ones, a prune-faced fellow with a snooty look, as though he'd just sucked on lemons. Who is he to look down on me as though I'm low and vile when he's the one plotting murder?"

"Randolph," Fionn muttered, but he knew they all had to be in on it. The Right Honorable Randolph Brennan had never had an independent thought in his life.

"That's the one. A sniveling cove, he was. But my wits must have fled, 'cause I never put it together that you were the Major Brennan they was after. Only once I saw ye carrying the young lady to safety did I take a closer look and realize ye were their quarry. So, now I'm thinking they have something to hide from ye, and they're worried as hell ye'll find out what it is and come after them."

Constable Angel regarded him thoughtfully. "Do you have any idea what he is talking about?"

Fionn shook his head. "None whatsoever." But he was curious to find out. "Ducky, I cannot leave my post. I have responsibilities, a hospital about to start construction, and I am also in charge of the regimental outpost here."

"Caw! We always knew ye'd make something of yerself. Most of us is dead or rotting in prison, but ye…ye've survived it all. We're proud of ye, Guv." The man's beady eyes brightened. "What are ye proposing?"

"Assuming Constable Angel permits your release, I propose you return to London and find out what the Brennans are so afraid for me to discover."

"And what will ye give me in exchange?"

"Your life back, for what you did is a hanging offense. You almost killed a viscount and the daughter of an earl. I'll also provide an honest job for you, if you return with information that proves true. However, about that job…if you so much as steal a spoon, I shall have you shot at dawn."

"Fair enough, Guv." Ducky reached out a dirty hand for Fionn to shake. "Muskrat and Squirrel are still on the streets. I'll enlist their help. Will ye promise jobs for 'em, too?"

"Yes," Fionn said, for they were part of his motley band of urchin thieves and he did not have the heart to let them down. "Same terms."

"Ye have yerself a deal. They'll be most appreciative." Ducky laughed. "See, I know some of 'em big words. Life on the street is hard, and to tell ye the truth, we're all weary of it."

Fionn turned to Constable Angel. "Will you agree to set him free? I know it is asking a lot of you, but…"

"Blister it, how can I? As constable, it is my duty to see him properly tried and punished."

Fionn cleared his throat. "It would not be your fault if he escaped."

"Oh," the constable said with a groan. "I'll be done for if word gets out. All right. For you, Major Brennan. I'll turn my back as the wretch breaks out." He cast Ducky a stern look. "Do you think you can do it on your own? I cannot lift a finger to help you."

"Course I can. Ye needn't bother to do a thing. I'll be off right after dark." Ducky turned back to Fionn, his dirty hand still outstretched. "Are we all right, Guv?"

Fionn shook the little weasel's hand. "Do not betray my trust in you, Ducky."

"Never, Guv. Ye did right by us and stayed loyal. We owe ye no less."

Guv was the name he used to be called in the days before Viscount Brennan came along and rescued him. It was short for Governor, for even at his young age he had shown leadership qualities. The street urchins used to follow him despite his never wanting to lead them. But they, including himself, had all been very young and in need of protection.

He was tallest and strongest, and probably smartest. So, he'd taken it upon himself to protect them as best he could.

Even once under Viscount Brennan's care, he took time to send them old clothes and whatever scraps of food the scullery maids were about to toss out. It was far from perfect, but for those who had nothing, it was a gift from heaven.

"Well, I suppose that solves this investigation," Fionn muttered, now heading back to the fort with the constable at his side.

They had yet to cross the street before they heard a clanging sound from Ducky's cell. In the next moment, they saw Ducky take off like a shot out of town. Indeed, he was out of sight in the blink of an eye.

He had managed to disappear so adeptly that Fionn suddenly wondered if the rogue had purposely allowed himself to be caught. While they questioned him, the little weasel also got the chance to see him up close and decide whether he wanted to shove a knife into Fionn's ribs or assist him.

Good thing he had decided to assist.

But what could the Brennan family possibly want to hide from him?

Constable Angel asked him the same question.

"Truly, I have no idea."

"Bother it," the constable muttered. "He said he would wait until dark to escape."

Fionn sighed. "I know, but he isn't too good at keeping to his word. Probably eager to get started now that he knows I was their target."

Yes, Ducky's word was a loose thing. Sometimes given and held to, but not usually. However, Fionn knew all his former friends would never turn on him. Nor would they ever renege on a promise to keep their sticky hands inside their pockets and not steal from anyone in Moonstone Landing.

While the constable pretended to chase after Ducky, Fionn returned to his office to finalize preparations for the start of construction.

He worked for several hours, and after a short respite for a quick meal, returned to his plans and sketches. The construction supplies had also been arriving over the course of the past week, including the needed supply of nails and beams.

He strode into the courtyard to help unload several wagons piled full of materials as they drew up. "Stack those beams in the stable."

He had decided to use the fort's stable as a storage ware-house, and weeks ago had made arrangements with Thaddius Angel, owner of the Kestrel Inn, to lodge the army horses in the inn's stable under the care of their ostler. Mr. Matchett was an unmitigated snoop, but he knew how to handle horses, and Fionn knew they would be in the best care.

The men under his charge began hauling the beams into the cleared-out structure. Fionn soon joined in the effort.

An officer in his position was not required to do more than supervise, but he enjoyed the physical effort, and his men worked better when they saw him put his shoulder to the heavy lifting along with them.

Now that the needed materials were arriving, he was eager for the actual work to commence.

After a few hours of labor, he returned to his quarters and hastily washed up, for he was due to return to Westgate Hall by early evening. From his open window, he could hear one of his sergeants drilling the men to keep them from remaining idle now that the unloading of the wagons was completed.

The day had grown hotter and the wind was nonexistent.

He frowned, not liking that his men were still in full sun and there was not so much as the gasp of a breeze around to grant them respite. He needed these soldiers fit for tomorrow and had no intention of allowing his subordinate officers to exhaust them. He understood that boredom often led to short tempers, and he did not want his men fighting over nothing.

But having them march in this heat was no answer.

He hurried back downstairs and stepped into the courtyard. "Sergeant Ames, take the men down to the beach for a swim."

"Yes, sir." The sergeant gave a deft salute. "Right, you scurvy knaves! You heard the major."

The men let out a cheer and moved as fast as Ducky had when disappearing from town.

Ames was a good man and managed to keep the men in order as they stowed their weapons and then trotted in an organized column down to the beach.

Having no desire to study their naked arses, Fionn retrieved Sophocles and rode out of town at a steady lope. He was too early for the supper invitation, but one of the things he liked most about Moonstone Landing was all its hidden coves. Dozens were tucked away along the coast and most were sheltered by rock formations that allowed for privacy.

Even the fort had its own private cove where the soldiers could swim without getting gawked at by the villagers. Not that any of his men would care, especially if ladies were doing the gawking.

All it took were a few large rocks to separate the fort's beach from the rest of the natural harbor. This was how the entire stretch of shoreline had also formed, soft sand beaches with overlooking cliffs and natural rock outcroppings that reached out like gentle hands toward the sea.

Everyone owning a manor house along the coast also got their stretch of private beach.

He rode to one of the more isolated spots and settled his large frame upon one of the flatter rocks in the outcropping. Trees dangled precariously overhead to cast shade upon him as he looked out over the glistening water.

A light breeze stirred the waves so that they formed white, foamy crests.

It was quite a sight, one he never thought to see while struggling to survive in the filthy streets of London. He closed his eyes and listened to those waves gently breaking against the rocks and lapping the sandy shore.

All was quiet save for the occasional caw of a gull or kestrel circling over the cove in search of fish for their supper.

He liked the solitude and the silence. It allowed him time to think.

Mostly of Chloe, because his brain could not seem to keep her out of his thoughts.

He also wondered what would happen between her and Lord Claymore. So far, she seemed to be resisting his attentions. Not that it signified anything, for she had only met the viscount today.

And nothing would change his own circumstances. No matter how elegant he might look in his uniform or how proper his demeanor, he was still a baseborn pauper.

Which made the news Ducky had related all the more confusing.

Viscount Brennan had died several years ago, so why were his heirs now trying to harm him?

Chapter Six

"CHLOE, WHAT ARE you doing up here?" Fionn asked, surprised to encounter her in his bedchamber at Moonstone Cottage. Several days had passed since his moving into the place, and a full week since the incident with Lord Claymore's runaway phaeton.

"I'm sorry. I did not expect you to be here. I thought your duties were taking up all your time."

"They are." He had looked in on Chloe the day following the incident, and then returned later in the evening to dine with her and her family. But ever since then, he had gone out of his way to avoid her, hoping absence might diminish his longing for her.

Unfortunately, that had not gone according to plan.

First of all, it seemed his heart would not allow it.

In addition, Dr. Hewitt had taken it upon himself to stop by his office every day to report on her improvement. His afternoons now consisted of staring distractedly out of his office window in anticipation of the doctor's appearance.

He craved every bit of news about Chloe, which was how he learned Lord Claymore had taken to visiting Chloe every day.

In fact, he knew everything about Claymore's daily movements. Everyone in the village, from Mrs. Halsey to Thaddius Angel to Mr. Bedwell, and a host of others, deemed it their mission in life to report the man's slightest sneeze to him.

"Are you going to let the viscount steal our Lady Chloe from you?" Mrs. Halsey had admonished him only yesterday while he was in the tea shop for a slice of her apricot pie.

Why did everyone believe he was in competition for Chloe's heart?

He wasn't. He could never be.

What was she doing here at Moonstone Cottage?

He stared at her, his body on fire as he took in her appearance. She stood by the bedchamber's small balcony, drenched in a circle of light, as though a flame-haired angel descended from heaven.

Her gown was of plain muslin and her hair was drawn back in a simple bun at the nape of her slender neck. However, there was no mistaking her elegance.

"I'm truly sorry, Fionn. I have no business being here. I thought it would be harmless…and I did not expect you back so soon."

He had just returned from a quick trip into town and brought two of his adjutants along with him. Those men were now downstairs preparing the final touches to the study, which was to be used by him as an architect's workroom.

It was still early morning, far too early for someone as genteel as Chloe to be up and about. He had not expected to find her in his bedchamber, looking so lost and forlorn as she gazed out across the shimmering waters of the cove.

Well, it was really the ghostly sea captain's bedchamber, and everyone still referred to it as that.

She cast him a hesitant smile and turned to leave. "I had better go. It was nice to see you, Fionn. Even if only for this brief moment."

"I would allow you to stay for as long as you wished, but my men are downstairs and it would hardly look proper." His eyebrow shot up to emphasize his concern.

Not for his sake, but for hers. To be caught alone with a gentleman in his bedchamber would ruin her reputation. He could never allow that to happen, especially now that she was being seriously courted by Lord Claymore. The man had been true to his declaration, remaining in Moonstone Landing to search for a suitable property and at the same time pursue Chloe.

Unfortunately, his friends had decided to remain with him. Fionn was not thrilled about that. He did not want Chloe getting too friendly with that lot, for the ladies—and he used the term loosely—had few morals and would be a bad influence.

"I know. It is quite improper." A light pink blush stained her cheeks. "I meant no harm. But this place calls to me as much as it calls to you. I thought you were gone for the day…and I only wanted to take a quick look around now that I am on my feet again."

"Then do so," he said, taking light hold of her hand. "It is not fair of me to rush you out. Stay as long as you need. You have as much right to be here as I do. More right, since you own the place. But what are you doing in this bedchamber particularly?"

She cast him a wry smile. "I wanted to have a final look at what I hope will eventually be my bedchamber. I long for it to be mine. But I can see you have already moved in, and it will be yours for the coming year. I meant to have a final walk through some days ago, but…" She glanced at her now-healed ankle. "Circumstances prevented it."

They stood together in silence, he still holding her hand because he simply could not let go of her.

She sighed and continued. "I have always thought this to be the most beautiful room in the cottage. The house was built for Captain Arundel, to his detailed specifications. Perhaps he had some architectural training as well?"

Fionn arched an eyebrow. "Any similarity between him and me is pure coincidence."

"I don't know. You were quite heroic the other day. And Captain Arundel is the village's very own renowned hero. Brioc Taran Arundel is his full name." She emitted a soft breath. "I came here to ask Brioc not to harm you."

Fionn laughed. "He's a ghost. Hardly likely to do me harm."

"Do not dismiss him or you will anger him," Chloe warned, but she was smiling, so he doubted there was much to fear. She had told him the story about the captain who had become a local legend after saving the children of Moonstone Landing from a shipwreck during one of the most violent storms the quaint village had ever seen.

He shrugged. "I am not afraid of ghosts."

Starvation.

Imprisonment.

Freezing to death.

Those had been his childhood worries. Ghosts were about as frightening to him as a picnic in the park.

She laughed. "That is because you have never encountered one. But I'm sure you will meet Captain Arundel and my Aunt Hen soon. They are inseparable, you know."

The sea captain had managed to rescue all of the children off the damaged sloop before getting hit on the head by a cracked mast and falling to his watery grave. After that, Chloe's aunt had acquired the beautiful home and bequeathed it to her nieces when she passed away.

Chloe was one of those nieces, the youngest and only one as yet unmarried.

Ever the romantic, she insisted her aunt and the sea captain had fallen deeply in love and their hearts were now bound together for eternity. Fionn did not want to believe such a thing was possible. He wasn't a cynic so much as desperately in love with Chloe and struggling to keep that fact a secret even from himself.

Why did she have to torment him by coming up here now? And why allow himself to hope for the impossible? He and Chloe were not the sea captain and her aunt.

He did not even believe in eternal love… Well, perhaps he did with Chloe. She was in his blood and in his soul. In the very air he breathed. In every beat of his heart.

How long before she accepted Lord Claymore's proposal? He wanted to hate the viscount, but he could not. The man was a decent fellow and not at all condescending.

"Take all the time you need in here," he said, his heart in palpitations as they continued to stand side by side on the bedchamber's small balcony, their arms almost touching. "I shall leave you to your thoughts."

"No, please don't go. Stay just a moment longer. There can be no harm in it."

He gave a gruff laugh.

He really had to go before he did the unthinkable. That bed was the perfect size for them.

Not to mention, Chloe was irresistible.

The sun struck her features in such a way that her eyes sparkled a particularly bright green and her hair was soft and molten.

He ached to pull those pins out of her hair and allow it to tumble around her shoulders, to slip the gown off her luscious body and delve… No, that thought needed to remain buried.

She turned away a moment to peer out the window, her gaze resting on the magnificent cottage garden and beyond to the shimmering expanse of sea, lost in her thoughts and unaware of his own. "This was the captain's bedchamber first. Then it became my Aunt Henleigh's chamber. After she died, we moved in and my sister Hen took it over," she said, her manner wistful. "She was the eldest, so by right the largest bedchamber went to her. Then she married and moved out, so Phoebe took it over. When she married, they realized I could not be left to live here alone. I was too young."

"It was the right decision. You were only fifteen. Not even of marriageable age. But you are of an age to marry now." Even if by some miracle Lord Claymore did not win her hand, it was only a matter of time before someone else came along and took her from him forever.

Fionn had no doubt she would be lost to him before the Season was even fully underway. Who would not want this beautiful girl?

She groaned lightly. "I dread being shoved onto the Marriage Mart. I cannot think of myself as living anywhere but in Moonstone Landing beside my sisters. Indeed, I would be happiest remaining a spinster so I can live out my days here."

"Has Lord Claymore not stolen your heart yet?"

"Do not mention him. You will only make me cry."

He inhaled sharply. "Chloe, has he said something…done something…?"

"No, nothing like that. He isn't so bad." She shook her head and laughed. "He's all right, just not for me."

"Too low a title? How about an earl? Your sisters have already claimed a marquess and a duke."

"There is more than one duke out there. Although Hen did claim the best one in the Duke of Malvern. And the Marquess of Burness turned out all right, despite his wicked reputation. He and Phoebe are so much in love."

"And you wish this for yourself?"

She nodded. "I do, but I doubt I will find this deep, abiding love in London. I see my sisters when they are around their husbands, and it is as though they cannot breathe for the joy of being with them. It is the same for their husbands with them. I think this is what Aunt Hen felt for her sea captain."

"And he for her." He had been looking at her as she spoke, but now turned to peer out across the scenic cove and its sparkling waters. "Your family will never force you to do anything you do not wish to do."

"I know. Well, I am not going to think about anything beyond this summer. Cormac's nieces are here, and we are going to have a lovely time. You are welcome to stop by whenever you wish. It can get lonely out here all on your own."

"You've kept Mr. and Mrs. Hawke on to look after the place. I won't be on my own. Even if I were, being alone has never bothered me. I have been on my own since the day I was born."

She nodded. "Until your benefactor took you in."

"He was the kindest man alive, but the members of his family are all repulsive creatures. They had yet to seal the lid on his coffin before tossing all my possessions out of his home and warning me never to return."

"Major Brennan," one of his aides called out, his footsteps clomping on the stairs. "Where shall we set up the maps?"

"I'll take care of it, Sergeant Ames. Just leave everything in the study for now."

A pretty blush stained Chloe's cheeks as his aide strode in.

"Oh, forgive me," the man said, now flustered. "I did not realize you had company."

Fionn introduced the sergeant to her. "This is Lady Chloe's home. She and her sisters own it. Lady Chloe, take whatever you need from here."

She shook her head. "I only came for one last nostalgic look at the house before you occupy it. Well, I was late in attending to it. But I'm here now, and isn't the view beautiful, Sergeant Ames?"

His sergeant nodded. "Indeed, my lady."

"Well, if you are done," Fionn said gently, "I'll escort you back to Westgate Hall."

She looked so pained, it tugged at his heart.

"I'll see myself back. It is a much shorter walk if I go along the beach. The tide is only now starting to come in. I ought to be safe enough."

He held out his arm. "Let me escort you."

"Afraid I will be washed out to sea?"

"Something like that," he said, returning her smile with one of his own. "Those waves can be treacherous."

"I won't go near them. I can hop over the rocks between the two properties."

"All the more reason to accompany you. That ankle of yours is hardly healed. You might slip and damage it again."

She sighed and took his arm. "Very well, I shall play the damsel in distress, since I always enjoy your company. You can tell me about your plans for the hospital you are building by the harbor."

They paused downstairs, and he showed her some of the architectural drawings.

"How clever," she remarked. "You've arranged the design in a U-shape with a central courtyard and all of it overlooking the water."

"We'll have three operating rooms once the hospital is built. We expect to receive an overflow of the more severely wounded soldiers whenever the hospitals in Plymouth and Bournemouth cannot handle them. Moonstone Landing's port requires very little expansion to accommodate our navy frigates."

"Have you thought about what to plant in your courtyard? Hen has established a society for the beautification of our local area. Phoebe and I were her first members, of course," she said with a mirthful chuckle. "Now most of the women in the village have joined. But this is what we do, come up with ideas to improve the aspect of every building, and we can certainly do the same for your hospital."

He folded his arms across his chest and listened to her go on about her ideas, not only because he loved the lilt of her voice, but because she was coming up with some excellent suggestions.

"Did you know that plants have healing properties? And that various scents can be quite soothing. Lavender and lemon, for example. Would you allow us to present you with ideas for your courtyard plants?"

He had not considered adding anything there, just leaving it as a grassy area with some benches. He was on a tight budget, and the hospital's interior was where he needed to spend the army funding. The operating rooms, supplies, beds. Trained staff. None of these came cheap, and he could not spare anything for flowers.

He stopped Chloe when she started talking about scented soaps. "Lye soap is army regulation. We are not running a club for London's elite. No Farthingale scented soaps or oils for us. It is simply not in the budget."

"But this is something our ladies' society can provide," she said with appealing passion. "It won't cost the army so much as a shilling. What is wrong with allowing us to donate these little extras? Flowers, soaps, and whatever else can make these wounded soldiers a little more comfortable. Extra blankets in winter. A few extra vegetables or meat for their soups."

Her eyes were now sparkling.

He hated to dampen her enthusiasm, but the army did not operate this way. Every change from their routine had to be approved by his higher-ups. "Come on, let me walk you back to Westgate Hall and we'll talk about it."

She sighed. "Don't you like any of my ideas?"

"I like them all."

"Then what is the problem?"

"It took years to get these hospital plans approved and now underway. I cannot delay this project because you are proposing changes to the courtyard. The entire tract of land must be leveled and the building's foundation needs to be poured and set before the cold weather comes on."

"So you will not allow us to help in any way?"

"I will listen to all your ideas once the hospital is built. But I am not changing a single brick or we'll be waiting another three years for construction to begin."

She nodded. "All right. But let us work within the scope of your designs. Why should the army care what we propose if we are footing the cost?"

"They shouldn't, but they will. Perhaps it is nonsensical, but it is the army's way."

They walked out of the house together and took the stairs down to the beach. The tide was already coming in and had flooded the sandy walkway between Moonstone Cottage and Westgate Hall. They would have to climb over the rocks separating their beaches.

It was not a particularly difficult climb, but Chloe had just recovered from a sprained ankle, and it still had to be tender. Not to mention her ribs might still be sore as well. This meant he needed to stay close and possibly hold on to her to make certain she did not aggravate her injuries or take a spill.

This would require putting his hands on her.

She sensed his reluctance and gazed up at him with pitying eyes. "Are you worried you will not make it over those rocks with your damaged leg?"

He laughed, the sound carrying on the wind and mingling with the whoosh and crash of waves now hitting those rocks. "No, I was worried about you. My leg is fine."

"I am wearing my sturdy walking boots and just need to hold on to the hem of my gown so as not to trip over it as I climb. Close your eyes, Fionn, if the sight of my legs offends you."

"Nothing about you offends me...that's what I'm worried about."

She cast him a soft smile. "That's the nicest thing I've heard you say to me in ages."

He raked a hand through his windblown hair. "You shouldn't be climbing, and I shouldn't be aiding you. What if you get hurt?"

"You will protect me, won't you?"

"Of course, but..." He shook his head and started up the rocks before the tide covered them as well. "Here, give me your hand. I'll pull you over."

He tried not to stare as she raised her gown and secured it to her belt. This left her shapely legs exposed to her knees. She took his offered hand and scampered up beside him. They repeated this routine twice more, he climbing further up and then reaching down to assist her, until they reached the top.

Now it was a matter of helping her down the other side, a trickier undertaking because the rocks were quite wet and slippery as waves began to crash closer around them. "Wait. Let me get a foothold, and then I'll help you climb down to me."

Except climbing down involved not quite the same logistics.

He was now required to stand beneath Chloe, which gave

him an unimpeded view of her bare legs. Her shapely derriere was outlined beneath the muslin fabric of her gown and practically in his face as she slowly moved downward with his assistance to secure her footholds.

One wave suddenly crashed too close, and she lost her footing.

"Bollocks, Chloe. I told you this was a bad idea," he muttered as she slid down the length of his body.

She held on to him for an aching eternity, her arms wrapped around his neck and her divine bosom flattened against his chest, before steadying herself and turning to regain her footing on those slick stones.

It was all he could do to keep his body from betraying him.

He kept an arm around her to hold her securely. "Don't look down or you'll make yourself dizzy. Just concentrate on me. Blast, this was a terrible idea. I could kick myself for allowing you to talk me into it."

And yet he lived for such moments when he could touch her, breathe her in, and wrap her in his soul.

"Honestly, I wish you would stop berating me or yourself. I'll be more careful. We are not exactly climbing a mountain. We'll be fine."

He was not going to be fine at all. Was there ever a woman created with a sweeter body? They should not have fit in any way, and yet they did to perfection.

"Please don't be angry with me, Fionn."

"I'm not."

"Nor angry with yourself. I did not think it would be this hard. It isn't really, only that these rocks are now so wet."

"And your ankle is not quite as healed as you pretend it is."

She merely grumbled in response.

He held on to her the rest of the way down and then released her to drop onto the sand. He held out his arms to assist her with her last jump. She lost her footing again and fell atop him.

"Blast it, Chloe." Fortunately, he was prepared for this and caught her…awkwardly.

His leg gave out, and he fell back harmlessly onto the soft sand. She landed atop him, somehow facing him.

Once again, he felt the soft give of her breasts against his chest.

Holy Mother.

"We must stop meeting like this," she teased, for they had been in this exact position after he'd rescued her from the runaway phaeton.

"I should have walked you the long way around and avoided the beach altogether."

"Nonsense, it would have added almost an hour there and back. You make for a lovely cushion, Fionn."

"Glad to be of service," he said dryly, and nudged her off him, for they were far too comfortable holding on to each other. Another moment, and he would kiss her.

He now had sand on his uniform and some in his hair. He quickly shook as much of it off him as he could.

She stood there looking as lovely as a water sprite with her windblown hair and dazzling smile. Some of the pins had fallen out of her hair, and strands of her lush mane were now tumbling over her shoulders and tousled by the wind.

After a moment, she realized her gown was still tucked into her belt and hastily lowered it to cover her legs.

He would not soon forget the sight of her lovely limbs or the feel of her body against his.

His heart was still in a rampant roar, and he was going to have improper dreams about her tonight.

He shook out of the thought. "Can you make it the rest of the way back to the house on your own?"

She nodded. "The more important question is whether you can make it safely back to Moonstone Cottage over those rocks? You can borrow one of our horses and ride back."

"Rocks will do for me." He turned away to climb back up them.

"Fionn, wait." She had started toward the beach stairs leading up to Westgate Hall but now hurried back to his side. "Will you let us do anything to help your soldiers?"

"With the hospital? Let me think about it, Chloe. I won't dismiss your offer, but I have to get the foundation excavated and footings poured first."

"All right." She nodded. "I understand. Will you join us for supper tonight?"

"I don't think so. Too much work to be done today."

She nibbled her lip. "Then tomorrow, perhaps. Our offer is always open to you. Join us whenever you wish."

"Thank you. I will keep it in mind."

"Please do. You are always welcome." She reached up and kissed him on the cheek, blushed profusely, then scampered across the beach and up the wooden stairs.

He watched until she disappeared from view.

Lord, he loved her innocence. She thought she was being quite brazen by giving him that peck on the cheek.

It should not have affected him, but of course it did.

He easily scaled the rocks and returned to his cottage.

He had become quite adept at scaling walls and leaping across rooftops in his younger days. Perhaps he was no longer quite as agile. But what he lacked in agility because of his damaged leg, he easily made up for in strength.

His adjutants had finished moving in the last of his work materials and awaited their next instructions. "Give me a moment and we'll ride back into town." He rolled up one of the maps that had been spread on the long table that now dominated the study. "I'll need this to make certain the excavation for the foundation is properly staked out."

He returned to the room that was now his bedchamber, noting the portrait of Captain Arundel that remained on the wall. Indeed, Chloe and her sisters had left this bedchamber as a sort of shrine to the man, for none of his furniture had been touched, even though two of the sisters had occupied the bedchamber themselves. He liked that it had been left with a masculine feel.

He had spent most of his life sleeping on the streets wherever he could find shelter. Then a few years of luxury beyond his wildest imaginings when taken in by his benefactor. But the streets had never left his soul. His bedchamber at his benefactor's house had a large, canopied bed, but he often chose to sleep on the carpeted floor beside it.

No doubt the maids had reported this behavior, but Fionn hadn't cared. He did not like sleeping on fine sheets and huddling under a silk counterpane.

But here, this chamber—there was something quite practical about it. Yes, the bed was large and had its canopy, as well. But it was just a solid bed with cotton sheets and a sturdy blanket. No one would criticize him if he chose to sleep in it or on the floor…or on the balcony on warmest nights.

He stared at the portrait of the sea captain. "Please don't chase me out. I need to be here."

Although he could not imagine why.

He was not going to court Chloe, no matter how deeply she was lodged in his heart.

This was as close as he dared get to her, residing in a house she owned and had once lived in. Later tonight he would probably do something stupid, like walk into the room she had occupied and inhale deeply in the hope of catching her scent.

It was in moments like this he felt so empty inside.

He was nothing more than a cipher, a puzzle never to be solved.

Who was he?

Who were his parents?

Were either of them still alive?

Why did they abandon him?

Chapter Seven

A S THE WEEKS passed, Fionn fell into a comfortable routine, rising early and heading to the hospital construction site at break of day because he wanted to get as much building done as possible before the summer heat exhausted his men and they lost their concentration. The foundation had now been poured and the building was starting to take shape.

This day was unusually hot as it wore on, so he and his men took off their shirts as they continued to toil under the heat of the blazing sun. The wind had died down and the sun now beat down on them with unrelenting force.

Despite the discomforts, the work was progressing smoothly.

Fionn was pleased, for they remained on schedule and were almost done putting up the outer walls.

"That's the last brick, Major Brennan," Sergeant Ames said, climbing down from the scaffold. "I don't think there's anything more to be done today."

"It's a good stopping point. We'll start fresh in the morning. Take the men off to the beach." Fionn grabbed his shirt and slung it over his shoulder, preparing to walk back to his office. He intended to return to Moonstone Cottage and swim there before having his supper and reviewing the schematic diagrams for tomorrow's scheduled work.

"Won't you be joining us?" the sergeant called to him.

"Not today. I'm heading back ho—" Dear heaven, he'd almost called Moonstone Cottage his home. Well, it certainly felt like home to him. "Er, heading back to the cottage. Summon me if anything urgent comes up."

"Yes, Major Brennan." The sergeant saluted Fionn and then turned to bark the orders every soldier had been waiting for. "Right, you scurvy knaves. We're off to the beach."

A cheer went up, and the men formed their columns as they marched off.

Fionn sauntered back to his office to pack up the architectural drawings used for today's work. He would need to review them as well in preparation for tomorrow's work. But as he entered, he realized someone was in his office.

He glanced around, wondering where his adjutant had gone off to and irritated the young soldier was nowhere in sight. "Blast it, Chloe. What are you doing here? Who let you in?"

"The guards at the front gate." Her eyes popped wide the moment she noticed he was shirtless.

She turned away with a squeal. "I had no idea you were... I... You see, I asked to see you, so the guards at the fort's entry pointed me to your office."

Blast again.

They must have recognized her and assumed she was to be let in.

Well, it was a correct assumption. He had put her on the list of those to be granted access to the fort. He simply hadn't expected her to come on her own or without advance warning.

"No one said anything when I stopped one of your soldiers on the stairs to ask for directions. I assumed it was all right to come straight up here. I didn't think there would be any harm. Nor did I wish to just appear on your doorstep again at the cottage. But I don't suppose this is any better."

"No, it's probably worse." He tossed on his shirt and quickly tucked it into his trousers. She was still turned away, no doubt mortified she had come upon him in his state of undress. "Why are you here, Chloe?"

She groaned.

He took her gently by the shoulders and turned her to face him. "Well?"

Her eyes widened again as she looked at him. "I wanted to show you my sketches for the courtyard. I know you think it is premature, but I hoped you might have a look and keep them in mind while you build. Stop frowning at me, Fionn. I think what you are doing is wonderful, and I would very much like to have some small part in it."

"You could have just sent your sketches over by messenger. This is no place for you, especially to stop by here on your own."

"Messenger would never do. I need to explain my ideas to you so you understand my reasons behind each planting. I've been wanting to talk to you for days, but no one in the family was available to accompany me here." She sighed and slumped her shoulders. "Sometimes I feel my entire existence is a waste. I do nothing all day and have a retinue of servants at my beck and call to attend to me as I do nothing. If not for Ella and Imogen, I think I would go mad with boredom."

"And what of Lord Claymore?"

She shrugged. "He comes by every day...he and his friends. He's all right. Quite the gentleman, in fact. But I don't fit in with his fast crowd."

"No, I didn't think you would."

"Will you look at my drawings?"

"I'll take them back with me to the cottage. I was about to ride over there in a few minutes. Did you come into town on your own?"

"No, I brought Imogen and Ella with me. We took Mr. Hawke's wagon. I left the girls at the tearoom having strawberry ices while I stopped in to give you these. I had better return to them now."

"Give me a moment and I'll walk over with you."

She cast him a smile that reached into her eyes and made

them sparkle. "You'll join us?"

He nodded.

"Join us for supper, too. At Westgate Hall. I know you are busy, but you needn't come early or stay late. We always enjoy having you with us."

He nodded again. "All right."

He left her side to return to the commander's quarters, where he quickly washed his hands and face, then donned a fresh shirt and put on his jacket, since he did not want to be seen outside the fort in anything less than his proper uniform. He grabbed the pouch he had been using to carry his plans and notes, and then strode back into his office, where Chloe was waiting. She had taken a seat beside his desk and now rose with a smile.

He'd left her no more than five minutes ago, and yet his heart swelled as though he were seeing her for the first time.

She stole his breath away.

He strode toward her and held out his hand. "Let me have your designs."

There was something about this lovely girl, an irresistible appeal to the soft curves of her body and the perfect way her bosom filled out.

Perhaps he should not have been looking.

But how could he not?

Her gown was simple, a pretty confection of palest rose, and she wore no jewelry other than a small heart necklace with a pearl at its center that rested becomingly at her throat. It drew one's eye to the delicate curve of her neck and the swell of her bosom.

Since the day was hot and his office particularly stifling, a small line of perspiration now trailed down Chloe's neck and into her bosom. He resisted the urge to lick it off her with his tongue.

Lord, his gaze had to stop straying there.

Of course, it could not.

Having spent much of his life surviving on the streets, there was a rougher part of him that urged him to take what he wanted…and he surely wanted Chloe.

But this was also the surest way to lose her.

Not that it should matter to him, since he had resolved not to marry her.

Blast.

He didn't know what he wanted.

He tucked her designs in his pouch along with some of his work, and then slung it over his shoulder. "Shall we go?"

She nodded.

"Where is Lord Claymore this afternoon?" he asked as they walked out of the fort and onto the high street.

"Looking at yet another property with his friends. I think he is searching for something quite specific. Not merely the merits of the property, but something that will capture his heart. I suppose we are all seeking something like this in life. Often it is a thing we do not realize we need until we've found it." She shrugged and shook her head. "They ought to be back soon and will be joining us for supper."

"I see."

"Now you are regretting your decision to join us. Don't you dare back out, Fionn. Please come as a personal favor to me. I would love to hear more about your progress on the hospital. Truly, it is infinitely more interesting than listening to gossip about people I don't know and feigning shock at their scandals. Lord Claymore will be interested in what you have to say. I cannot vouch for his friends, however."

"They are a pretty useless lot."

She nodded. "The ladies talk about you all the time."

"In rather crude terms, I expect." He arched an eyebrow. "Did they encourage you to drop in on me unannounced?"

"No, that was my own clever idea," she said, tossing him a wry grin. "It never occurred to me that… Well, I did not imagine you worked without a shirt on. I suppose I got more of you than I bargained for." She blushed. "I am truly sorry."

"Chloe, my only concern is for you. I don't want to see your reputation tarnished."

"Do you think it is? I doubt anyone but you saw me."

"You'll be fine this time. Just don't tell anyone about it, all right?"

"Of course." She looked up at him as they approached the tearoom. "I will not breathe a word. But seeing you shirtless is easily the most exciting thing ever to happen to me."

"Other than almost being squashed beneath Lord Claymore's phaeton wheels?"

"That was a bit too much excitement for me, but I meant the most exciting thing in a good way."

"Good?"

"Oh," she said with a light groan. "I suppose it makes me a bit of a wanton. Do you mind terribly that I ogled you?"

He laughed. "No, I don't suppose I do. But surely your life has not been all that dull. How can it be now that you have a viscount courting you?"

She shook her head. "I've told you, he is not for me. I do like him, for he is a gentleman and intelligent. But I have no feelings for him in a romantic way. Nor do I think he has them for me. He likes me very much, but I do not think I stir his passions."

Fionn tried not to chuckle again. "Chloe, do you even know what that means?"

"Stirring one's passions? Probably not, since I am completely inexperienced. Do you know that I have never even been kissed? Lady Gemma and Lady Sarah say it is something I ought to try, and I will enjoy very much."

He frowned. "Do not be goaded into doing something foolish by that pair."

"I hope I have better sense than that. But do you not think it is time I experienced something as simple as a kiss? I would like it to happen soon. Not with just anyone, mind you. A first kiss must have meaning. It has to be filled with wonder and be memorable enough to last a lifetime."

He did not think it was an appropriate conversation for them to be having, especially since *he* was aching to kiss her. But he found her innocence quite charming and could not resist hearing more. "You certainly have definite ideas about it."

"Should I not? Am I being silly?"

"No, Chloe. You are merely being curious."

She nodded. "I would never waste a kiss on the likes of Lord Hollingsworth or Lord Danson. Ugh, they are such…wastrels. I suppose that's the best way to describe them. I don't understand why Lord Claymore views them as friends. Nor do I wish to kiss Lord Claymore, for that matter."

"Well, you'll know who it shall be when the time is right. You'll find that someone special."

"What was your first kiss like, Fionn? Did it feel special to you?"

"No, Chloe. I was far too young when I had my first experience, and it went well beyond mere kisses. I did not grow up as you did. I almost starved on the London streets. When winters set in, I almost froze. I had no parents or siblings to protect me. I had no house. No warming fire. No regular meals. No decent boots or coat. No gloves. There came a point I was so beaten down, I considered selling my body in exchange for food and shelter. Other boys were doing it. This is common enough for those who live on the streets. One does whatever one needs to survive."

She placed her hand lightly on his forearm. "Oh, Fionn. I've done it again, haven't I? Been frivolous and thoughtless, never once thinking how you must have suffered. I am so sorry."

"Don't be, Chloe. You and your family have always been kind to me. You are not responsible for the way I was treated as a child. There are thousands who were worse off, and many of them did not survive."

Fionn studied her expression and saw that she was fretting.

He placed a hand over hers as it rested on his forearm. "I love that you genuinely care about people. You cared enough to sketch out designs for the hospital courtyard."

"It was nothing. Truly, trivial. I did not mean to waste your time."

"You haven't. I will look at them tonight and think of your proposals as we construct."

"Is there anything more I can do? Perhaps not in the construction, but something for the patients. A concert? Tea and cakes? Do you think it is possible?"

"Yes, not only for the patients but also for the men under my command. We can speak of this tonight. Just be aware, nothing may actually happen until the hospital is built. Come on, I'll treat you to one of Mrs. Halsey's pies. Or would you prefer a strawberry ice? The heat is blistering. That's what I think I will have."

"Me too." She graced him with another of her smiles that sent his heart soaring and at the same time tore it to pieces.

He considered himself more a realist than a philosopher, but these feelings he had for Chloe went beyond one's normal understanding of daily life. It felt to him as though his life was made up of threads, some coarse and some silken. Chloe was obviously a silken thread. Each time he met her, she wove herself more deeply into the fabric of his being.

He did not know how else to explain this impact she had on him.

He could almost see their threads interweaving with each encounter, as though it was a palpable thing one could touch. A tapestry of their lives. He felt the strength of these growing bonds between them and saw beauty in the patterns he and Chloe could weave together.

But there was a lot of darkness within his own threads, too, many unknowns about his life. There would always be shadows lurking on the edges of anything they created.

"Ella. Imogen. Look who I've brought back," Chloe said with a cheerful smile.

The girls greeted him with equally open-hearted warmth.

"Are you enjoying your strawberry ices?" he asked them, unable to stifle his own smile.

"Oh, yes," Imogen said, her lips and tongue blotched strawberry red. "Very much."

He ordered the same for Chloe and himself then took the chair beside hers. "Have you done anything interesting today?"

Ella nodded. "We walked along the beach with Chloe and hunted for sand glass. We found some in the most beautiful colors. Then we drew sketches in the garden. Tomorrow Chloe is going to take us on an excursion to a smuggler's cave."

He frowned. "Alone?"

"Papa might join us. Mama has been feeling a little tired lately, so he said he might stay with her if she isn't feeling better by then. Uncle Cormac and Aunt Phoebe are busy, too."

Chloe shot him a cautioning look. "It isn't far, and Mr. Hawke can drive us, if you don't mind us taking him from you for the day. You're usually in town and have no need of him."

"Of course, it is best that you take him." He had no idea their mother, Charlotte, had not been feeling well. He hoped it was nothing serious. Obviously, Chloe was trying to distract the girls. "Will it be an all-day excursion?"

"Just for the afternoon," Chloe said. "The cave isn't far. We might have a picnic before we explore."

"Will it be just you three? What about Lord Claymore?"

"No, just us." Chloe did not explain further, and he did not wish to pry in front of the girls. Even though Claymore appeared to be pressing his suit, it also appeared Chloe had not changed her opinion of him.

"Would you care for company? Mind if I join you? I don't like the idea of you three wandering alone in a darkened cave."

The girls cheered. "Yes, please do."

Chloe's eyes lit up. "That would be lovely. But do you have the time to spare for us?"

"Yes, the hospital walls need to properly set before we start on the roof. Tomorrow will be taken up mostly sawing beams. I'll need to supervise those first few beams to make certain they are cut to the exact dimensions. After that, the men will work from those specifications to ensure the rest are all cut properly."

The girls were excited about the excursion.

Perhaps he should not have offered to accompany them, but he was glad he had.

While the girls ran off to select some tarts to bring home for their mother, he turned to Chloe. "We can discuss all your ideas tomorrow after exploring the cave. I think my men could also do with a diversion before the month is out, perhaps a concert or afternoon tea to reward them for their work. Do you think you could help me plan something for them?"

"Yes! You know I would be thrilled to help."

He nodded as the girls scampered back. "We'll discuss this in more detail tomorrow as well."

"Thank you, Fionn," she said, her smile soft and exquisite.

They finished their ices and left the tea shop with the girls now excited about tomorrow's excursion. He saw them into their wagon and then returned to the fort and construction site for a final inspection before riding to Moonstone Cottage.

He had agreed to join the Marquess of Burness and his family for supper tonight and wanted to look his best. Not that he was vain about his appearance, but since Lord Claymore and his friends would also be in attendance, he wanted to make a good show of himself.

He told himself it was for Chloe's sake, but it was mostly for the sake of his own pride.

The parish assembly ball, which was really no more than a church dance, was also coming up in a couple of days. He had promised Chloe a dance. In truth, he did not want to attend and hoped she had forgotten about the waltz they were supposed to share. He'd talk to her about it tomorrow.

He was lost in his thoughts on the ride to Moonstone Cottage, but his mount knew the way by now and needed no guidance. He remained lost in his thoughts as he washed and shaved, and all the while pondered what to do about his feelings for Chloe.

This push and pull never left him, this wanting her and knowing he was the worst thing for her.

Well, he would see how tonight went. He had not seen her with Lord Claymore in quite some time and was curious about how the two behaved around each other.

All that mattered to him was Chloe's happiness.

As for himself, he had been on his own all his life. It would not bother him to spend the rest of his days unattached. He was used to the loneliness and isolation.

Nor did he care to seek out female company. No one was ever going to replace Chloe in his heart.

Lord Claymore and his retinue were already at Westgate Hall enjoying the view from the terrace when he arrived. Chloe's sisters and their husbands were also present. The men had glasses of brandy in hand, and the ladies were sipping sherry.

"Major Brennan, how lovely to see you again," Chloe said, being the first one to approach him once Melrose announced his presence. "The girls had a lovely time with you today."

"I'm sure they will tomorrow as well," Lord Stockwell said, entering just behind him and shaking Fionn's hand in greeting. "My wife hasn't been feeling well, and I did not want to worry the girls. Your accompanying them tomorrow relieves me greatly. I need to remain here with my Charlotte. Indeed, I won't remain down here for long now, since I don't want to be away from her side at all this evening. Dr. Hewitt is here and taking a look at her."

"We tried not to make an issue of it for the sake of the girls," Chloe said quietly. "We told them the doctor had come to look in on me and thought he may as well stop in and see their mother, since she appeared to have a cough and a few sniffles. But we are worried it is a little more serious than that."

Lord Stockwell nodded, his expression careworn.

"I'm sorry, Lord Stockwell," Fionn said. "I sincerely hope it turns out to be nothing and Lady Charlotte recovers quickly. As for your girls, I will take good care of Ella and Imogen tomorrow.

You have my oath on it."

The marquess now approached him and handed him a brandy. "You know our other guests."

"Indeed, I do." Fionn bowed over the hands of Lady Gemma and Lady Sarah, and nodded to their brother, Lord Hollingsworth, and their already drunk cousin, Lord Danson.

The women regarded him hungrily. The lords regarded him with disdain.

However, Lord Claymore was his usual genial self. "Good to see you, Brennan. Seems that hospital construction is moving along well."

Fionn nodded. "We've had a run of good luck with the weather. I only hope it holds out a little while longer. I'll breathe easier once the roof is in place."

"There must be a lot to do."

He nodded again. "Yes, but I have good men working under me, and they know what they are doing. The army's corps of builders are experienced in the various trades."

"And what of the regular infantry soldiers under your command?" Phoebe asked.

"They do not have these skills, but they have the muscle required for the more basic tasks. It is my hope some of them can be trained in the various trades through this construction project, training that might provide them with a source of income once they are discharged from military service."

"I suppose it will keep them from begging on the streets," Lord Danson grumbled. "Demmed nuisance it is. One can hardly make one's way through Covent Garden without being accosted by all manner of beggars, thieves, and cutpurses."

Chloe cleared her throat. "My lord, what are they supposed to do when they have no food or shelter and no means of support?"

"Then they ought to find a means of support," Lady Gemma said with a shrug. "I saw an old woman begging outside my modiste's shop on my last visit there. It was exceedingly uncomfortable. Fortunately, the constables chased her away."

The Duke of Malvern was also there with his wife, Hen, and now jumped into the conversation. "It is a serious situation, one I hope we'll address when Parliament is next in session. I know I will have the support of Burness, but what about you, Claymore? Where do you stand on the matter of caring for these old soldiers? Or the widows left with nothing."

"Oh, gawd. Widows and orphans again." Lady Sarah groaned. "Oh, do save this conversation for later when you men are having your port. Have you gentlemen not been going on about this problem for years now, and nothing ever seems to get resolved? Just put them somewhere and be done with it."

"Ship them off to Scotland," Lady Gemma said with a giggle. "Then they shall be Scotland's problem."

"Not quite, since Scotland and England have been united since King James of Scotland took over the English throne after Queen Elizabeth's death," Lord Claymore remarked. "For the most part, we are paying out of the same coffers."

"We are?" Lady Gemma seemed utterly surprised. "When did this happen? Was it recent?"

Chloe shook her head. "A little over two hundred years ago."

"Demmed nuisance," Lord Danson remarked, holding out his glass for a refill.

"Indeed," Lord Hollingsworth said, smoothing out his silk waistcoat.

Phoebe cleared her throat. "Isn't it a lovely sunset?"

"Yes, quite," Lord Claymore said. "This is the sort of view I hope to find. I've been shown several very pretty properties, but none as pretty as Westgate Hall. I've heard Moonstone Cottage is also quite lovely."

"It isn't for sale," Chloe said immediately.

"I am quite aware," Lord Claymore responded, casting her a wry grin. "No one shall gain that property unless they also gain you, Lady Chloe. I believe you and that cottage are quite inseparable."

Melrose rang the dinner bell just then, sparing all of them from Chloe's response.

Fionn lagged behind to allow Lord Claymore to escort Chloe into the dining hall. The Marquess of Burness hung back with him as well. "What do you think of Claymore?"

Fionn arched an eyebrow. "What does it matter what I think of him? Isn't Chloe the one whose opinion matters?"

He nodded. "Yes, but I would also like to know what you think of him."

Fionn shrugged. "I don't really know him beyond a few conversations. Surely you and the Duke of Malvern have a better sense of him than I do."

"Not really. Neither Cain nor I did much to recommend ourselves to Polite Society. We were hellraisers and traveled with a fast set. Mostly vain idiots such as his friends seem to be."

"You cannot fault him for the friends he keeps," Fionn said with a grin. "You've told me yourself that your taste in friends was just as bad."

"Oh, much worse." The marquess chuckled. "Phoebe had a word for me and my unsavory friends. She called us vile and accused me of being a bigger idiot than Claymore. She's right, of course. Took me a long while to come around and straighten up. Phoebe did that for me. I took one look at her and fell madly in love. I knew the moment I set eyes on her that I had to be a better man, or she would never have me."

"Then Claymore is ahead of the game, isn't he?"

"Yes, I suppose. But he should be doing better with Chloe. She isn't giving him a chance."

"Not giving him a chance? Or does she know in her heart he isn't right for her? If she doesn't want him, then do her sisters really want to push her at him?"

"No, they never would. But neither do they want Chloe wasting her life pining for someone she can never have."

So this was what their cozy little chat was really about—Fionn's unsuitability for Chloe. "Are you warning me to back off?"

This was what Fionn *had* been doing, but he did not care to be told he had to do it.

"No, you mistake my meaning. I suppose I am rather inelegantly asking what your intentions are toward Chloe."

"I have none, if that is what you are worried about."

"I am only worried about Chloe's happiness. Your plans are set for tomorrow, and I will not interfere with them. In truth, you are doing my brother a great favor by joining Chloe and the girls. I know they will be safe in your company."

He nodded. "Upon my oath, I will guard them with my life."

"But after this, I think you must keep away from Chloe."

"Is this what Chloe wants?"

The marquess had been grinning, but his expression now turned grim. "It is what Chloe needs. She will never look at another man while her dreams are filled with you. I—"

"There you two are," Phoebe said, bustling to her husband's side and taking his arm. "You're supposed to be acting as host. And you, Fionn…please, you must tell us all about this hospital you are building. If I have to listen to Lord Claymore's friends prattle a moment longer about their idle, useless, mindless London lives, I shall scream."

"I shall do my best, but the topic is more likely to put you all to sleep rather than fascinate anyone's imagination."

"You are far too modest. By the way, did my husband pump you for information about Lord Claymore? He is a bit of a puzzle, I think. An intelligent man who surrounds himself with these idiots. What do you make of him?"

"I cannot say."

"Well, do let us know if you have any insights. Cain has written to his Bow Street Runner asking for information on him, but that report should take a few weeks to prepare. In the meanwhile, I hope you stay close to Chloe. I know you are busy and this may be an imposition, but she likes you and trusts you…as do we all. Hen and I are worried about her being out alone with him and his circle of friends."

The marquess groaned. "Phoebe, he cannot."

"Why ever not?" She stared at her husband. "Oh no…you didn't. What stupid thing did you just tell Fionn?"

Fionn thought it was his duty to intercede. "Your husband's concern is for Chloe, and he is right. I know she likes me perhaps more than is wise, and this is blinding her to more suitable men. I've just assured your husband that I will not court her, so you needn't concern yourself—"

Phoebe's gaze turned fiery—it was the only way to describe the fierceness suddenly in her eyes. "You have no intention of courting Chloe?"

"How can I? She is an earl's daughter, and who am I?"

"But you like her?"

He hated others knowing his feelings, but what was the point of hiding it from Chloe's sisters when he would likely need to enlist their aid in helping Chloe move on and find a proper suitor?

"Fionn, do you like her?" Phoebe asked again, pressing him for an answer he was reluctant to reveal.

Finally, he gave a curt nod. "More than is wise." Now that he'd admitted it, he wanted to take a dive off the nearest cliff. "I can make up some excuse to leave, if this is what you now wish. After tomorrow's excursion, I need never see Chloe again. I think it is best, although it might take some convincing on her part."

Phoebe was staring at him with her mouth agape. "Are all men as stupid as you and my husband?"

Chapter Eight

CHLOE'S HEART WAS in a flutter as she stood with Ella and Imogen in the courtyard of Westgate Hall shortly after the noon hour, all of them wearing their sturdiest walking boots and straw bonnets. Their gowns were plain and of durable muslin. They wore no adornments, no silk ribbons or lace that might snag or get ruined in the dank cave.

She watched Fionn and Mr. Hawke approach in the wagon, easily making out their forms. Fionn was especially easy to notice, for he was big and muscled, and radiated a manliness in his casual pose. He had one booted foot on the footboard and was leaning back in his seat, his arms outstretched and resting along the back boards of the driver's bench while Mr. Hawke drove the wagon into the courtyard.

It had rained a little this morning, nothing more than a light sprinkle that passed quickly and showed few signs of ever having happened. The air held little dampness, nothing more than the familiar scent of the sea.

Ella and Imogen were hopping up and down and waving as the wagon drew up.

Their father had come outside to see his girls off and was the first to step forward to greet Fionn when he jumped down from the wagon. "Thank you again, Major Brennan. My little ducklings are thrilled beyond measure to explore the smuggler's cave. Cook has packed a picnic luncheon for you all." He motioned to the footman loading a large basket into the wagon. "Eat hearty, my darlings. Any pirate will tell you that smuggling is hard work."

His daughters giggled and each hugged him tightly before scrambling onto the wagon.

Fionn chuckled. "Lady Chloe and I shall make proper knaves of them."

He then turned to Chloe and assisted her into the wagon, placing his large, warm hands about her waist to give her the slight lift up. His touch shot tingles through her body, and she felt her cheeks heat.

He did not seem to notice, for he had already moved on to assist Phoebe's maid onto the driver's bench beside Mr. Hawke. Those two were to serve as chaperones for the outing. Fionn then hopped into the back of the wagon with her and the girls, settling his large frame beside her as she sat opposite the girls. "We are all in, Mr. Hawke, and ready for our adventure."

The girls squealed in delight and turned to wave at their father, continuing to call out to him until the wagon clattered out of sight of Westgate Hall.

Imogen, with her typical sensitive nature, turned sad once she could no longer see her father.

"What is wrong, sweetling?" Chloe asked.

"I hope Mama is all right."

Chloe reached over and gave her hand a little squeeze. "She will be. Do you recall just a few weeks ago when I was stuck in bed because of my sprained ankle?"

Imogen nodded.

"And look at me now, able to hop about better than a frog."

Fionn cast her a soft smile.

Ella managed a small smile, too, but it quickly faded. "Papa would have come with us if he weren't so worried about her."

Chloe wished his daughters were not quite so perceptive. "You know how much he loves you girls and your mama. To see any of you under the weather is very hard on him. And doesn't your mama always take excellent care of you? Is she not always by your side at the slightest worry? He feels he can do no less for her."

Ella nodded. "He always calls her *my love* and gives her kisses when he thinks we are not looking."

This was what Chloe so desperately wanted in a husband.

Her sisters had found this same thing with their husbands. Apparently, so had Imogen and Ella's parents. How wonderful it must be to feel so swept away by one's spouse, so breathless and intoxicated by their every smile. Of course, it would also plunge one to the depths of worry if the person you loved so dearly was ailing.

But was it not all worth it to accept the bad along with the extraordinary good?

She glanced at Fionn and was surprised to find him looking pensively at her. She cast him a hesitant smile.

He turned to the girls. "You know your mama wants you to have a good time. She will feel bad if you are so worried about her that you do not allow yourself to have any fun. So, no more frowns or sad faces. Today you are fierce pirates entering a smuggler's cove to stash your booty in a cave. What is your pirate name to be? Remember, you are fierce marauders and afraid of nothing. Imogen, you go first. Is there a name you would like for yourself? Or shall I think one up for you?"

"You think one up," Imogen said, a smile forming on her little bow lips.

"All right, let me think… Well, your Uncle Cormac calls you and Ella his ducklings, so this is what you shall be. Captain Deadeye Duckling, feared plunderer of the Irish Sea."

Chloe and the girls laughed heartily.

"And mine," Ella said, now bouncing on her bench. "I'm a duckling, too."

"Indeed," Fionn said, his manner austere. "Captain Pegleg Duckling, scourge of the Barbary Coast."

He had the girls in gales of laughter as he playfully growled and put on a pirate's voice, punctuating his phrases with *argh* and *matey*.

"What shall Chloe be called?" Ella asked, still bouncing on the bench.

"That's an easy one," he said, turning to Chloe and giving her a wink. "She's the Moonstone Marauder, fierce queen of all oceans, lakes, and puddles."

The girls were squealing with glee again.

"And you, Major Brennan?" Ella asked with a giggle. "What is your pirate name to be?"

"Must I be other than Major Brennan? After all, someone has to keep you scurvy pirates in line."

"No, no," Imogen insisted. "You have to be a pirate, too. Give yourself a name. Everyone must have a name."

Chloe saw the flicker of pain in his eyes.

Everyone must have a name.

Except he didn't have one.

He was a foundling left on an orphanage doorstep with no idea of his true identity. He'd gone from one of the horrid orphanages straight to the workhouses then escaped onto the streets before he'd reached the age of eight.

All he knew of himself was that no one wanted him.

Chloe could not help aching for him, so she quietly took his hand. He entwined his fingers in hers and gave her hand a light squeeze before easing it out of her light grasp.

This big, brawny soldier, who oozed confidence and charm, had a painful hole in his heart that would never heal until he discovered who he was. Chloe wanted to tell him that the past did not matter, for how was he ever to discover his identity all these years later?

To her, none of his past mattered. He was brilliant and valiant and had worked his way up from nothing to become the man he was meant to be. It took such inner strength to overcome the disadvantages he had faced all his life.

Not only overcome those disadvantages, but become a good

and honorable person instead of turning bitter and resentful.

She did not care where he came from, only who he was now. "I think he must be Captain Beauregard Handsome, pirate prince of Valhalla."

He laughed heartily and at the same time groaned. "No, absolutely not."

"Yes! Yes!" the girls cried.

"Pirates can be handsome," Ella insisted.

"And you are ever so nice looking," Imogen said with her innocent truth, bobbing her head in agreement.

He turned to Chloe with a helpless look.

She grinned and bobbed her head too. "Ever so nice looking."

Mr. Hawke chuckled. "Mrs. Hawke will have a good laugh when I tell her. Enjoy the moment, for in a few years you'll start losing your hair, growing a pot belly, and sprouting a forest of hair out of your ears and nose. In other words, you'll look like me!"

They reached the site of the cave within the hour, and Mr. Hawke drew up the wagon in a flower-dotted meadow that sloped slightly down to the sea. There was not much of a sand beach at this spot, just fields of grass and a copse of trees with silvery leaves not far from the edge of the water where seedlings had somehow taken root.

They spread their blanket in the shade of those white bark trees whose silver leaves shimmered and sounded like fairy laughter whenever the wind tinkled through them. Just beyond, at the bottom of the gentle slope, was where the land met the deep blue sea. A column of rocks jutted out into the water, and among those rocks was the entrance to the cave.

The tide was ebbing, so they would be able to walk through the cave without getting their feet wet, but they dared not tarry too long with their picnic luncheon or have to deal with the tide coming back in.

Chloe felt Fionn's gaze on her as she began to set out the contents of the basket. "There's chicken and potatoes, cold ham, and freshly baked bread. Oh, and some apples and cheese for lighter fare." She removed her straw hat and set it aside as she dug deeper into the basket. "And strawberry tarts. Oh my. How splendid."

The girls were giggling again as they removed their dainty walking boots and wiggled their toes in the grass.

Chloe offered a plate to Mr. Hawke and Phoebe's maid, a shy girl by the name of Molly. "That basket is for you, Lady Chloe. Mrs. Hawke prepared one for Molly and me. Once you've finished, we'll pack up your basket and then have a bite to eat ourselves while you explore the cave."

It did not sit right with Chloe, but she knew better than to protest. Mr. Hawke and his wife had been in service at Moonstone Landing for a decade, and despite their genuine fondness for her and the girls, it was obvious they were not about to become chummy with those they deemed above their station.

Molly, being young and shy, was never going to contradict Mr. Hawke on this matter, so Chloe was not going to insist. Still, she felt awful about it.

She briefly thought of Lord Claymore and his friends, knowing they would call her a nitwit for stewing over the comfort of servants. But how could she ignore their circumstances?

She watched a moment as Mr. Hawke unhitched the horses and led them to a stream that meandered through the meadow down to the sea. Molly sat upon a rock in a shady spot in the copse of trees and kept an eye on the girls...and Fionn. A lot on Fionn. Who could blame her? It was all Chloe could do not to sit there gaping at him, either.

The man was too splendid for words.

The girls nibbled on chicken legs while she took a piece of thigh. Fionn cut himself a piece of chicken breast and began to eat it. Terribly naughty thoughts swirled in Chloe's mind the moment he sank his teeth into the tender meat. She wanted to turn away before he caught her blushing, but his gaze was on her and had her riveted.

She could not move.

When had eating a chicken ever been so naughty?

But…dear heaven…she felt as though he was eating *her* with his every bite. When he ran his tongue over the crispy chicken skin to lick up the delicate spices Cook had rubbed into it, she almost knocked over her lemonade. She caught her glass in time to prevent a spill, then guzzled the lemonade and gave herself a coughing fit.

Fionn set down the remains of his breast and came to her side to hold her until she calmed. "Better now, Chloe?"

She leaned her head against his shoulder, feeling spent and humiliated. "I hate chicken."

He laughed. "It was the lemonade that got you."

She was almost certain he then placed a light kiss on her forehead. But it was soft as a whisper, and she could not be sure.

She eased away and dabbed her lips with her table linen.

His gorgeous silver eyes held tender amusement. "Diamond of the first water, that's what you are," he said, and tweaked her nose.

Her face was flush from all the coughing, and she imagined her nose was a bright red, too. Not quite the tempting siren, and certainly no *ton* diamond.

They quickly finished their meal, all of them inhaling the strawberry tarts that must have been baked fresh this morning and acquired from Mrs. Halsey's tea shop. Afterward, she helped the girls on with their boots, and they all made their way to the stream to wash their hands.

Imogen had strawberry crumbs at the corners of her lips, so Chloe dipped her handkerchief in the crystal water and gently wiped off the crumbs. "Let's go explore," she said, tucking the damp handkerchief in her belt.

Mr. Hawke and Molly waved as they marched off.

The girls were little gazelles and easily made it down the slope.

She commented on it while standing hesitantly at the top of

the incline that appeared much steeper now that she was staring down at it.

Fionn paused when he noticed she was not following them. "You can do it, Chloe. Just mind your ankle."

"It is all healed."

"But it will take nothing to sprain again. Is this what has you worried?"

She nodded, knowing she was not as secure in her footing as the girls and needed Fionn's help to make it onto the sandy strip without falling. He guided her down while holding on to both of her hands. "There you go." His voice was deep and reassuring, shooting tingles through her as she inched down the incline. "See, you made it just fine."

"With your help. One would think I was an eighty-year-old matron. Some dreaded Moonstone Marauder I turned out to be." She would have slid down the entire way on her rump if he had not been there to steady her. The girls might be gazelles, but she was more of a clumsy donkey.

He tucked a finger under her chin, tipping it upward slightly so that their gazes met. "You are fierce and beautiful, my Moonstone Marauder. Fearsome queen of oceans, lakes, and puddles."

She could not help but smile. "You are obviously suffering from too much sun, and it has boiled your brains."

"Not at all. Chin up, and be proud of your title." He made certain she was on solid footing before letting go of her hands.

She smiled, truly loving how gentle he was with her. "I am entirely in your debt...Captain Handsome."

He groaned. "My men will be ruthless in their teasing if word of my pirate name ever gets out."

"I'll never tattle, and I shall make the girls take an oath of silence. I'll make a pirate ceremony out of it. They will love it."

As expected, the tide had gone out. They were now able to walk to the cave's entrance without having waves wash over them.

It was not unusual for visitors to explore the various caves discovered along the coast. Constable Angel maintained this one on behalf of the town of Moonstone Landing and sent a man out every few days to make certain no one had gotten trapped inside.

There was a cupboard at the entrance where one might find lanterns, flint, rope, and even some apples when in season.

"Wait for me to light the lantern," Fionn said, and held the girls back when they tried to run in. "We'll be in pitch darkness within ten steps of the entry. Imogen, you are going to hold my hand at all times. Ella, you are to do the same holding on to Chloe's hand. You must always watch your footing and never let go of your partner's hand. I want your sacred pirate oaths on this."

The girls nodded. He knelt beside Imogen, for she was to go first. "Repeat after me. I, Captain Dead-eye Duckling…"

Imogen parroted his words with an adorably youthful earnestness.

"Shall never let go of my partner's hand…"

"Shall never let go of my partner's hand," she said in her sweet, little voice.

"Or ever wander off alone…"

"Or ever wander off alone."

"I give my sacred promise…"

She bobbed her head. "I give my sacred promise."

Fionn then repeated the oath for Ella. "I, Captain Pegleg Duckling…"

To Chloe's surprise, he asked her to repeat the oath, too. "But—"

"Will you dare defy me, Moonstone Marauder?"

"No," she responded, and took her oath. "Your turn now, Captain Handsome."

He growled low in his throat and then did the same, speaking with solemnity. Then all four of them spat into their palms and shook hands.

The girls were thrilled.

Chloe whipped out her damp handkerchief to clean off everyone's spittle, but Fionn stopped her with the stern arch of his eyebrow. He motioned for her to put the handkerchief away.

She supposed he was right, for the girls would equate washing off the spit as washing away the vow.

The cave was not very deep, but anyone could get disoriented in the dark. Who knew what new hollows the pounding waves might have carved out of the sturdy rock? It all felt quite eerie as they edged their way deeper into the cave.

She was glad Fionn led the way and had the lantern in hand, as well as a firm grip on Imogen, who looked up at him with so much trust, it made Chloe's heart ache for the sweetness of it.

The lantern's flame flickered each time a gust of wind swept through the cave. How lost they would be if it sputtered out.

It did not help that the wind made a ghostly howl as it traveled through the cave and seemed to bounce off the dank, mossy walls. But it all added to the sense of adventure.

This was also why Fionn insisted on their staying close to each other, especially little Imogen, who was now clutching Fionn's hand with both of hers.

It wasn't long before the cave passage opened up into a larger, cavernous area, no doubt where the pirate smugglers hid their crates of illicit wares. Fionn gave the girls a little of the cave's history. "The coast of Cornwall has been a pirate haven for hundreds of years. Imagine what it must have been like back then, their sleek ships sailing into the cove under cover of night, soundlessly dropping anchor, furling their sails, and then dropping their rowboats into the black waters."

The girls stared up at him, rapt as he continued the story, looking very much the fierce and handsome pirate in the amber light of the lantern's glow. The light accentuated the manly lines and fine hollows of his face. "They only sailed in on the new moon, for they dared not be seen by the silver glow of a full moon. Royal guardsmen patrolled the coast looking to nab these pirates as they unloaded their booty."

"Were they ever caught?" Imogen asked breathlessly.

"Aye, matey. Some were. But it did not deter the others, for there was too much plunder to be had in smuggling. Crates filled with merchandise were piled upon this very spot where we are standing."

Imogen and Ella looked down at their feet.

Fionn grinned at Chloe and then continued. "The cave was in use even as little as a decade ago, while we were at war with Napoleon's forces. French lace, perfumes, and wines were banned here in England. But no one wished to give up those luxuries, so smugglers replaced the legitimate importers who could no longer bring in those wares."

"Would the crates not get wet when the tide came in?" Ella asked.

Fionn nodded. "An excellent question, and the answer is…sometimes. The pirates would stack their crates on low tables so that the rising tide did not reach them. Usually the tides are strongest at the full moon and weakest in the new moon. But storms are a force of nature and do not wait for the turning of the tide or the phases of the moon. On occasion, a severe storm would hit and completely flood the cave."

Imogen's gaze remained on Fionn. "What would the pirates do then?"

"Lick their wounds, salvage whatever they could out of their losses, and go plunder more merchant ships for their booty."

They took a turn around the cavern, taking note of messages scrawled into the rocks. "One-armed Wills was here," Chloe murmured, reciting one of the inscriptions.

"Uncle Cormac has only one arm," Imogen said. "He used to be so angry about it all the time, but he doesn't mind so much now that he is married to Aunt Phoebe."

"I overheard Papa tell him that marrying Aunt Phoebe was the first smart thing he'd done in years," Ella said in a whisper that resounded through the cave.

Chloe laughed. "Your Uncle Cormac was an utter donkey

before he met my sister and fell in love with her."

Imogen nodded. "Mama called him an insufferable arse."

"Imogen! You mustn't repeat what Mama said. She used a bad word. But she likes Uncle Cormac a lot better now."

"Yes," Imogen said earnestly. "She likes him much better now that he got rid of his naked ladies."

Chloe tried to stifle her laughter, but she wound up sounding like a snorting sow instead.

Incredibly, Fionn managed to keep a straight face, although she saw the amusement in his eyes and knew he was working hard to hold back his own burst of laughter. He held it back the entire walk back to the cave's entrance and said nothing while the girls ran up the slope to be met by Mr. Hawke and Molly at the top. He kept a straight face while the girls disappeared from view over the rise, but their high-pitched voices could be heard telling Mr. Hawke and Molly about their pirate adventure.

Only then, once he and Chloe were alone, did he let out a deliciously deep and hearty chuckle.

His mirth set hers off again, and she joined him in the laughter. "Poor Cormac—his ears must be burning."

"I'm sure." Fionn doused the lantern and replaced it on the hook beside the cupboard, then he stowed the flint and rope exactly as he'd found them. "All done. Ready to go?"

His smile was captivating and his expression tender.

Chloe realized this was a moment not to be wasted, for when else would she ever be alone with him? Should she not take advantage of this fact?

She knew what she wanted from him, for who would ever be a more perfect candidate to give her a first kiss?

She watched him secure the items taken into the cave and make certain they were in order for the next party to go exploring. He moved with a lithe grace, his body lean and magnificent.

Kiss me.

Please, kiss me.

How was she to ask him such a thing?

What if he refused her?

She must have had the oddest expression, for he regarded her a moment and then frowned as he caressed her cheek. "Chloe, are you all right?"

She nodded.

"No, something's not right. What is it?"

She took a deep breath. "I had a nice time with you. A wonderful time."

"So did I." He cast her the softest smile. "Those girls are little treasures. The marquess will have a fit when he learns what they were saying about him."

"He'll take it in stride because he knows what he once was. Anyway, who is going to tell him? Certainly not I." She placed a hand lightly on his arm. "You cannot tell him either."

"No, I never would. I'm no tattler. That would break my sacred pirate oath."

She could not help but return his smile. "That's right, *Captain Handsome.*"

"Oh, bollocks," he said with a groaning laugh. "That name."

"It suits you. The girls thought it was very clever." She covered her mouth as she began to giggle, unable to remember when she had ever enjoyed an afternoon more. It was because of Fionn, of course. She hoped he was having as spectacular a time with her.

She thought he might be, for she had never seen him so lighthearted or relaxed.

He took her hand, the gesture so natural she did not think he realized what he was doing, only that he instinctively wanted to hold her.

She felt the air crackle between them.

"Come on, Moonstone Marauder," he said, his voice suddenly gruff and gritty. "I'll help you to the top."

So there was to be no kiss. Only this brief touch of their hands.

She tried to hide her disappointment. "Fionn…"

He paused to stare at her. "Something is wrong. Tell me what it is."

How could she let on? She would truly die of embarrassment if he refused. But nor would she ever have her answer if she remained silent.

She cleared her throat. "It isn't that something is wrong, but that it is very right...ah, um, very right...between us. Is it my imagining? Am I mistaken in thinking that... Dear heaven. Why is this so hard? Do you have any idea what I am talking about?"

"Yes," he said, frowning lightly as he studied her more closely. "Unfortunately, I do. All the more reason why we ought to get back to the others now."

He started to turn away, his obvious purpose to walk off and put the matter to an end.

Well, there it was.

"Unfortunate? Is this all I am to you? I did not think you disliked me that much. Perhaps not dislike, for that involves actual feeling. Indifference, for that requires nothing on your part. I'm so sorry. I never meant to make you feel awkward. It's just that..." She was going to keep rambling because she was so humiliated. "I have no experience in such matters...and obviously, I misread our friendship. I only hoped for a kiss...that's all. I'm so very sorry. You go ahead. The girls must be wondering what happened to us. I'll be along in a moment. I cannot just yet."

He had taken no more than two steps before turning back to face her and making a sound that resembled a groan. "Blast it, Chloe. Are you going to cry?"

"Yes." She nodded. "Again, I am so sorry. It's just that the moment felt so perfect for my first kiss, and I wanted it to be you. How could it ever be anyone but you?"

He groaned again. "I cannot let this happen."

Was that a hint of yearning in his voice?

No, probably irritation, because she wanted to be kissed and he did not want to kiss her.

"What can you not let happen? My tears or our kiss?" She

shook her head and wiped her eyes, feeling like a foolish infant. "Please, just go away. I'm truly sorry I ruined our lovely afternoon."

"Stop apologizing to me."

"I cannot help it. It is all catching up to me now, and all my feelings are spilling out. I have tried very hard not to like you. Do you think I want to flutter and tingle whenever you are around me?"

He arched an eyebrow but said nothing.

"I don't know why this should happen, because you have done nothing to encourage me. Quite the opposite. Fionn, you ignored my letters. You have avoided me at every turn since coming back to Moonstone Landing. You no longer want to be my friend, and this tears me apart more than anything. What have I done to offend you?"

"Nothing, Chloe. Dear heaven…" He raked a hand through his hair. "You have done nothing but be sweet and kind to me."

"But I must have. Why else would you be horrified at the thought of kissing me? And yet there are times we fall back into our easy friendship and I am certain you like me. There are times you look at me and…and I simply melt. But it never lasts long, and then you hide from me for days. Do you not see how you are crushing me?"

She gave a mirthless laugh, short and pained, in the face of more silence. "You are frowning at me again. I'm sorry. I—"

"Chloe, for pity's sake. Can't you see you have done nothing wrong?" He sounded agonized. "Put your hands on my shoulders."

"Why?"

"Do you want your kiss or don't you?"

"I do." She did as directed and rested her hands upon gloriously hard muscle.

A feral heat sprang into his eyes, a look she liked very much. "Perhaps we both need this. One kiss. Nothing more."

Her heart took leaps as he tucked a finger under her chin and tipped her head upward to meet his gaze.

She nodded. "That is all I am asking."

An errant wave lapped at their boots.

"Close your eyes, Chloe," he said in a whisper, and crushed his lips to hers.

Chapter Nine

F IONN HAD NEVER felt a softer mouth on his than Chloe's.
Nor a sweeter one.

Nor had he ever experienced a more perfect moment.

He always knew it would be like this with Chloe.

The girl was magic.

He allowed himself this one indulgence, losing himself in the wonder of her luscious lips that sank against his with innocence and ardor. Their light, beautiful touch ignited a dangerous flame in the deepest recesses of his heart, one he had to douse soon. It never escaped his memory that he was kissing an earl's daughter.

Kissing her.

It was an exquisite mistake that roused every aching sensation he had worked so hard to suppress. But this would always remain one of the sweetest moments in his life, and he was not about to cut it short.

The sun beat down upon his shoulders, the heat soothing and mild.

Waves broke upon the shore mere inches from them, their ebb and flow a timeless rhythm as vital as the beating of their hearts.

The air was as pleasant as any he'd ever breathed, a mix of salt from the sea and sweet gorse wafting down from the meadow.

Indeed, this day had turned out perfect.

The moment even more so.

Chloe.

Chloe.

His dreams were filled with her.

But this was real, so achingly perfect and real.

His lips sank deeper onto hers, pressing against their shapely fullness with a desperate yearning.

Just one kiss.

No one would be hurt by it.

She tasted as sweet as the strawberry tarts they'd had for dessert.

He inhaled the intimate scent of her body, sunshine and lavender meadow flowers, so lovely and perfect as it blended with the warm breeze that surrounded them and the salt of the sea.

A shudder tore through him as her breasts pressed against his chest.

Their bodies were made for each other.

He wanted more than this one kiss, but this was all he dared allow. Even this was a step too far and should never have happened…should not be happening.

Yet how could he resist?

His heart had always belonged to Chloe, in friendship first, but now in the way a man desired a woman. He meant to keep the kiss brief and now end it, but how did one end a touch of heaven?

He found he could not.

So he continued to kiss her sweet mouth and allowed dreams to form that could never be. Dreams that would end when their lips drew apart.

Not yet.

He deepened the kiss, desperate to blot out the years of tormenting ache and deprivation.

In kissing Chloe, it was as though a floodgate had opened within him, and all the feelings he had denied throughout his life now came spilling out. The hopeless future of the street boy he'd once been. The cruel, heartless strength he had needed to survive, for he'd fought like a lion for every scrap of food and grabbed whatever he needed to live into the morrow.

All his experiences had shaped him into the man he was today.

The man upon whom Chloe had chosen to bestow her first kiss.

He should not have allowed it for so many reasons, the most important one being Chloe's welfare. This kiss could lead nowhere. It did not change the circumstances of his deprived life or her privileged one.

And yet it did change something profound between them.

He used to find comfort in being the boy who guarded his heart and never let anyone in. But Chloe had found her way in, pouring light into the darkest parts of him.

He kissed her until she moaned into his mouth, her angel lips now completely surrendering to his. He wanted to conquer this beauty who had effortlessly captured his heart, wanted it and her for these few moments.

But who was he to demand any of it?

What could he ever offer Chloe when he did not know who he was or what dwelled inside him?

If she dug beneath the uniform, she would find nothing more than a name someone had made up for him—Fionn Brennan. He was a man with no answers.

Just an empty uniform covering an empty heart.

He drew away slightly and kissed her throat, needing another moment to gather the strength to release her completely. He suckled the pulse at the base of her throat, gently teasing and wrapping his lips on it before taking a step back.

Her eyes had been closed, but they now opened to stare at him.

Her dark emerald eyes dazzled in their softness and their beauty. Tears now formed in them, for this was Chloe, and he knew this would happen. She wore her feelings on her sleeve. "Fionn," she said in a breathy whisper, "that was wonderful."

"We had better join the others."

He saw the hurt in her eyes over his response, but he wasn't going to encourage this madness beyond one kiss. While Chloe's sisters, having married for love, wanted the same for their beloved younger sister, the brothers-in-law knew better.

It took more than love to make a happy marriage, especially to one of the Killigrew girls who were raised in elegance. How could he ever compete with wealth and a title?

Chloe thought she was above it all, but she was not. She had never endured real hardship, and he was not going to be the one to introduce her to it. Life as an army wife might be fine for other women, but not for one who had grown up in London's elite Mayfair and now had a duchess and a marchioness for sisters.

He took her hand and led her up the slope, ignoring the softness of her skin against the rough pads of his blistered palms.

She darted from his side when they reached the top and ran into the copse of trees. "Chloe, where are you going?" He took off after her.

But she merely intended to dunk her handkerchief in the stream. After wringing it out, she hurried back to the wagon. Mr. Hawke, Molly, and the girls were already seated on their benches, and the picnic basket had been neatly stowed.

Heat burned through him as he placed his hands around Chloe's waist to help her up. She did not thank him or look at him, but immediately asked the girls to put out their hands. She wiped each with the dampened handkerchief and then wiped her own hands.

He climbed in beside her. "We're all settled, Mr. Hawke. Drive on, if you please."

Clouds were beginning to gather on the horizon, and they had a good hour before they would reach Westgate Hall. He did not want the girls or Chloe to be caught in the rain.

As the wagon rattled along the path toward the main road,

Chloe gently took his hand. He glanced down, noting the disparity between them. Her hand was soft and small, while his was big and roughened from toil. "What are you doing?" he asked.

"Cleaning your hands, too. We all spat into them."

"It is nothing." He had put his hands into far worse, endured festering wounds formed from broken blisters when working as a chimney sweep's monkey, among other things. He'd been only six years old at the time. As the boys around him began to die off, he knew he would have to make his escape and somehow survive on the streets.

But Chloe did not need to hear this story.

He held out a hand. "All right."

She took gentle hold of it and ran the cool cloth over his calloused skin. Once done, she took his other and did the same.

"Thank you, Chloe," he whispered.

"Same, Fionn. Thank you for a perfect afternoon. *All* of it."

He sighed and cast her a wry smile. "My pleasure. *All* of it."

They reached Westgate Hall moments before the first raindrops fell.

Fionn hopped down and helped the girls alight. "Run straight inside."

Melrose was waiting at the front door and held it open for the two little ones. One of the footmen helped Molly down, and she hurried in after Imogen and Ella.

That left only Chloe.

Her eyes sparkled, no doubt because she had now received her first kiss and was quite pleased by the result. "I won't delay you," she said, giving him her hand. "The heavy rain will come soon. Thank you for a beautiful day."

"I enjoyed it, too."

He had watched her run inside and was about to hop up front with Mr. Hawke when the Marquess of Burness came hurrying out. Of course, Chloe had turned back and was now on his heels. "Don't leave yet, Fionn. Come into my study. Cain is here as well. We have something important to discuss with you."

"Very well." He motioned for Mr. Hawke to take the rig back to Moonstone Cottage. "I'll cut through the beach afterward." It was the shortest way home.

He marched in with the marquess and Chloe, knowing this important matter could have nothing to do with the kiss he'd just given her.

That would be a confrontation for later on.

"Cormac, what's happened?" Chloe asked, showing every intention of meddling in his business.

"It is Fionn's private business," her brother-in-law said, waving her away.

"Why can I not hear it, too? Am I not his best friend? Indeed, I think I must be his first and oldest friend in Moonstone Landing." She tipped her chin up and defied any of them to deny it, even the Duke of Malvern, who was waiting for them in the study as they walked in.

The duke decided to set down the law to her. "Go away, Chloe. This is not open for discussion."

"That's right—I am not discussing it with any of you. I am staying."

Fionn raked a hand through his already windblown hair, wanting to laugh at her presumption, but also knowing she was right. He had never allowed anyone this close to him before and he trusted her to the depths of his soul. Nor had he ever kissed anyone with the ferocity of love he felt for her. "I have no objection to her remaining."

"There." She settled on one of the well-padded maroon leather chairs, pleased she had proven her point. "What is this about?"

The marquess sank into the large chair behind his desk. "You ought to tell him, Cain. This Bow Street Runner is your man."

Fionn fixed his gaze on the parchment the duke was holding in his hands.

"All right." The duke cleared his throat. "I sent word to my Bow Street investigator, Homer Barrow. Cormac and I wanted him to investigate Lord Claymore."

Chloe sat up straight as a rod. "What has this to do with Fionn? Doesn't this have more to do with me? You wanted to know what sort of man Claymore was on the chance I fell in love with him. Is this not so? You should have asked me, and I would have spared you the expense. I am not in love with him and will refuse his offer should he ever propose to me."

Both of her brothers-in-law moaned.

"Must all you Killigrews be so headstrong?" Cormac said with a grunt.

Cain cast her a wry smile. "Well, we did not think of asking you, did we? No matter, it is done, and he seems to be the genuine article. A good man by all accounts. His finances are in good order and appear to be efficiently managed by him. He is a loving son to his mother, who is now the only surviving parent. Nor does he have any brothers and sisters, so he is feeling the pressure to find a wife and sire heirs."

Chloe was not moved. "It won't be with me."

Cormac leaned back in his chair and sighed. "Phoebe said as much, but are you sure? He is a viscount, Chloe. Wealthy. A man of good character. Ladies also seem to find him handsome."

She nodded. "Indeed, he seems quite cozy with Lady Sarah and Lady Gemma. What am I to think of a man who claims to court me and yet keeps those lady friends on the side? Not that I am accusing them of any immoral behavior."

"But you are," the duke said with another wry smile.

"Well, it can hardly be overlooked, can it? I have no proof, and it is none of my concern. Nor should it be any of yours. I am certain he will find himself a lovely young lady to marry, hopefully one who will love him for himself and not for his rank or fortune. I only hope it will not be either of those ladies. I do not like to speak ill of anyone, but...if he truly is the sort of man who will hold to his wedding vows, then I think marriage to either of them will not make him happy."

Cain nodded. "Let's hope he has the wisdom to see this for

himself."

"I agree," Chloe said. "But it still concerns me that he has not dispatched those Hollingsworths back to London. Why would a man of solid good sense ever consider them his friends?"

Fionn exchanged glances with the other men.

Chloe noticed and frowned. "What?"

He wasn't going to tell her that Claymore was probably thinking with his lower parts and not his brain. Bedding both Lady Gemma and Lady Sarah might be a pleasure he was not yet willing to give up. Sex did that to a man, turned his brain to pudding. The upper crust strolled about with their fine airs, but they were no different than any other creatures.

The man could be the handsomest, wealthiest, and most sought-after bachelor in England and Chloe would not be impressed. That Claymore was likely having intimate relations with one or both of his lady companions while courting her was a deathblow for him in her eyes.

Nor did it speak well of him in Fionn's eyes, no matter what glowing attributes of the man were indicated in Mr. Barrow's report. Even he, lowborn as he was, would never have kept up such an arrangement, never touched another woman while he courted Chloe.

He wasn't even courting her and would not consider another woman.

She sighed to regain his attention. "And I still have no idea how Fionn is brought into this."

"I am getting to that now." The duke turned to Fionn. "While investigating Claymore, Mr. Barrow encountered your friend, Ducky."

"Oh, blessed saints." No good would have come from that encounter. "Did he try to pick Mr. Barrow's pocket?"

"You'll be relieved to know he did not," the duke replied, looking down at the parchment still in his hands. "But this Ducky person did confide to Mr. Barrow that he had stumbled onto something regarding Viscount Brennan's testamentary bequests."

Fionn leaned forward, eager to hear more. "Does he say what Ducky found out?"

"No, your friend would tell him nothing more other than to say something 'squidgy' was going on. Mr. Barrow is now asking me if he ought to assist the man in pursuing the matter."

"Of my inheritance?" He glanced at Chloe, now wishing he had not allowed her to remain in the study with them. He needed to talk to her brothers-in-law about matters of finance and did not want to do it in front of her.

Well, he supposed it did not matter. Chloe knew he had nothing to his name.

"Viscount Brennan's solicitors told me what I was to receive. In fact, I did receive the distribution and have now put much of it toward residing in Moonstone Cottage for the year. It was a generous bequest on the viscount's part. I did not expect anything at all, for he'd done so much for me during his life. Is your Bow Street man suggesting there is something amiss?"

"He is only saying perhaps there is. Mr. Barrow has a nose for this sort of thing. And by the tone of this letter, he did not think your Ducky competent to get at the truth on his own."

"That's for certain," Fionn said with a snort of laughter. "One can never accuse Ducky of having brains. I'm amazed he is still alive."

He now turned to Chloe, who was also leaning forward and eager to hear more. Obviously, she had no intention of quitting their conversation.

"I know you will consider me rude, Lady Chloe...but I need you to leave."

"Why? Don't you want my opinion?" She noted the determination on his face, the implacable frown, and took offense. "Fine. Work it out among you *men*. It is the way of things, is it not? We women are shut out of everything, even though we are more perceptive of feelings and usually know a thing or two that you, being *men*, have not worked out."

She tipped her pert nose in the air, rose, and then slammed

the door on her way out.

The marquess chuckled. The duke groaned.

Fionn sighed. "Are all the Killigrew sisters like this?"

"Yes," the marquess said. "You should have seen Phoebe at her best. Thoroughly blistered me, but then, I was a complete arse and deserved it."

The duke settled back in his chair and propped his hands behind his head. "Hen adored me from the start. Still worships me. But she is no wilting flower. She stands up to me whenever she disagrees with me. Of course, she always wins because she has a very sensible head on her shoulders and will not take me on without good cause."

"I will make it up to Lady Chloe," Fionn said. "I do value her opinion, but this is too personal a matter. It sounds like Ducky has latched on to something, but I meant it when I said he isn't very bright. I'm not sure he will ever figure out what is going on if left on his own to solve. Nor are any of his confederates all that clever, either. They survive by being nimble and able to pick pockets, not by their abilities at mathematics or science."

He paused a moment and shook his head in contemplation. "How much does your man charge? I'm not sure I can afford his fee."

The duke regarded him thoughtfully. "I'll strike a bargain with you. I shall pay Mr. Barrow's fee, but—"

"No, Your Grace. I cannot let you do this."

"The name is Cain. We've been over this before. No formality among friends and family."

"I am honored you consider me a friend, but I cannot accept your footing the bill."

"I shall pay it, but you shall pay me back if Mr. Barrow uncovers a greater inheritance that is due to you."

Fionn still declined. "It is unlikely. You are only throwing your money away on me."

"I do not see how I am. I disagree with your odds. In fact, I think it is highly likely Mr. Barrow will turn up something."

"I want in on this," the marquess said. "I'll put up half of Mr. Barrow's fee. Same terms as you've made with Cain. You pay us back if you gain something. If nothing comes of it, then you owe us nothing. Believe me, I've squandered far greater sums on the stupidest bets…of course, not now that I am married to Phoebe. My stupid days are a thing of the past. Do not be stubborn because of misplaced pride. Yours is a worthy undertaking. I am certain Phoebe and Hen would approve as well."

"Why? Because they think I want to marry Chloe?" Fionn asked.

"Don't you?" Cormac asked.

"My point is, I am not going to marry her. I would not insult your families by doing so."

"What makes you think we are insulted?" Cain asked.

"Did the both of you not warn me away from her just weeks ago? Not that I blame you. How can I ever be considered suitable for someone like Chloe?"

"We were only concerned about your sincerity. She cares for you very much, and we did not want to see her hurt by you."

"I never would." Fionn gripped the arms of his chair. "I would die for that girl."

Cain sighed. "That's what my wife said when boxing my ears for ever mentioning it to you. She called me an idiot for doubting you love her."

"My wife called me an idiot and an arse. You are of far better character than I ever was," Cormac muttered.

Fionn managed a grin, thinking of Imogen's comment earlier in the day, but it quickly faded. "Do not indulge your wives in their romantic notions. Being penniless and raised as a foundling is something I shall never be able to overcome. Nor will I ever accept charity from either of you, or Chloe, who is an angel, and the man who marries her will be the luckiest on earth."

Cormac was now frowning at him. "And it will not be you?"

"How can it be? I do not even know who I am."

Cain crossed his arms over his chest. "All the more reason

why you must take us up on our offer. Something about your past may be discovered. If you will not do it for your sake, then do it for the sake of Chloe."

Fionn's every thought was about her. Was it not obvious? Marriage to him would deprive her of everything she deserved.

"You are both quite generous. But…may I think about it and give you my response tomorrow?"

Both men nodded.

"Thank you. By the way, how is Lady Charlotte doing? Her girls were quite worried about her."

The marquess ran a hand through his hair. "We're not certain yet. John may need to take her back to London. Dr. Hewitt is a good man, but I don't think he can compare to our family physician, George Farthingale. The man is brilliant. Phoebe and I will keep the girls with us, if it comes to that."

"Then it sounds quite serious. I am truly sorry. Let me know if there is anything I can do. I am building a hospital, after all."

The marquess appeared genuinely pained. "Thank you, but we shall keep our hopes up. She took care of me for years as I was recovering from my war wounds." He glanced at his missing arm. "I was a beast to her…to everyone, but especially to her, since she was the one who had to deal with me every day. This is my chance to make it up to her. I dread that it may be needed."

Fionn strode out of the study, his intention to take the shortcut along the beach to return to Moonstone Cottage. Melrose was at his post by the door, and Chloe was standing right beside him with her arms folded across her splendid chest while impatiently waiting to question him.

"You cannot leave just yet," she said, pointing to the window. "The rain is coming down in torrents. It should pass in about twenty minutes. I think Mr. Hawke will have made it safely back to the cottage before it started. I hate to think he was caught in the downpour. Come into the library and tell me what is going on."

He shook his head. "You know we cannot be alone in a

room."

"We shall keep the door open."

"What I have to say is private, and I am not going to discuss it with an open door." He glanced out the window again, willing the rain to stop.

It came down harder. Thunder rumbled in the distance.

Chloe cast him a smug grin. "Trapped."

"Yes, for the moment. But I am still not going to discuss the matter with you. Perhaps I will talk to you about it tomorrow. I have to think on it first."

"All right," she said, her voice quite gentle. "Come into the library with me anyway. Melrose will bring in a tea cart for us while you wait out the rain. I'm sure we can think of a dozen nonsensical topics to occupy us."

"No, Chloe." He peered out the window yet again. "It appears to be stopping."

"I have never known darkening thunder clouds to represent a storm clearing. Do not even think to go down to the beach now, or you will be struck by lightning on the water. You owe me a waltz at this week's upcoming church dance. How do you intend to keep your promise if we find your charred remains on the sand tomorrow?"

He grinned. "A bit of an exaggeration, don't you think?"

"Not at all. Who is to worry about you if not me?"

"Chloe, this is getting out of hand." He took her by the elbow and led her into the library, not particularly caring who overheard him. "You are not my wife."

"Yet."

"Not ever. I will not deny my feelings for you, since I cannot seem to hold them back and they spill out in a flood. But it does not change anything between us. I am still a nobody, and you are still an earl's daughter."

She had a stubborn look on her face, but he noticed her eyes start to water.

All the better. A little hurt now would save her a world of hurt later.

"I am still a prideful arse and will not take a pence from you. I cannot do it. I *will* not have my wife support me. Yet we can never live on my earnings."

"Others do it. Many officers are married."

"To women who are commoners. Look at this house," he said, pointing out the finery. "And what of the duke's home, St. Austell Grange? It is even finer. Where am I to put you? In a two-room cottage in the fort?"

"We could live at Moonstone Cottage. You are there already."

He began to pace across the library's carpeted floor. "Leave it be, Chloe. I am already in agony over our situation. Let me do the right thing."

He had her in tears now.

He had two options at this moment—to take her in his arms or walk out.

He chose to walk out.

The rain poured down on him and a lightning bolt almost did fry him as he cut across the beach to return to Moonstone Cottage. He felt the sizzle of the sand beneath his boots, and a jolt run up his bones as the bolt struck close upon the water.

He stalked into the cottage and went straight up to his bedchamber, carelessly tossing off his boots and soaked uniform. He dried himself off with a drying cloth and then wrapped it around his waist and stretched out on the bed.

After a long moment of staring up at the ceiling, he turned to gaze at the portrait of Captain Brioc Taran Arundel.

The blasted portrait was staring back at him, as though the sea captain himself was following his every movement.

"Moonstone Landing's hero," he muttered, still sprawled upon his bed. "Did you really wait around for Chloe's aunt, Henleigh?"

Of course, a portrait could not talk.

But he continued to talk to it anyway.

"How long do you think before Chloe tires of waiting around for me?"

Chapter Ten

C HLOE COULD NOT contain her excitement on the night of the church dance. She had agonized over her selection of what gown to wear, always keeping in mind Fionn's concerns and determined to show him she could survive without all the luxuries her easy life had provided. Of course, she was not going to dress as a pauper.

But why overload her gown with silk ribbons and lace trim?

Nor would she overdo the jewelry. A simple necklace with a teardrop pearl.

"Chloe, are you not ready yet?" Phoebe asked, gliding into her room and looking every bit the marchioness.

"Almost. I'm just putting on my slippers." They were satin slippers to match the sea green of Chloe's gown.

She had spent days giving thought to striking just the right balance, so her heart sank when she arrived with her sisters and brothers-in-law only to find Fionn missing from the soldiers in attendance.

Every officer under his command was here, along with one of his drill sergeants she recognized. It was bold of her to approach him, but the hall was a crush, so who would notice? She would pretend to have encountered Sergeant Ames along her way and stopped to greet him out of politeness.

The man blanched as she addressed him, and he fumbled

over a bow. "Lady Chloe…um, a pleasure. I hope you are enjoying the evening."

She nodded. "We've only just arrived. I am delighted to see officers of the regiment in attendance. I suppose Major Brennan was delayed?"

The man's face turned a beet shade of red. "Yes…ah, well. I do not think he will attend."

Chloe's heart began to beat a little faster, a mix of ache and anger. "Not attend? Surely that cannot be so. He is commander of the fort. He cannot dismiss this important gathering out of hand."

What she meant was, how dare he shrug her off? Had he not felt the impact of their kiss?

She sighed. "Of course. He must be very busy with all that is going on with the hospital's construction."

But he had promised to share a waltz with her.

He had *promised*.

She greeted several other officers, exchanging a few pleasantries and comments about how well the construction was proceeding, and then moved on. None of the officers were going to request a dance, since she was the daughter of an earl—as Fionn often went out of his way to point out—and no one was going near her.

It was not long before Lord Claymore and his entourage arrived.

He somehow spotted her across the crowded dance floor and strode toward her, an engaging smile on his face. His friends, on the other hand, would rather be caught peeling potatoes than dancing here.

"Lady Chloe, do assure me that your dances are not all taken," Claymore said before raising her gloved hand to his lips and giving it a lingering kiss.

"No, they are all quite free." She had no intention of putting on airs and pretending she was in any way the belle of the ball. Cain and Cormac had danced with her because it was their brotherly duty. But for the most part, she would be left standing off to the side with her sisters.

Lord Hollingsworth or Lord Danson might have asked her out of politeness, but she certainly hoped they wouldn't. She did not like them, and they did not like her.

Lord Claymore claimed the first waltz of the evening.

He had barely placed a hand around her waist before he began making conversation, although it felt more of an interrogation even as he spoke with a smile. "I heard Major Brennan escorted you and Lord Stockwell's daughters to the Moonstone cave yesterday."

"Yes, and we also had a picnic luncheon in the meadow near it. Lord Stockwell was to take us, but his wife is not feeling well and he decided he ought to stay with her. It was wise to get the girls out of the house before they began to worry about their mother."

He frowned, looking genuinely concerned. "Is it something serious?"

"We are not certain yet."

"Let me know if there is anything I can do to help. I mean it, Lady Chloe. I am more than willing."

She nodded. "That is very kind of you. I will let Lady Stockwell know you asked after her."

He twirled her effortlessly amid the crush of dancers. "Please do."

"How is your house hunt going?"

He shook his head and groaned lightly. "Not too well."

"What is it exactly you are looking for?"

"Perhaps that is the problem. I don't know, but I think I will when I see it."

"Are you trying to recapture a memory of an earlier happy time? Or a feeling of that happy moment?"

"I don't know."

"It could be that you are looking in the wrong place."

He laughed and gave her another twirl. "Are you trying to be rid of me?"

"Not at all, but it does strike me you are holding on to two separate worlds." She nodded toward his friends, watching as Lady Gemma refused a handsome captain's offer to dance. "That of the *ton* elite and that of the real world."

"You do not like my friends."

"Do you?"

He chuckled. "Sometimes I do. They are out of place here."

"Why don't they leave?"

"Because I remain here."

"Why do *you* remain here?"

"At this point, I think because of you. I've seen all the properties to be had in and around Moonstone Landing, and none of them have leaped out at me. But you hold me here in the hope something more might develop out of our acquaintance."

"Lord Claymore, I will only marry for love. By this I mean a true and committed marriage. Do you see my sisters and their husbands?"

He followed her gaze. Hen was chatting with the vicar, and Cain stood beside her with several officers from the regiment. But Cain took a moment to look at Hen, and his entire face transformed.

"Do you see the way he looked at her just now?"

Claymore nodded.

She turned to Cormac and Phoebe and pointed them out with a bob of her head. Phoebe had just finished helping Mrs. Halsey set out more orgeat punch and cakes, and was now weaving her way through the crowd to her husband's side.

That same transformation occurred as Cormac watched her approach him.

"My lord, did you see that, too?"

"Yes."

"What I have not seen is you looking at me this way. Forgive my impertinence, but if you want my opinion...which I shall give whether you do or not," she said with a laugh. "What you are looking for is not to be found in a quaint village or in a property but in the young lady who will steal your heart. The one who will have you staring at her the way my brothers-in-law look at their wives. But that young lady is not me."

Their waltz was coming to an end, and Chloe was pleased by the way it had turned out. "Hold out for true love," she urged. "You see it exists and how wonderful it can be."

He shocked everyone by giving her a heartfelt kiss on the cheek once the dance ended. "You are indeed someone special."

She was unprepared for the gesture, although it came as more of a surprise than a shock. It was a very sincere and gentle kiss. She did not consider it improper at all. It might have gone unnoticed had he not been one of England's most eligible bachelors. Now everyone in attendance thought this meant a betrothal announcement was imminent.

Which it decidedly was not.

Lord Claymore escorted her back to her sisters and then strode across the room to rejoin his companions. Lord Danson's nose was a bulbous, red thing that served as a beacon should anyone wish to find him…assuming the dolt remained standing. The slightest breeze would knock him over, for he was already deeply in his cups and weaving on his feet.

Lord Hollingsworth was ogling a young widow who had recently moved to Moonstone Landing by the name of Lady Dowling, but the lady in question did not seem to be interested in what he was offering.

Lady Gemma and Lady Sarah had been standing near their brother, but they were now making their way out of the hall…as were two of Fionn's captains.

She had been distracted watching these assignations unfold and gave a cry of surprise when her sisters each grabbed an arm and began tugging her in opposite directions. Phoebe won out because she had always been the most determined of the three of them. "Did he just propose to you?"

"No."

"Then why did he kiss you?"

"I gave him some sage advice, and he was most appreciative. It was a farewell kiss, if you must know."

Hen now gripped her elbow as she studied her. "Then he is not going to marry you?"

"No. Besides, you already know I was not going to accept him even if he had proposed."

Phoebe shook her head. "And you are quite happy about it?"

"Yes. It is a weight off my shoulders. I do not love him."

Phoebe now stared at her. "Not everyone falls in love at first sight as we did. I think it isn't so much that you do not care for him, but that you care for someone else more. Where is Major Brennan?"

Chloe tried to hide her distress. A failed endeavor, because her sisters knew her too well. "He promised me a waltz."

"There are only two on the list for this evening," Hen said, "and you've already danced one."

Cormac joined them at that moment. "What happened? The room is abuzz with the oddest rumor, no doubt wrong, since Chloe looks nothing like a blushing bride-to-be."

"Claymore did not propose to me," Chloe repeated, hoping she would not be required to fend off questions all evening. "We are friends and shall stay friends, that's all."

He tossed Phoebe a naughty grin. "Men do not want to be friends with pretty young ladies. Chloe, you are too innocent for me to tell you what they really want to do, but you get the gist. So the bounder had no intention of offering for you after all?"

Chloe shook her head. "He did wish to propose. I cut him off and explained to him why it was all wrong."

"Then that look of despair is for someone else?" Cormac took a sip of the ale he had in hand. "I cannot imagine who."

Her shoulders slumped, for Cormac's comment was sarcastic and he knew exactly who was at the root of her distress. "He promised to dance with me."

"But he is not here. Shall Cain and I go fetch him?"

Her eyes widened in alarm. "Don't you dare! Am I not pathetic enough? I will not have you drag him here. Besides, he is too strong for even the two of you to handle. He is a street fighter and will lay both of you low before you even have the chance to raise a fist to him. Which is precisely the problem. He refuses to court me because I am too lofty for him."

"You are, Chloe," Cain said, now joining them. "He will always see himself as someone's discarded by-blow. It does not matter that he has made something of himself. Sadly, the very traits that make him worthy also prevent him from offering for you. Perhaps you ought to reconsider Claymore."

Hen punched him in the shoulder. "Perhaps we ought to come up with a plan to change Fionn's mind."

"You'll only chase him away if you press him," Cormac said. "He isn't ready to listen, and there is nothing you can do about it. I should know—took me three years before I came around to accepting Phoebe...or rather, stopped hating myself long enough to sober up and stop destroying myself. These feelings run deep. You cannot overcome them with cute female plots. I don't want to make it sound hopeless, Chloe. But you have to realize what you are up against. He may take years to come around."

"Or not come around at all," Cain added as yet another word of caution.

When the orchestra began to play the last waltz, Chloe simply wanted to run away and hide. But Cain's estate manager, a charming older gentleman by the name of Charles Weston, approached her for the dance. He was now married to their cousin, Prudence, who must have heard the news from her sisters and insisted Mr. Weston assume the protective mantle.

He had the good sense not to offer her advice, although he was quite clever and might have had a helpful insight. She gave it a moment's consideration and then asked him, "Mr. Weston, since everyone else seems to have an opinion on what I ought to do, I thought perhaps you might have one, too."

"I wish I did, Chloe. But the heart is a terribly fragile organ. It can also be temperamental and fickle."

"Are you suggesting I am pining for Major Brennan simply because he will not have me?"

"No, my dear. In truth, I think you have shown wisdom beyond your years in choosing him. Most young ladies of your age would have set their cap for Claymore and been quite happy with their choice. But you know who you are and what you need. You are not one to be pushed into something that does not feel right to you, no matter how tempting it appears on the surface."

"My life would be a lot simpler if I cared for Lord Claymore."

"Not really. There is not enough of a spark between you to hold you together as anything more than dear companions. Men stray when this is all they have. Of course, Claymore would have been extremely discreet about it and remained an attentive husband. Many people are happy with such an arrangement, but you would never be. You feel things too deeply. You always have, even as a little girl."

She would not call Mr. Weston's advice helpful so much as encouraging. What he had said about her was true. She did feel things deeply and knew her own mind.

More important, she knew her own heart.

And her heart wanted Fionn.

His heart wanted her, too. At the very least, he needed her.

How was she going to convince him to get out of his own prideful way?

Chapter Eleven

FIONN SAT ALONE on the terrace at Moonstone Cottage, hoping to drink himself into oblivion. He had purposely stayed away from the church dance tonight, needing to drink at least another bottle of brandy to convince himself he was doing the right thing in breaking his promise to Chloe.

She had been nothing but hopeful ever since he had agreed to allow the Duke of Malvern to follow up with his Bow Street investigator, Mr. Barrow, about the "squidgy" inheritance matter. Since when could anyone trust anything Ducky told them?

Nothing was going to come of it, for Viscount Brennan had died years ago. Whatever might have been learned back then was likely destroyed or securely hidden away. Chloe would ultimately be heartbroken.

Nor did he like that the duke and the marquess were footing the costs. He was determined to pay them back no matter the outcome of the investigation, no matter how long it took him to gather the funds.

He had only agreed to the investigation for Chloe's sake.

And also for the fact that his washbasin kept toppling off his bureau until he finally promised Captain Arundel's portrait that he would permit Mr. Barrow to proceed on his behalf.

The washbasin miraculously stopped toppling once he had made that promise.

He refused to believe it was a ghostly doing. After all, it was ultimately the right decision and one he would have reached eventually because Chloe was so broken up about their situation and her sadness destroyed him.

Her hopefulness destroyed him even worse.

Was it not worth the expense of an investigator to put finality to her dream of wedded bliss between them? How else would she move on?

He did not know how he ever would.

But his feelings weren't important, only hers. So he had agreed to the duke's proposal.

However, until there was proof of a greater inheritance or some explosive secret of his birth revealed, he saw no point in encouraging more of a friendship between him and Chloe.

For this reason, he had broken his promise to waltz with her tonight, purposely remaining home instead of going to the church dance. His gut was in a knot over it.

The Hawkes were at the dance, so he was quite alone in the cottage and now soaking in the familiar solitude.

He had been born alone.

Grew up alone.

And would die alone.

This was his fate.

He finished his glass of brandy and poured himself another.

The night was hot and damp. Or perhaps it was just that one felt overheated when drinking oneself into oblivion.

There were very few clouds in the sky, so he did not think it would rain anytime soon. Indeed, the night sky was clear enough to put on a dazzling display of stars. Perhaps he was already too drunk and seeing double…or triple.

What did it matter?

He had stripped down to his breeches, grabbed that bottle of brandy, and was determined to drink himself into a stupor. Anything to stop thinking of Chloe.

To stop aching for her.

Before entering his obscene state of inebriation, he had thoughtfully lit a lantern and placed it on the kitchen's window ledge. It would cast just enough light onto the terrace—where he now sat, if one could call his slouch a proper way of sitting—to keep him from tripping over the furniture once he decided to walk inside.

He was in no hurry to disappear into the house. First, he was probably too drunk to make it up the stairs tonight. It was very possible he would sleep on the grass and wake to find himself surrounded by the early-morning mist.

Second, he already felt too closed in by his thoughts. He liked the outdoors, the light breeze off the water and the way it wrapped around his skin. The air he breathed was refreshingly clean and fragrant.

Of course, the scent of flowers permeated the air and reminded him of Chloe's delicate scent.

Had he poured himself another drink?

His glass looked empty, so he poured again and was about to put it to his lips when he saw a ghostly vision rising from the beach stairs. First that blasted basin kept toppling off his bureau and now this? "What the…?"

He blinked.

And blinked again.

A woman in white, and she was still there.

He staggered to his feet, stupidly thinking he could chase the vision away if he showed no fear and approached it.

But as he stumbled across his garden toward those beach steps, the vision seemed to be coming toward him with an equally determined purpose. An angry ghost, he could tell by her strides.

Were hauntings supposed to work this way?

The glorious vision was now directly in front of him, within arm's length, to be precise, and she was glowering at him.

He felt the sting of a slap across his face.

The brain matter between his ears rattled, but that unexpected jolt had the remarkable effect of clearing his thoughts and his eyesight. "Blessed saints, Chloe. You should not have come. What are you doing here?"

She was sobbing and heaving breaths while her hands were fisted at her sides. "You gave me your word and then you broke it."

"For your own good. Do you think any of this is easy for me? Look at me. I'm so drunk, I am not even sure you are here in front of me. Are you real or an illusion? You look exquisite, by the way."

"Says the man who cannot see straight," she muttered. "And look at me. Can you not see what you have done to me?"

"That slap was a helpful hint."

"Fionn, I am brokenhearted." Tears streamed down her cheeks.

"And I am angry that you might have drowned walking over here. Does your family know where you are? What time is it? Must be after midnight."

"It is. Everyone's asleep, but how could I close my eyes? I had to slip away."

"To confront me and tell me what a wretch I am? As you can see, I have beaten you to it." He glanced at his bottle and then raked a hand through his hair. "You cannot stay. I'll walk you back."

"You'll fall down the stairs and break your neck. I walked over from the beach on my own and can make it back the same way once I am ready."

"You'll drown."

She rolled her eyes. "I am not in danger of drowning. The tide is out."

"But it won't be for long."

"What I have to say to you won't take long."

He was numb enough to accept whatever chastisement she intended to serve up, and probably wouldn't remember a thing she'd said by morning. "You look beautiful, by the way."

"You've already told me."

"I have? When?"

"Less than a minute ago."

"Oh." His gaze raked over her. "What are you wearing? It looks deliciously skimpy."

To his fuzzy eyes, it looked like a gown of ivory silk that clung to her exquisite curves. Her hair was unbound and in a wild tumble down her back, the ends curling in a becoming fashion about her womanly hips.

What a body on this girl.

"I have on my nightgown and robe. It is absolutely proper."

He laughed. "You are here after midnight. In seductive night-clothes. It is not—"

"Seductive? How is a plain cotton nightgown and a robe buttoned to my neck in any way seductive?"

"You could be wearing a sack of burlap and still put my body in a thrum." Why was he not drunk enough to overlook every tormenting detail of her appearance? "Go on. Start yelling at me. Get it all out." He needed to finish drinking himself into uncon-sciousness.

She sobbed again and began to pound on his chest. "I love you."

This was not what he'd expected to hear, although he knew she did, and this was the crux of their problem.

"Do you hear me, you dolt? *I love you.*"

He did not know what to say, so he wrapped her in his arms, groaned in wretched agony, and then kissed her as though he was going to die if he did not take enough of her in. He hadn't meant to, but his brain was in a fog and he did not know what else to do.

So he kissed her again, inhaling her and sucking her in as though she was the very air he breathed.

Obviously, he had not thought it through.

Then again, perhaps it was not such a bad idea to kiss her when he was drunk to the point of passing out and his breath reeked. How could she like such kisses?

He pressed his open mouth again to the tight purse of her lips. He was too drunk to control his tongue as he tried to stick it in her mouth, hoping to do it gently because he never wanted to hurt Chloe, just make her not like his kisses. When she resisted opening her mouth, he wound up drooling over the edges of her lips.

He knew what had to be running through her mind. She was not being kissed by a man so much as a slobbering dog.

Well, he wasn't trying to be romantic. He was trying to prove he was an oaf and chase her away.

Nor did he manage to control his hands, which were now roaming freely over her body and should have earned him another slap. Remarkably, she did not protest when one of his hands found its way downward to cup her nicely rounded bottom and the other cupped a nicely rounded breast.

What felt like a volcanic explosion tore through him.

Dear heaven, she excited him.

He muttered something into her mouth while he continued to slobber kisses over her face and body. He could not make sense of what he was saying. He hoped she could not either. Especially if he was stupid enough to utter an *I love you* back to her.

A desperate *I love you*, because being drunk had not suppressed his feelings but sent them gushing out.

She moaned as he trailed kisses down her neck and into her cleavage.

Blister it! Had he somehow managed to undo those buttons at her throat? How?

Never mind.

He fumbled with the rest of them because he was going to burst every organ in his body if he did not tug that robe off her this very instant.

He now had only the nightgown remaining as an obstacle.

Was he insane? Drunk or sober, he should not be undressing her. Nor should she be allowing it.

He moved his face off her cleavage, trying to behave. But he noticed her lush, heaving breasts straining through the thin cotton fabric, and began to lick those magnificent peaks through it as well.

Only after licking the fabric did he think of easing the nightgown off her shoulders to get at those two luscious and creamy prizes. He wanted to taste her skin.

"Chloe, you haunt my dreams. You torture my heart." Where had his glass and bottle gone? And now his head was reeling. His body began to sway like a moored boat on a rising storm tide.

"Fionn, no! I forbid you to pass out. Do you hear me? Do not pass out."

He responded by falling backward onto the soft grass and taking Chloe down with him.

He braced himself for the sting of another slap, but she was laughing.

"Are you no longer mad at me, Chloe?"

"No, you pathetic thing. Would I be laughing if I were?"

"I couldn't bear it if you were. And I cannot bear it that you are not angry as hell with me. I did not dance with you tonight because I needed to push you out of my life. It is for your own good."

She caressed his cheek. "Since I am now flat atop you, I would say your plan did not work out quite as you hoped."

"I will adjust my plan to make it work once I am sober."

She kissed him softly on the lips. "Don't bother. Nothing you do or say will ever make me stop loving you."

"Nothing? Are you not in the least disgusted with me? I am drunk. I purposely broke my promise to you. I am a nobody with no name and no family."

She kissed him again. "Do you think you can get up?"

"I don't know. You are atop me." He caressed her cheek. "Lord in heaven, you feel so good."

"As though I was made just for you?"

He nodded.

"I am rather comfortable atop you, too. You are exquisitely muscled. But you must get up now. Let me help you." She scrambled off him and tried to put her shoulder under his arm to haul him upright. "Goodness, you're big."

"And you are sweet and little, and the most beautiful girl I have ever seen...and I've seen plenty. Done plenty. Even when I was obscenely young and should have been tucked in bed and had bedtime stories read to me. But you...sweet heaven, you are so beautiful inside and out. Your heart. Your body. Your kindness. You are perfect. The loveliest thing in creation. My head's still spinning. You had better not move me. I may cast up my accounts."

"Don't you dare. But you must get up."

"Why?"

"Because I am not going to let you break your word to me. We are going to dance."

He laughed. "Several problems with that idea. First, there is no orchestra. Second, even if I could stand up, I doubt my legs will move in any coordinated fashion. Third... Oh, hell."

"What is the third issue?"

"I will do a terrible job of it and disappoint you."

"Breaking your word is the disappointment, not the grace with which you spin me around your garden. I expect you will be incredibly ungraceful. We might even topple a time or two. But it is more important that you keep your word. I shall have my dance."

He wanted to tell her that he loved her more than anything on this earth, but even drunk he knew this admission would trap her forever. She would never move on. Never find the happiness she deserved.

He did not know how he did it, but he managed to get to his feet and stay upright. He also managed to hold Chloe in his arms and spin her very slowly to a waltz tune he made up in his head.

After making it through what barely counted as a proper waltz, he kissed her breasts and kissed her perfect mouth, and then he toppled into oblivion.

HE AWOKE THE next morning to a light mist over the water and the hint of a sun trying to break through the tendrils of gray.

The grass beneath him was damp with dew. Several ladybugs were crawling up his arms.

He sat up and clutched his head to stop the hammer pounding in it.

A bottle of brandy and an empty glass stood upright on the wrought-iron table on the terrace. Had he left it there? The chairs were all neatly aligned, as though no one had sat in them or toppled them as they rose. He was almost certain his chair had toppled as he struggled to his feet when seeing the vision of Chloe.

He rolled to his knees and then to his feet and made his way to the beach stairs. There were no telltale signs of Chloe. No little footsteps in the sand or silk ribbons trapped between rocks.

He was shirtless.

Had she been in his arms?

He inhaled, hoping to catch her scent on his skin. To his frustration, he could not tell. All he could smell was his own foul breath.

Worse, he did not know if Chloe's appearance last night had been a fantasy. Had he really kissed her breasts? Sweet heaven, they were lovely…but had he kissed them?

Only one way to find out.

He had to see her today.

It was Sunday and no work would be done on the construction, so he had time to pay a call on her.

But he was so spent by the time he made it upstairs to his bedchamber, the first thing he did was retch into his chamber pot.

He could have sworn he heard ghosts laughing, one a deep

chuckle and the other a light, feminine titter.

He wanted to tell them to go away, but simply did not have the will to do anything more than collapse onto his bed.

It was noon by the time Mrs. Hawke clomped up the stairs to make certain he was still alive. "Oh dear. You look awful."

"Good morning to you, too." He groaned. "Is it Monday yet?"

"No, Major Brennan. You look as though you were caught in a grist mill, ground up, and fed to the cattle. Can you sit up? I'll prepare a posset for you that will clear out your innards."

"I think I've already done that." He motioned to the chamber pot into which he had retched no less than three times. "I'll carry it downstairs and empty it. My mess, my responsibility to clean it up."

"You just worry about sobering up. You have business to attend to over at Westgate Hall."

He frowned. "What business?"

"Lord Claymore danced with Lady Chloe last night and brazenly kissed her cheek. It is all anyone is talking about. They say he proposed to her."

No wonder she had come to him last night in tears.

Or had he dreamed her up?

He had better find out.

He felt much better after he'd washed, dressed, and put solid food into his stomach. Nothing fancy, just plain scones that he ate dry. No jam or cream on them. The mere thought of those embellishments curdled his stomach.

By early afternoon, he no longer looked like something the cows had digested and then spat out. He rode over to Westgate Hall, not certain what he was to say to Chloe. Why had she not told him about Lord Claymore's proposal?

Perhaps she had and he'd said something stupid in response.

Chloe was just coming up from the beach with Imogen and Ella when he rode into the courtyard. She looked glorious in her beach attire, a pale pink gown of homespun cotton and a large straw hat that hid most of her fiery curls and accentuated her big eyes.

She whispered something to the girls. They waved at him and hurried off inside.

He kept his gaze on Chloe as he dismounted and handed his reins over to the groom. His gaze remained on her all the while he strode toward her.

She looked about for a place to hide, but they were in an open courtyard and he was too close now for her to do anything about it.

Her face turned flaming.

So she had been with him last night, and he had slobbered all over her body. "Take a walk with me."

She held back as he took her arm to lead her down to the beach. "But I just came from there."

"I know. However, you cannot go inside looking as you do or everyone will know something happened between us."

She touched her hands to her cheeks. "Am I blushing?"

"Chloe, you are on fire. I did not think it possible for anyone to turn that shade of red."

She groaned. "It is all your fault. You should not have touched me."

"I know, and I apologize for it. All my defenses were down because of you…and then you appeared before my very eyes, the most beautiful apparition I had ever seen. I don't think I remember all of what I said or did, only that I was doing a lot of licking."

She tried to suppress a burst of laughter, but couldn't. "At first, it was horrible. But then it turned out to be quite wonderful. Sadly, I doubt you remember the best parts."

His heart hitched. "Just what do you think were the best parts? Blessed saints, what else did I do?"

"I am still *unspoiled*, if that is what concerns you." She cast him a vulnerable smile. "I would not have stopped you had you tried. But I think your noble character prevented you from doing more than exploring my bosom in painstaking detail. I could have stopped you, but I found the sensations fascinating."

"This is worse than I thought," he said with a groan. "Chloe, why did you come to me when... What is this I am hearing about you and Claymore?"

"Ah, this is what has you riding over here. What did Mrs. Hawke tell you? Or was it Mr. Hawke?"

"Mrs. Hawke. She said he proposed to you, and you accepted."

"He did not propose, and I did not accept. I think he meant to, but I cut him off before he could. He kissed me on the cheek out of gratitude."

Fionn arched an eyebrow. "Gratitude? What man is grateful for being rejected?"

"It never got to the point of rejection, since I stopped him before he could ask. I explained all the reasons I was wrong for him and what he ought to be looking for in a wife."

"He was likely heartbroken but chose to be a gentleman about it."

"I truly do not think so. He would never drink himself into oblivion over me as you did. Nor would he ever kiss me as though I was the very air he breathed...even if it was a bit slobbery." She grinned impishly. "Half the time you missed my breast and kissed my armpit."

"Chloe!"

"But it was quite delicious when your aim was on the mark."

"Dear heaven."

"The more of a fool you made over me, the deeper I fell in love with you. So I think you have to stop denying the obvious and work with me to come up with a solution, because I will not marry anyone but you."

"I am not going to hold you to that."

"I am not asking you or giving you the choice. This is a promise I have made to myself." She emitted a ragged sigh. "Do you have any idea how deeply I am in love with you?"

"Yes." Because he felt the same and probably loved her even

more deeply than she did him. She had taken many people into her heart, her parents and sisters. Ella and Imogen. Her brothers-in-law. Probably a dozen others. Her heart was cluttered.

His wasn't. Indeed, it had been achingly empty until she came along.

Viscount Brennan had taken him in but never thought of him as anything more than a ward. Fionn did not want to diminish the man's kindness, for he had been generous beyond measure. But he had not been taken into the man's heart, not ever considered as a son. The only one who had ever shown him that kind of permanent love was Chloe.

He thought of it as a forever love, because nothing could shake him from this feeling he had for her.

He took her hand and placed it on his arm. "Come on, let's go inside. How is Charlotte doing today?"

"No better."

He gave her hand a light squeeze. "Let me know if there is anything I can do."

"I don't suppose you are a praying man?"

"No, but I'll put in a word for her anyway." He was not religious—how could he be when all he saw around him in those early years was abject misery? But lately, he was beginning to wonder. He now had a profession and had risen nicely in the army ranks. He had just let Moonstone Cottage, a house he considered to be the most beautiful in England. It was not the finest by any means, but it felt like home, and he had never had this feeling anywhere else before.

Home.

Perhaps because it was Chloe's, and he loved her.

"Since you are here, join us for tea," she said, distracting him from his thoughts.

Well, it was Sunday. He had nowhere else to be. Nor did he wish to be anywhere else but beside Chloe.

He nodded and escorted her in.

Cormac was alone on the terrace when Fionn walked out

there. Chloe had run upstairs to change out of her beach wear and check on the girls to make certain they did the same.

"Fionn, good to see you." Cormac set down his glass and extended a hand to him. "We missed you last night. But I suppose you heard the gossip by now."

"Yes, Chloe told me what happened."

"Have a seat. Care for a lemonade?" He motioned for one of his footmen to pour Fionn a glass. "That's all I'm drinking after last night. Imbibed a bit too much. By the look of you, I'd say you did, too."

Fionn settled into a chair with his fresh glass of lemonade. "I might have overindulged a bit."

Cormac grinned. "Yes, those Killigrew girls will do that to you. Claymore probably tied one on after Chloe rejected him. What are you going to do about her?"

"We'll see what Mr. Barrow has to say about Viscount Brennan's legacy. In the meantime, nothing has changed." He said no more as Imogen and Ella scurried out to join them. Cormac's brother was not far behind and greeted him warmly.

Fionn could tell by his expression that nothing had changed regarding Charlotte's condition. It would not be long before he returned to London with his wife to seek out expert medical advice. His daughters would be devastated.

The burden of distracting them would likely fall on Chloe, because Phoebe had her own children to deal with as well as other obligations in running the house.

An idea formed in his mind when Chloe, after joining them on the terrace for refreshments, suddenly disappeared into the parlor to sit at the pianoforte and play a few songs for the girls. She played surprisingly well and had a decent singing voice.

Was there *anything* about her that he did not like?

Ella and Imogen, it turned out, also had charming voices. If it became necessary to distract the girls, he would ask Chloe to help him organize a concert for his regiment, and perhaps open it up to the villagers as well. Moonstone Cottage was the perfect location for this sort of affair, and there was already a pianoforte in place for Chloe to use.

The Hawkes would be overjoyed having her and the girls around. Chloe had lived there with her sisters for many years and only been required to move out because Hen and Phoebe had married while she was too young to remain on her own.

He proposed the idea to Cormac, who heartily agreed with it. "Charlotte is not doing well at all. We're going to give it another day or two at most, and if there is no sign of improvement, John will take her back to London."

"It will be hard on the girls."

Cormac nodded. "Fortunately, they are used to spending their summers with us. But nothing can replace the love of a mother."

Fionn wouldn't know, never having had one. But he had seen the way Chloe and her sisters cared for their loved ones and understood this was how it should be. He did not regret the path his life had taken, since it had brought him to Chloe.

Brought him to her doorstep and then stopped him cold.

He understood most marriages were entered into for the advantages to be gained. It was fairly common for a bankrupt nobleman to wed an heiress. But they had a title and a history to those titles to contribute in exchange for a whopping sack of coins.

Perhaps he would be worn down over time and accept the bounty he was offered, even though he had nothing to offer in return.

He wasn't there yet. But what a jest it would be if his old friend, Ducky, turned out to be the savior who uncovered the solution to his dilemma.

Could Viscount Brennan's loathsome relations have hidden something important from him?

Chapter Twelve

A S THE SUMMER progressed and it was now nearing the end of August, Fionn began to resolve himself to the fact nothing was going to turn up regarding Viscount Brennan's inheritance or any secrets to Fionn's identity.

While he had never expected Ducky or Mr. Barrow to discover any startling information, he could not help but feel disappointed. There had been no word to the good or bad from either of them.

He strode out of the fort and headed to the neighboring work site to supervise the last touches to the hospital roof. There was still much to be done, for only the skeleton of the building had been put in place. The windows would be next, and then the flooring. But the roof was the most urgent work that had to be completed while the weather cooperated.

The interior construction would commence over the course of the winter, and the harbor expansion would likely commence sometime in late spring of next year, unless something happened to disrupt the schedule.

Sergeant Crane walked up to him as he arrived at the site. "The men are asking when the next recital is to be held?"

Fionn arched an eyebrow and grinned. "Next week, in all likelihood. What's going on? Since when are soldiers eager to stand around holding dainty cups of tea while listening to a piano recital when they could otherwise be at the tavern enjoying an ale?"

"You weren't at the last recital, Major Brennan."

He nodded. "I was in Plymouth, as you well know, giving a report on our progress to General Hayward. What happened in my absence?"

He had only returned last night and intended to stop by Westgate Hall on his way back to Moonstone Cottage later this evening to catch up on all the news.

"Since you were not there to assist her, Lady Chloe invited some of her friends to join her and Lord Stockwell's daughters. I am a happily married man, sir. But I must tell you, one was more beautiful than the other. Especially Lady Dowling. She's the widow who keeps mostly to herself, as would be expected of a gently bred lady recently out of mourning."

Fionn shrugged. "I know who she is, but I never paid particular notice."

"None of us did, for she always wears those hideous veiled bonnets that hide most of her features. But she wasn't wearing her bonnet at the recital. The men are hoping she'll be helping out again."

He laughed. "I ought to have known their sudden desire for culture was nothing more than a prurient interest in women. I'll ask about her next time I see Lady Chloe."

Sergeant Ames happened to be passing and caught his last words. "Sir, Lady Chloe is with Lord Stockwell's daughters at the tea shop, if you happen to be looking for her."

"I wasn't, but thank you for mentioning it." Fionn had missed Chloe while off in Plymouth and was eager to see her again.

Aching to see her.

Why not stop in at the tea shop to catch up on any relevant news? Besides, what harm could there be?

Well, of course there was harm. They could not look at each other without their hearts bleeding.

He didn't care.

He had to see her.

The day's construction was coming to an end, and his sergeants would be marching the men down to the cove for their daily swim. He certainly did not need to supervise them.

He took another few minutes to finish up with his inspection of the day's work and make notations for his report before heading off to the tea shop in the hope of finding Chloe still there.

Foremost on his mind was Lady Stockwell's condition.

He hoped the family had received good news from her London doctors, but life was not always kind to good people, and there was no telling the outcome. To distract the girls from worrying about their mother, Chloe had now held two recitals at Moonstone Cottage for his soldiers.

The arrangement suited everyone, keeping the girls occupied and distracted, and giving Chloe a reason to visit the cottage every day.

She was happy because all she ever wanted was to be at the cottage.

He was pleased because all he ever wanted was to be with Chloe.

He had also come up with another project to keep her returning to the cottage, one he knew would tantalize her. Last week, while searching his bedchamber for a set of keys he was certain he'd placed upon the bureau but must have fallen and rolled somewhere, he had come upon a secret door in his bedchamber that none of the Killigrew sisters or the Hawkes apparently knew about.

Inside was a treasure trove of family documents belonging to their ghostly sea captain, Brioc Taran Arundel.

He had yet to discuss this newly found treasure with Chloe, for he had made the discovery the morning he was to leave for Plymouth. But now that he was back, he meant to pursue it.

He intended to ask for Chloe's help in cataloguing these papers and then figuring out what to do with them. The cottage belonged to her and her sisters, and therefore the trove of documents would by rights belong to them.

Chloe happened to be seated alone in the tea shop at a corner table beside the window overlooking the street. It was the same table where he'd carried her on the day she was almost trampled by Lord Claymore's phaeton. He was never one for expressing feelings, never had a reason to feel anything for anyone. But the sight of her as she sat lost in her thoughts, the sun spilling in through the window and wrapping her in a golden light, completely overwhelmed him.

She looked lovelier than ever.

His heart began to pound as he watched her absently staring out the window to where the girls were now playing with some of the local children in the village green across the road. She had a cup of tea in front of her and absently took a sip of it.

She was so lost in her thoughts, she was unaware he had walked in.

He nodded to Mrs. Halsey's daughter, who was working behind the bakery counter, and then continued toward Chloe, drawing out a chair and taking a seat beside her.

Her eyes glittered and her smile beamed the moment she realized who had been so bold as to join her at the table without invitation. "Fionn. I'm so glad you're home. When did you get back?"

"Late last night." His own lips twitched upward at the corners in a smile, and he could not seem to stop smiling.

This is what it means to be loved.

He surely loved Chloe in return.

Why was he allowing his stupid pride to stand in the way of their happiness?

In the same moment he had this thought, he also recalled the reason. He could never afford to buy her the beautiful gowns or fine jewels she always wore. Not that she walked about like a jeweler's display. Quite the opposite—she never wore anything ostentatious. Simple earrings and a heart locket usually, and this was all the jewelry she had on now.

Her gowns were never frilly or overly adorned, either. But they were always of the finest materials. Whether silk, muslin, or wool, the fabrics were top quality, as were the lace trims on most of them.

He set aside thoughts of Chloe because they would start to whirl around and around in his head, solving nothing and making him feel like a dog chasing his own tail.

"How was Plymouth?" she asked.

"All went well. General Hayward appeared quite pleased with the progress and signed off on the next round of purchases." He motioned to Mrs. Halsey's daughter to bring him a cup of tea, which she promptly did and asked if he would like anything else. "The tea is all, thank you."

"Next round?" Chloe asked, pursing her lips as she continued their conversation. "Does the army not fund the entire project all at once?"

"No. The protocol is to submit our reports at every phase. They pretend to understand what those reports say. Then we hold our breath until they sign off and give us the funding for the next step."

"What would happen if they did not sign off?"

He took a sip of his tea and then set his cup down. "Moonstone Landing would be sitting with an unsightly, half-built hospital, and some pretty broken-up roads."

"Good heavens, that is awful."

"I worked hard to make certain all was in perfect order before we dug into the soil with the first shovel to commence work."

"I have no doubt. No wonder you were so adamant about not changing a single brick. You were not jesting when you said it could undermine the entire project."

"In truth, these projects usually go smoothly when one understands the protocol and expectations."

"As you do. You are awfully clever, you know."

"Hardly," he said with a grin. "I would call myself methodical. By the way, I found something at the cottage that I think will interest you."

"Truly? What is it?"

He noticed the girls now running back and did not want to say too much in front of them. Not that the trove of documents was a secret, but it was no one's business yet. They might have been hidden in that secret space for a reason. "I'll stop by tonight and tell you more. Will you be up to visitors?"

She nodded. "For you? Always. I have no plans."

"Good."

The girls were excited to see him again and greeted him warmly. Following on their heels was Lady Dowling, the woman who had managed to charm his entire regiment. She was wearing her usual veiled hat, so he did not see much of her face. However, he took notice of her body, which was quite voluptuous.

He sensed she was studying him behind her veil.

Well, he was used to women eyeing him just as she was likely used to men eyeing her. He would mention her to Chloe tonight, since he had promised his men to ask about her and would likely be hounded until he gave them an answer.

"See you tonight, Chloe." He left the tea shop and strode back to the fort.

By early evening, he had caught up on the most pressing items requiring his attention. The rest of it could wait until tomorrow. He stretched his large frame to relax his taut muscles, then rose and made his way to the Kestrel Inn stables, which now also housed the army horses, since their own stables were still being used to store the building supplies.

The ostler was an amiable but chatty fellow who loved to gossip. Fionn could tell by the man's look that he had a juicy tidbit to report. "Major Brennan, have you heard? Lord Claymore's coming back here next week."

A pang of irritation tore through him at the mention of the viscount. Not that he was jealous, but…why was the viscount coming back to Moonstone Landing? It had to be for Chloe.

"Any reason given for his return?"

"Thaddius Angel was the one what got the letter reserving his rooms, so better ask him. But my guess is because of the pretty Killigrew lass, Lady Chloe. Anyone could see he was taken with her last time he was here. And then everyone thought he had proposed and she had accepted because of that kiss."

Fionn tensed, unhappy about the reminder. "I understand it was merely a polite kiss on the cheek."

"A man like that don't feel polite over a beautiful girl like her." The ostler continued to chatter as he saddled Sophocles. "Mrs. Halsey thought for sure you were going to propose to her first, but I suppose the duke and the marquess were having none of that. Rank is rank and blood is blood, and there's no getting around it."

He paused to await a response from Fionn that he was not about to give. "Good evening, Mr. Matchett. I'll see you in the morning."

"Right, Major Brennan."

Fionn gave Sophocles his lead while he lost himself in thoughts of Chloe. What he should do was propose to her and then spend the last of his inheritance on a special license in order to marry her before the week was out.

But it felt wrong, as though he would be cheating her out of a choice. He never wanted to trick her or push her into something she might regret soon after.

Chloe was at the entry, standing beside Melrose, when he rode up to Westgate Hall. "I was afraid you might get too caught up in your work and not stop by. I'm so glad you did. Tell me all about Plymouth and your latest discovery."

She led him into the summer parlor, which was cozier than the main parlor where the marquess and marchioness entertained visitors in elegant style. She motioned for him to take a seat. The chairs in this room were designed for comfort rather than formality. He sank into the soft cushions with pleasure.

"Would you care for a drink?" she asked, ever the considerate hostess.

"Cider or lemonade if you have it. I'm not about to touch brandy for a while yet."

"I cannot imagine why." She laughed lightly. "I won't soon forget that night."

He ran a hand along the nape of his neck. "And I am still struggling to remember half of the stupid things I said or did."

"They weren't stupid. For the first time, you allowed me a glimpse of your honest feelings. You are always so composed and in full command of yourself. I never know what you are truly thinking or feeling. It was nice to see the unguarded part of you for once."

"Right, once and never again."

"Well, I hope that is not so. Have you eaten yet? I assume you have not."

"I'm sure Mrs. Hawke will have left something for me in the kitchen."

"Have something here now. There's always plenty at our table." She rang for Melrose and asked him to bring cider and light refreshments. Then she turned back to him and settled in the chair beside his. "Cormac and Phoebe will be down shortly. They are just tucking their children into bed. Ella and Imogen as well. They've had a busy day."

"Any news on their mother?"

"She's holding steady last we heard, so I suppose that is something. The girls are worried, of course. We all are, because it does not seem there has been any improvement."

"I'll keep her in my thoughts."

Melrose returned with a cart laden with food and pitchers of cider and lemonade. He knew Chloe thought of him as special and made the extra effort to entertain him in style, but this was exactly what he did not want. It only served as a reminder he could never maintain a household at this level.

But this elegance and bounty was all Chloe knew. She thought it was normal for all families to have this, which it was for her.

"I heard from my men that your last recital was a great success."

She poured him a glass of cider and smiled. "I think Lady Dowling was the success. I could have been blowing a trumpet straight in their ears and your men would not have noticed me. I had no idea she was so pretty beneath that veil."

"Nor did they." He took the offered glass and drank its contents down quickly, for he had developed a thirst after a long, hot day. "I have been requested to ask if she might attend the next recital. In truth, all your friends were much admired, and my men would enjoy seeing them all."

"But Lady Dowling dazzled. I know, we all saw the effect she had on your men. I will ask her. She is shy, and I don't think she realizes quite how beautiful she is. Or perhaps she does and this is why she is still wearing her veiled hats whenever she goes out. I don't think it is because she is grief-stricken. From what I've heard, the marriage was one of convenience, not an all-consuming passion."

"Who told you it was not a love marriage? Moonstone Landing's resident gossip, Mr. Matchett?"

She laughed and nodded.

"He's probably wrong more than he is right. Well, enough about the dazzling widow. I really came by to tell you about a secret compartment I found connected to Captain Arundel's bedchamber. It is not very big, not the size of a room. More of a secret cupboard."

Her ears immediately perked. "How is it possible? Where is it located exactly?"

"Behind his bureau. I suppose no one ever moved any of his furniture after he died. The chamber looks untouched."

"We purposely left it that way. None of us had the heart to change a thing about the room. How did you find this secret place? And was there anything hidden inside?"

"Yes, it had boxes of documents that I hope you will help me sort through. They are yours, of course, since you own the house.

As for how I found this compartment, the answer is quite odd."

She inhaled lightly. "Was it the ghost's doing?"

"One might think so if one believed in such things. I had placed keys atop the bureau... I know I set them down there. Somehow, they wound up on the floor behind the bureau. I could not get to them by reaching behind it, so I moved the bureau aside."

"That is confirmation enough for me. Our Moonstone Cottage ghosts must have led you to it, don't you agree?" She cut a slice of ginger cake and handed it to him. "I'm sure they had a purpose."

He cast her a wry smile. "Well, I'll leave it to you to figure out what it is. Assuming they even exist or had any involvement whatsoever with this accidental discovery. I truly don't know what to believe, except there was no way those keys jumped off the bureau on their own."

"Fionn, this is so exciting. I would love to have a look at those papers. They must contain something important, or Captain Arundel would not have led you to them. May I start tomorrow?"

"Yes, if you wish. I'll be heading to the fort shortly after sunrise and won't return until evening. Bring the girls with you, if you like. Make a day of it."

"Thank you, I will. I'll pack up our beach attire and art supplies so we can break up the day if they begin to fidget. They are my charges for the summer, and I am doing my best to keep them entertained, but I doubt they will find searching through documents very much fun. I know I will need to distract them. It is so hard on them because they know their mother is ailing."

He reached over and took her hand. "Call on me if ever you need my help, Chloe. I can only imagine the fear those poor, sweet girls are feeling."

"I try my best to keep them hopeful, but it is harder to do as the days pass and we receive no good news." She sighed and shook her head to dismiss the sad thought, but he knew it was not easy on her either. She ached for those girls and felt helpless to make things better. "Would you like another slice of cake?"

He'd devoured the first slice, not realizing how hungry he was. "Sure."

She served him and then prepared a plate of game pie that looked quite fresh and must have been left over from their supper. "I suppose I've done it backwards, offered you the sweets before the meat."

"It all ends up in the same place," he said, patting his stomach. "By the way, Mr. Matchett told me another bit of gossip as he saddled Sophocles for me. It seems Lord Claymore is returning next week. He wrote to Thaddius Angel to reserve a suite of rooms."

"I hadn't heard." She pursed her lips and frowned. "I do hope he isn't bringing his friends along."

"Our resident gossip did not know the details other than he was coming back."

"I wonder why he would. I don't think he's found a property, and he's already seen most of what is available around here."

Fionn sighed. "I should think the reason is obvious. He's coming back for you."

"I hope not. I haven't changed my mind. I'm afraid my heart is still yours, even if you are reluctant ever to have me."

"You know my reason for hesitating. I suppose you received no word from Mr. Barrow or Ducky."

"No, nothing yet."

He set aside his plate and leaned over to take both her hands in his. "I have no idea what I said that night. I'm sure I blurted something foolish as I was slobbering over you."

"You needn't panic. Every word was unintelligible. I think you were trying to recite a Shakespearean sonnet to my beauty."

"I didn't think I knew any," he said with a soft laugh. "But if I did, they would all be dedicated to you, Chloe. I won't pretend I don't have feelings for you. My deepest fear is that those feelings won't last. Not on my part but on yours."

"On your part, too. You'll despise that I can dip into my inheritance every time I want something that is more than you can provide for me on your wages. You'll despise that by marrying you, I shall be the poor sister, the deprived sister. You already despise that you don't know who you are and the best you can give me is a made-up name. Let's not talk about it here and now. But we must talk it out eventually."

"I know. Perhaps after Lord Claymore's visit."

"Ever the gentleman, determined to keep silent and allow my choices to remain open for me."

She was right, since this was exactly what he intended.

They said no more as Cormac and Phoebe joined them.

Fionn did not remain long afterward, for no one had anything helpful to add regarding Ella and Imogen's mother or Mr. Barrow and Ducky's quest, which was looking more and more like a wild goose chase.

He returned to the cottage and went to the kitchen to put away whatever repast Mrs. Hawke had left out for him. Having come close to starving as a child, he had never been able to let food go to waste.

There were many things he had not been able to let go.

Oddly, he sensed Chloe understood, even though she had never experienced the same hardships and deprivations. Perhaps this was why he was so drawn to her, for her perception and the gentle way she seemed to soothe his unsettled soul.

Once the food was put away, he went upstairs to his bedchamber and stepped out onto its balcony to observe the night. The stars shone overhead, a sight that never ceased to amaze him. The moon was also bright and cast its silver reflection upon the water.

He stared out for a long while, hoping Chloe might show up again, a beautiful vision in her nightclothes.

But she did not, which was sensible on her part. He would never want her to make her way alone on the beach in darkness.

He stripped out of his clothes, all but his breeches, and then washed up. The night was warm, so he decided to sleep on the balcony.

He loved the sense of freedom.

For some reason, it also made him feel closer to the sea captain. Mrs. Hawke had told him the man often slept out here on summer nights. And the captain had led him to those boxes of documents hidden in the compartment behind the bureau.

Why had he not led Chloe's aunt, Henleigh, to them when she purchased the house? The two of them had supposedly fallen in love, and he would have kept nothing from her. Nor did he see fit to reveal those boxes to Chloe or her sisters.

Which led to Fionn's next and most puzzling question...why him?

What connection could he possibly have to those boxes?

Chapter Thirteen

"CHLOE, YOU'VE TAKEN on the entire responsibility for Ella and Imogen," Phoebe said, coming into Chloe's chamber as she was still abed early the next morning. "Cormac and I are going to take them from you for the next few days."

Since she was only now stirring awake, Chloe took a moment to yawn and sleepily sit up in bed. "But you have so much to do already."

"And you have helped to ease our load tremendously. However, they are his nieces. His precious ducklings, as he calls them. He feels he has been remiss with all that has been going on and is now determined to spend time with them. We've foisted the responsibility onto you for the entire summer, and it isn't fair."

"You know I enjoy them. I've never regarded them as a duty." Chloe adored the girls, but she could not deny it would be convenient to be on her own for the next few days. Those boxes Fionn had discovered were calling to her, and she was eager to dig into them.

She would have brought the girls along to assist her, but they were too young to hold the concentration required to spend entire days going through them. "Where do you plan to take them?"

"To the Falmouth fair."

"Falmouth? But you will never make it there and back in a

day."

Phoebe nodded. "Which is why we shall be gone three or four days in all. The girls will have Cormac's undivided attention, and I think they'll be thrilled. They sorely need the distraction, don't you think?"

"Yes, most definitely."

"But will you be all right on your own?"

"Oh dear," Chloe said with a broad grin, "the entire house, mine to do with as I please? What agony!" She fell back against her pillows and laughed. "I could wail and declare I will miss you terribly, but I don't think you would believe me. So I will stick to the truth. Time alone would be bliss."

Phoebe gave her a sisterly tickle. "I'm delighted you won't miss us in the least."

Chloe gave her a quick hug. "Of course I'll miss you. But I have a new project I am undertaking that will require all my concentration."

"Ah, those hidden boxes Fionn Brennan mentioned last night?"

She nodded.

"Or is the real project Fionn himself? I hope this is not a ploy on your part to have him propose."

"I do not need to scheme against him. He will come around in time because I know he loves me, even if he is too thickheaded to admit it. All I wish to do is go through each and every one of those boxes. I'm sure they contain important documents concerning Captain Arundel. The biggest question for me is, why did the captain choose to reveal them to Fionn and not us? And why now?"

"That is a fascinating puzzle. Oh, drat. I would love to help you, but I won't be able to do anything until we return from Falmouth. Hen can't either because she has the annual St. Austell Grange tea party to prepare for next week. The entire village will descend on her, and she's fallen behind in the planning."

"I'm sure Prudence and her Mr. Weston will help out. They

are both quite capable, and Prudence certainly has time on her hands," Chloe said of their cousin who had married Cain's estate manager for practical reasons but seemed to have fallen in love with him over time.

It was a good match, proof that two people could be quite happy even if theirs had not started out as a deep and abiding love.

But Chloe knew herself too well. She thought too much with her heart. For this reason, she could not marry anyone but Fionn. "Well, I'll stop over there to help her once I finish at the cottage, but it won't be tomorrow, because I want to get a solid start on those boxes first."

"Will Fionn go through them with you?"

"No, he'll be gone by the time I arrive, and I will be gone by the time he returns. Even though Mrs. Hawke makes for a proper chaperone, tongues will wag if it becomes known we were at the cottage together, especially with you and Cormac gone."

Phoebe now sank onto the bed beside her. "That is wise. Just remember this is how it ought to be. You are to leave if he returns early."

"He has to oversee the hospital construction, not to mention his regular work as fort commander. I'll probably be gone hours before then."

"All right. But do not be angry with us if Cormac insists on Prudence keeping you company while you are at the cottage. Hen can manage without her. It is more important that your reputation is protected."

"Nonsense, I need no such thing. Let her help Hen with her party. I hope your stubborn husband doesn't insist on it. First of all, Fionn is irritatingly honorable. He is never going to take a step out of line because that might lead to a forced marriage, and we all know this is the last thing he wants."

"Chloe, if he doesn't want to marry you, then how can you be all right with this?"

"He does want to marry me, but it must be on his own terms.

He's so worried our marriage will fail because of who he is…which is entirely the point, because he does not know who he is. I'm wondering whether Captain Arundel revealed those boxes to him because they concern him."

"Well, Imogen did see a resemblance between them."

"It must mean something. And little Imogen is never wrong about these things. She picks up on everything." Chloe threw off her covers and scrambled out of bed. "I'll help you get them ready for your trip and see you off before I head over to Moonstone Cottage. But what about your boys? Are you going to take them with you?"

"Yes, we are taking the entire entourage. Their nannies are quite excited about the excursion. We'll all manage. Our boys are always better behaved when playing with Ella and Imogen. Besides, Cormac and I would miss them too much if we were apart from them even for a day."

By late morning, the girls gleefully piled into Cormac's shiny black carriage along with Phoebe and Cormac, and their two boys Cormac jokingly referred to as the devil twins because they were little imps. The carriage was an imposing, highly polished conveyance with the Burness crest emblazoned on it and led by a pair of sturdy matched grays.

Chloe stood in the courtyard and waved to them until they disappeared from view.

The nannies, Phoebe's maid, and Cormac's valet rode behind them in an impressive second carriage that was also piled high with all their bags. One would think they were leaving for a month and not a few days.

More important, this left Chloe free to do as she wished for the next three or four days. Well, she was hardly going to throw wild parties. She had those documents to read and also an upcoming recital to coordinate.

Oh, and a request had been made for Lady Dowling.

Chloe would seek her out later today, for a mere message asking for her assistance at the recital might be politely declined.

Requests were much harder to decline when made face to face. The woman was not a recluse and would likely be in town later today to take tea at Mrs. Halsey's shop. Chloe and the girls had often seen her there.

She resolved to take a ride into town in the late afternoon to seek Lady Dowling out. This way, she could also stop in at the fort to talk to Fionn if she had any news to report on her findings.

Since the documents had to be old and musty, she chose to wear one of her sturdier muslin gowns, a pretty forest green that was unadorned save for a fichu that demurely covered her bosom and was held in place with a cameo brooch.

She added a few flower clips to hold her stylish chignon in place. However, she merely held her sun hat in hand because she did not want to flatten her elegantly styled hair. After all, what was the point of making all the effort if the attractive outcome was only going to be covered up?

She marched downstairs, excited by the prospect of spending the day at Moonstone Cottage. "I'm off," she said to Melrose as she breezed past him.

"Lady Chloe, shall I send a footman to escort you home?"

"Not necessary. Mr. Hawke will drive me back in the wagon. I might have him take me into town first." She walked with a spry step down to the beach. The tide was only now starting to come in, and she was easily able to avoid climbing over the rocks, since the sandy walkway was not yet flooded.

She made it to the cottage with ease and walked in through the kitchen, since she had come up the beach stairs and wanted to shake any sand off her before she traipsed through the house. Mrs. Hawke was moving about the kitchen at her usual bustling pace when she strode in. "Good morning, Mrs. Hawke."

The woman cast her a gracious smile. "Good morning, Lady Chloe. The major said you would stop by today. He's brought down some boxes and put them on the dining room table for you. He thought you would be more comfortable sorting through them there. He also told me to mention that he has plenty of paper and graphite pencils in the study. You are to help yourself to any supplies you need."

Chloe smiled. "That is very thoughtful of him."

Mrs. Hawke grinned. "Well, you know he likes you. He would give you the world if it were in his power."

Chloe blushed.

"Would you like a cup of tea? It looks to be thirsty work."

She shook her head. "No, I'll be fine. I'm afraid to spill anything on those papers."

After greeting Mr. Hawke as well, she went into the dining room and immediately set about to work.

She quickly saw these were important family documents, not only of Captain Arundel's but also those of a brother and a sister who had died before him.

Chloe used some of Fionn's paper to sketch out a family tree and used a second sheet to prepare a timeline of events. She did not know yet if they would be of any purpose, but something might reveal itself as she put the Arundel family history in order.

It did not escape her notice that Arundel was an important name in England. Perhaps she could do a little scouting on her own these next few days. There was an Arundel Castle. It was the home of the Duke and Duchess of Norfolk, and residence of the Earl Marshall of England at one time.

Arundel Castle was presently home to the Howard family, one of England's most respected and powerful dynasties. However, Chloe had no idea what connection the castle or the family could have to her ghostly sea captain. The castle was in the southeast of England, while Moonstone Landing was all the way southwest.

Yet the fort was known as Fort Arundel, and that could not be mere coincidence.

How was she ever to explore the castle when it would take her three days to get there and another three days back? It was impossible to ride over in an afternoon. But Fionn could stop there on his way to or from London, assuming there was some connection to be discovered.

In the meantime, she would ask Cain if he knew any members of the Howard family. Dukes likely knew each other because there weren't too many of them, and one would think they would meet often of necessity because of their elevated rank. Cain, if pressed to think about it, might find a similarity in appearance between Fionn and some member of the Howard clan, particularly one of the recent dukes.

She could not imagine anyone in that noble family looking as fine as Fionn, for he was tall and had the muscled strength of a warrior. She could easily see him as a valiant knight on a steed, carrying the Howard banner into battle.

She shook out of the thought, for her mind had already strayed from her ghost sea captain to one of England's most powerful families. In truth, there was nothing more than her active imagination leading her outside of Moonstone Landing.

Was it not better to stay focused on Fionn and the sea captain? The documents, not idle speculation, would lead her down the path she needed to go.

After six hours of uninterrupted work, quite pleased by her progress, she set aside the graphite pencil and studied the neatly ordered piles of documents. As she worked, she had been separating the documents into those she had read and those not yet read. Of those read, she further separated them according to family relation. Those relating most to the sister and brother were put in separate piles from those relating to the sea captain.

She considered leaving Fionn notes on what she had done. However, it would take too long to write everything down, and she hoped to see him in town shortly anyway, since she dared not remain at the cottage much longer. Tongues would wag if Fionn returned and the town gossips learned she was still here.

She rose from the table and entered the kitchen to seek out Mrs. Hawke. "What can I do for you, Lady Chloe?"

"Would it be an imposition to leave the papers on the dining room table? I have put them in a particular order and they should not be touched."

"Oh, I'm sure it is fine. Major Brennan rarely eats in there, especially when on his own. I don't expect he'll be bringing any of his officers home with him, or he would have sent word."

"Thank you. I'll return bright and early tomorrow morning to resume sorting through them." She bade the woman a good day and asked Mr. Hawke to hitch the wagon to take her into town.

"Shall I wait for you, Lady Chloe?" he asked.

She nodded. "Yes, Mr. Hawke. I think you had better. I shouldn't be too long, and you can drop me off at Westgate Hall on the way back."

When they got to the village, she had him pull up in front of Mrs. Halsey's tearoom in the hope of finding Lady Dowling. She walked in and cast Mrs. Halsey a bright smile. "Good afternoon, Mrs. Halsey."

"Good afternoon, lamb. Where are the girls today?"

"They're off to the Falmouth fair with Lord Burness and my sister. You should have seen them giggling with excitement. Has Lady Dowling been in—" The breath caught in her throat when she noticed the lady in question seated at her usual corner table, only this time she was not alone.

Fionn was with her.

Both of them were lost in conversation and hadn't noticed her walk in.

"Lamb," Mrs. Halsey said gently, "he only came in a few moments ago. She is the one who called him over."

The kind words did little to cheer Chloe.

Fionn was seated beside the dazzling Lady Dowling, who had lifted the veil from her hat so that all could see just how beautiful she was. And he appeared to be rapt, because he was paying no notice to anyone else.

Now, the pair of them were laughing over something witty Lady Dowling must have told him.

Chloe did not know what to do.

She suddenly felt inadequate and stupid, a young woman not even in her first year out while Lady Dowling was older—but not old enough to look wizened—and far more sophisticated.

For that matter, so was Fionn quite sophisticated in his own way. Perhaps better described as streetwise and experienced.

She was nothing more than a naïve ninny.

Her only claim to womanly experience was one kiss that Fionn had been reluctant to give her. How could she march up to them as though nothing mattered when suddenly everything mattered?

She did not know much about Lady Dowling other than she had been born a commoner and married quite well, if one's standard of measure was rank and fortune. Love was irrelevant in such arrangements. Her husband had been a minor lord, but still of sufficient rank to be addressed as such, and thereby making her a lady.

This was the sort of woman Fionn could marry...one who was elegant but not raised in elegance. One who may have once made a meal in a kitchen or hung out a wash or swept a room. One whose fortune was modest and who did not have siblings married to dukes or marquesses whose wealth he could never match.

This was whom Fionn would feel comfortable marrying.

Chloe clutched her stomach as it began to twist painfully and churn.

She had to leave. It hurt too much to watch them together and know they were a perfect fit.

She started for the door to make her escape, but Fionn caught up to her before she had taken two steps. "Chloe," he said softly, "I was hoping I might catch you here."

"You knew I was at the cottage."

"Yes, but you always come into Mrs. Halsey's shop with the girls at this hour. I didn't think you would stray from that routine. Why did you turn away and suddenly walk out?"

"You seemed busy. I did not want to disturb you."

He glanced around. "Where are the girls? Did you not bring them with you?"

Of course, he did not know Cormac and Phoebe had taken them to Falmouth. She quickly told him of the fair. "So I was able to work without distraction on those papers."

"That is fortunate. Let's finish with Lady Dowling and then I'll walk you back to my office so we might speak privately." He held out his arm to escort her to their table, his smile utterly charming as he addressed the merry widow. "I was just about to mention to Lady Dowling how much my men enjoyed her company at the last recital."

Chloe nodded. "This was my purpose in coming into town. I was hoping to find you here. Would you mind helping me out again? Of course, I will completely understand if you cannot. It must be quite an imposition, and you needn't feel any obligation whatso—"

"It would be my pleasure," Lady Dowling said.

"Oh."

"I haven't been in company in a very long while, and I think it is time I started. How kind of you to think of me, Lady Chloe."

"Not at all." Indeed, not at all kind. Especially now that Chloe wanted this beautiful woman to disappear in a puff of smoke.

Lady Dowling cast her a warm smile. "Would you care to join us for tea?"

Us?

Had Fionn all along meant to meet the widow here?

"No, I really must get back to Westgate Hall. I only intended to stop by in the hope of finding you here and asking you about the recital. I don't wish to intrude on you and Major Brennan. I can speak to him another time."

Fionn frowned. "I was just about to leave. Is there not a matter you wish to discuss with me?"

"It isn't important and can be left for another day. I really must be off. Mr. Hawke is waiting in the wagon to take me home, and I don't wish to impose on him more than I already have."

"I'll walk you out." Fionn took her by the elbow, not giving her the chance to protest as he led her out.

"What is the matter with you?" he asked the moment the tea shop door closed behind them.

"Nothing."

"You are as jumpy as a frog hopping from lily pad to lily pad."

"I have a headache and wish to go home." She broke free of his gentle hold and climbed into the waiting wagon. "Enjoy your tea with Lady Dowling."

He regarded her with the most confused expression. She could sense his gaze boring into her back on the entire ride up the high street.

She held back her tears until she returned to Westgate Hall and ran up to her bedchamber. Only then did she allow herself a good cry.

She cried so much she actually gave herself a blistering head-ache, and then promptly fell asleep in the hope of shaking it off.

She woke up an hour later to the sound of someone pound-ing at her door and then heard agitated voices. She recognized dear Melrose, who had his voice raised. "You cannot barge up here! Sir, it simply is not done!"

"Chloe," Fionn said with a growl, giving her door another pounding. "Make yourself decent. I am giving you to the count of ten and then I am coming in."

She had taken off her walking boots and let down her hair, but otherwise she was properly dressed. She marched to the door, threw it open, and glowered at him. "You have no right to be up here. Melrose, cart this man away."

Fionn scowled at the butler. "Do not dare put a hand on me unless you wish to lose it." However, he then gentled his tone. "You know I will never harm Lady Chloe."

Chloe sighed. "It is all right, Melrose. No need to summon the footmen."

Fionn raked a hand through his hair as he took in her appear-ance. "I was worried about you. Why did you run off like that?

And then Melrose said you had gone straight to your room clutching your stomach."

He really was worried about her?

"I'll be all right," she said, the defiance draining from her. "I'm sorry if I worried you. Melrose, escort Major Brennan to the terrace and have one of the footmen bring out a pitcher of lemonade. I'll be down in a moment."

Fionn hesitated, obviously concerned she might bolt her door and not come down, but then he nodded and followed Melrose downstairs.

She donned her walking boots and tied her hair back with a ribbon, since she had taken all the pins out and did not want to bother doing up her hair again. She washed her face and held a damp cloth to her eyes to blot away some of the redness in them.

What was she going to tell Fionn? That she had turned into a jealous harpy?

He was pacing on the terrace when she came out to join him, too lost in his thoughts to immediately notice her standing there. The breeze, which usually turned cooler as the sun began to set, had cooled very little. The air felt quite damp, a sign of impending rain. Chloe hoped it would arrive late in the night and be done by the time she made her way to Moonstone Cottage in the morning.

Fionn stopped pacing and turned to her. "Will you now tell me what happened?"

She decided upon the truth, since he was going to figure it out soon enough anyway. He listened without interruption while she began to explain her feelings upon seeing him with Lady Dowling and his ease when laughing with her. "There you were, seated beside this woman whose life may have not started out easy, and who would understand your deprivations better than I ever could. In that moment, I saw myself as you must see me. A pampered youngest child who understood nothing of life. I had to leave. I felt so humiliated."

"This is my fault," he muttered, "because of the way I've held you off. I only went to Mrs. Halsey's shop thinking I might find you there because it had become your routine with the girls. I had no idea they had gone off to Falmouth. I didn't see you and was about to leave when Lady Dowling called me over."

"That's what Mrs. Halsey said."

"Because this is all that happened. All Lady Dowling wanted was to ask me if I could put in a word to you about having her help out again. That's why you caught us laughing. I had just told her you were going to seek her out to ask her this very thing."

"But the way she was looking at you…"

"I know, Chloe. I am not blind to how women look at me. Don't judge her too harshly. She wasn't about to proposition me. I think she was merely trying to be friendly, hoping to get back into a social life but shy in going about it."

Chloe snorted. "Shy?"

"Perhaps uncertain about it rather than shy. Maybe hoping something might come of our acquaintance. And by that I do not mean a romp in the sack. I expect that, like you, she is hoping to find love."

"With you?"

"No, not with me… Or if so, then I am only one possibility among many others. You have no idea… It doesn't matter. My point is, you are the only one who has my heart, and no one else will ever entice me to stray from you. I mean it, Chloe. Other men may have it in them to move on, but I am not made that way. One woman. Filling my heart. For a lifetime. And that woman is you."

She sank into a chair. "Don't say that. I still want to be angry with you."

"I know, and I still deserve it. Others would find themselves fortunate to have captured the heart of an heiress, but this is the very reason I hold back. I cannot come into a marriage empty-handed. I have to give you something in return."

"You would give me love. That is more precious than anything else."

He sat beside her, resting an arm on his thigh as he leaned toward her. "I know it is. And this is all the more reason why I am desperate to preserve it."

"We are going around in circles. You are so afraid to lose me that you will give me up without ever trying."

"I am trying, Chloe. The last thing I ever want to do is give you up. I have pared down every blasted requirement I had made up for myself, and all I am trying to do now is give you one elusive thing that I can bring into a marriage. *One thing.* Even something as paltry as a name that is my own. All I've managed so far is to become indebted to your brothers-in-law for helping me out on some wild possibility that Viscount Brennan's kin tried to cheat me out of more of my inheritance. Gad, I could kick myself for allowing myself to be swayed by Ducky. He wouldn't know a clue if it bit him on the arse. And now I have you so overset, you've spent the last hour in tears."

"It was my doing, not yours." She saw that this discussion was bringing him pain, so she changed the subject. "Do you wish to know about my day? Besides my running out of the tea shop like a demented chicken?"

He cast her a wry, mirthless grin. "Of course. Better than keeping my mind on how badly I've hurt you. Did you find anything of interest in those documents?"

"Just scraps of information, nothing that leaps out at me yet. What do you know about Arundel Castle or the Duke of Norfolk?"

"Nothing, other than he was pivotal in approving this hospital project. Before you jump out of your chair and look for a hidden connection, let me assure you there is none to me, although there obviously could be one to our ghostly Captain Arundel. Norfolk is the lord in charge of a committee responsible for approving or denying all construction projects for the army."

She told him about the family tree she was constructing for the sea captain's family and her timeline of events that she had gleaned from those documents. "I am doing this in the hope it leads me to a connection to you. Do you not find it interesting that the sea captain's sister was called Fiona?"

"And you think there is a connection because I am called Fionn? That was just a name given to me at the orphanage."

"An unusual name, you must admit. What if it was not merely picked out of the air? What if you were given it because this was your mother's choice?"

"A mother who abandoned me."

He spoke with such bitterness, it made her heart ache for him. "We don't know yet what happened. You cannot assume she left you, certainly not willingly. All I am saying is there must be a connection, or else these documents would not have been revealed to you."

They spoke for a little while longer about other things, less painful topics, until Fionn finally rose. "Chloe, night is falling. I had better go."

She rose to walk him out. "Will I see you tomorrow?"

He sighed, ending with a soft groan. "I think I will avoid the tea shop for the next few days. But you will always find me at the fort or the hospital site if you need to seek me out. Or have Mr. Hawke send word to me, and I shall meet you wherever you like."

"All right. Seems everything we spoke about during this visit brought you unbearable pain. I'm so sorry, Fionn. But I sincerely believe the truth will free you from your torment. I want this so much for you, just to see you truly happy…or at least, finally at peace with yourself."

He caressed her cheek.

She sensed there was something he wanted to tell her—indeed, she suspected he wanted to tell her that he loved her.

Her fear was not about his feelings for her.

Even in her jealous harpy moment, she did not doubt her importance to him or that he loved her…although it would be nice to hear him say it once.

Her fear was always that he would do a foolishly noble thing for her protection and give her up. Her happiness mattered most to him, and he would not hesitate to sacrifice his own desires if he thought she would be better off for it.

Well, she'd got his prideful requirements down to just one, and that was a big step forward toward a marriage proposal. She thought even holding back for that one thing was a pointless endeavor. There was no magical talisman to a happy union. Even if he had come to her with a title and fortune of equal stature to her brothers-in-law, who was to say theirs would be a happy marriage?

She had seen her parents and now her sisters in their marriages. It took devotion, commitment, and a willingness to put the other ahead of their own needs. Sacrifice. Those requirements applied no matter how rich or titled someone might be.

She supposed the real question worrying Fionn was, how much would she sacrifice for him? Her answer was anything and everything. But he thought there were limits to her ability to sacrifice for him.

Perhaps he was right to be cautious and force her to think about the realities of their marriage. Becoming the wife of an army major and learning to do without the luxuries she had always had within arm's reach would be an adjustment.

She was not going to be pigheaded about it and deny the obvious. Even though she and her sisters had led simple lives after their father's death, all she ever had to do was ring for a maid if she wanted something. Nor did their meals magically appear with the snap of their fingers, for they always had a cook in their employ.

A maid and a cook, that was all. But it was still more than most people could ever afford.

She sighed.

Learning to fend for herself would be a challenge she realized while standing alone in the courtyard, watching him ride off on Sophocles in the fading light.

What would those boxes turn up tomorrow?

Chapter Fourteen

FIONN STOOD IN his office the following morning and stared at the blackening clouds gathering strength overhead. He had never seen any quite so dark or amassing with such menace, and knew they signified a bad storm on the way. The clock on his mantel had just chimed ten o'clock. The day's construction had started a mere two hours ago, but he knew it would have to be cut short and his men now put to work protecting the building materials and safely tying down their equipment.

He strode to the hospital site and ordered the men to stop their labors and immediately start covering everything they could find. Tools, supplies, hoists. The wooden beams meant to reinforce the existing roof supports were most important and needed to be protected, for they would be useless if they got wet. Rot would set into the wood, and having to replace them with new beams would cause months of delay.

Indeed, one bad storm could set back the entire timetable for as much as a year.

He worked beside his men for the next hour to secure all their building materials, and once that was done, called over Sergeant Crane. "Constable Angel might need help," he said, now shouting over the blustery wind. "Send some men over to him, and send Cray and Folger to the Kestrel Inn stable to watch over our horses for the duration of the storm. The other men should return to the barracks and remain them there until the storm passes."

"Aye, Major Brennan." The sergeant turned to the soldiers and barked the orders, which were met with relief from most, since they had been working hard to lay the foundation and get as far along in the construction as they could before the cold weather set in.

Fionn assigned a few more men to remain on guard in the watchtower and report if anything collapsed. "Just make note of any damage, but do nothing else unless a life is in imminent danger."

His lame leg could always feel changes in the weather, particularly an oncoming rain. But this approaching rain was much more than a mere shower. His leg hurt worse than anything he had felt in a long while. There was nothing any of them could do, or should do, but stand ready to assist the villagers, if requested, and be prepared to repair any damage once the storm passed.

He wasn't about to allow his men anywhere near the framed-out structure before the weather calmed, for he would then have a collapsed building and dead or injured soldiers to dig out.

Fionn thought about Chloe.

She was likely at the cottage and not paying attention to the looming storm.

He had given his officers their instructions, and the sergeants had ordered the last of his men to the safety of the barracks. There was nothing more for him to do but wait out the impending torrent.

Since he was not going to accomplish anything more today, he left the fort and rode at a gallop for home. Leaves swirled around him, and several tree branches had already broken under the force of the particularly fierce wind as he neared Moonstone Cottage.

Chloe smiled up at him when he strode in. "Fionn, what brings you here? I did not expect you."

"Nor did I, but there is a tempest brewing and I need to get you safely home before it hits." He glanced around, for the cottage felt remarkably silent. "Where are the Hawkes?"

"They went to St. Austell Grange to help Hen prepare for her party."

"So you were left alone?"

"Yes."

"All alone?"

"Honestly, I am not a child. I can be trusted on my own. Unsupervised." She grinned. "That is usually what 'alone' means."

Blessed saints. "I'm glad I rode back. Come on, leave everything as it is."

"But the documents—"

"Can wait until tomorrow. They've been hidden for years. Another day or two won't make a difference." The dining room windows rattled as a violent gust suddenly struck the panes. He hurriedly secured the shutters, then he and Chloe made quick work of securing the others throughout the house.

"There isn't time to lose," he said when they returned downstairs after closing up the last of the bedchambers. "You'll ride with me on Sophocles. It's the fastest way to get you home."

"What about the beach? I can walk—"

"Are you mad? You'll be washed out to sea. The cove must be flooded by now, every last grain of sand underwater and the waves ten foot in height. Come on, do not sit down or think to pick up your parchment and pencil."

"Where will you go after you drop me at home?"

"Probably back to the fort now that I know the cottage is secured. I trust my officers to handle any mishaps, but I ought to be on hand as commanding officer. However, I may run out of time and simply have to ride back here."

He took her by the hand to lead her out of the cottage, his strides long so that she had to take two of her own to keep up with his one. He then lifted her onto Sophocles, and had just mounted behind her when the skies opened up without warning.

Not even a few drops or a light, steady rain to signal the start of the storm.

He could hardly breathe for the water suddenly pouring down on them and knew Chloe had to be struggling, too.

This was no mild summer rain but a deluge of biblical proportions. It was as though someone stood above them unrelentingly tossing tubs of water down on their heads.

The sky was now black as night. The wind was howling with gale force. Lightning flashed in the distance over the water, and then one bolt struck so close to them that Fionn could hear the ground sizzle.

Sophocles panicked.

"Bloody, bleeding hell." Fionn turned the frightened mount around, holding tight to Chloe as the beast began to rear and buck.

It took all of Fionn's strength to keep him under control long enough to get him back into the stable. "Well, that's it. You and I are trapped here for the duration. This storm is going to be really bad." He dismounted and helped Chloe down, then unsaddled the beast. "Sophocles is trained for battle," he said, easing the skittish stallion into his stall. "If he is scared out of his wits, then there is reason to be worried."

While Chloe stroked and soothed his horse, Fionn took a quick moment to climb up to the loft and secure its sturdy doors.

"Should we just stay in here with Sophocles?" she asked when he hopped down from the ladder.

"No, back to the house. I'm sorry, Chloe. All I've accomplished is getting us soaked." Perhaps he should have stayed in town, but then she would have been left to fend for herself. The girl did not know how to boil water or light a fire or cook a meal. She did not even know how to warm a meal that was already cooked and left in a pot. How could she have survived the night alone here? Worse, what if she had decided to make her way home on her own and taken the shortcut from the beach?

No, he'd done the right thing in coming to her, even though

they were now trapped for the duration of the storm.

Unfortunately, there was no question word would get out and her reputation left in ruins. There was no help for it—he would have to marry her. Not that it mattered to him. He wanted to marry her, ached to have her as his wife. But this would force his hand and make him come to terms with the one thing that had held him back from courting her in the first place, his bringing nothing to the marriage.

Since neither the duke nor the marquess objected to him as a suitor, he knew it was only his stubborn pride standing in the way. The Fates seemed to have lost patience with him, just as Chloe had, and they were now making the decision for him.

There was not a chance of keeping their time together in Moonstone Cottage quiet. The town gossip, Mr. Matchett, was going to make certain the whole town knew.

"Take my hand, Chloe. We're going to make a run for the house." He peered into the courtyard and noticed it was already flooding. "Blast, wait."

He had heard enough about the sudden squall that led to the death of the cottage's ghost to know how fierce and dangerous this one hanging over them had to be.

He removed his jacket and handed it to her. "Hold it over your head."

"What about you?"

"I'll be fine." He wrapped an arm around Chloe and tried to shelter her as much as possible as they raced back into the house.

The wind blew the door out of his grasp and slammed it wide open the moment he released the latch. He pushed it shut as soon as he and Chloe made it safely inside. But a blast of wind had howled through the house while the door was open and now sent all her neatly sorted papers flying off the table.

Dozens floated about the dining room.

Chloe cried out and ran from one end of the room to the other to catch them before they hit the floor.

Great.

He had not been able to take her home.

The papers were now in a mess because he'd made her leave the house.

They were both soaked to the skin, his jacket doing nothing to shield her from the deluge.

And they were trapped alone in the house.

He may as well drop on bended knee and propose right this moment, because there was no getting around the inevitable. "Chloe, did you happen to leave any clothes here that you can change into?"

She was still hopping about and trying to scoop up all the loose papers. "No. I moved all of my belongings out just before you moved in."

He sighed. "I'll give you something of mine to put on."

She paused in her gathering and stared at him.

Her hair was soaked and puddles were forming at her feet as water dripped off her wet gown. He saw her expression change the moment she realized what being alone with him signified. "Fionn…?"

"My officers know where I was going."

"Will they keep quiet about it?"

He nodded. "The Hawkes won't say anything either, but there is a house full of servants at St. Austell Grange who know the Hawkes were there helping out your sister and not here with you when the storm hit. Someone is going to put two and two together, likely Mr. Matchett, because he knows I rode out just before the storm hit."

"What shall we do?"

He took the papers out of her hands and set them carefully on the table. "Come upstairs, Chloe. I'll help you out of those wet clothes."

Her eyes grew wide.

He kissed her softly on the mouth. "I will marry you if word gets out."

She shivered lightly. "Is that supposed to make me happy?

The wonderful thing about being a well-connected heiress is that men will court me even if I am ruined. You are the only one who disdains my wealth."

"I don't disdain it. I just…" He raked a hand through his wet hair. "Look at whom your sisters married. How am I supposed to feel when compared to them? I can never give you all they are able to give their wives."

He took a moment to light a lantern because the house was now in a gray gloom. Then he wrapped her hand in his and led her upstairs to his bedchamber.

She stood shivering amid the lantern's golden glow.

He wanted to wrap this bedraggled angel in his arms and kiss her into forever, but he was also soaking wet, and both of them were dripping on the carpet. He turned away to withdraw one of his shirts from the wardrobe and toss it on the bed. "That's for you."

He then removed the cameo brooch and fichu she had strategically placed at her bosom for modesty, his fingers grazing the soft swell of her breasts because it was unavoidable. In any event, that he took such intimacies no longer mattered, since she was to be his wife.

His wife.

"Turn around, Chloe," he said in a raspy whisper. "The clips are falling out of your hair. Let me undo it." He sucked in a breath as those fiery curls tumbled over her shoulders in a wet tangle. "Let me get you undressed, and then you can comb out your hair."

He gently drew her hair to one side, and then began to unbutton her gown. As it loosened on her body, he saw that she also had on a corset and chemise.

"I'm so sorry, Chloe. I was frantic with worry and only meant to be sure you were safe. We will now certainly be forced to marry." He kissed her softly on the neck while he unlaced the corset, his fingers seeming to have a mind of their own as they caressed her skin. "I do want to marry you."

She was hardly breathing and said not a word.

Neither of them had expected this, and it had to be a little overwhelming for her.

He did not remove any of her clothes after untying them, not the gown, nor the chemise or corset, because a naked Chloe was more temptation than he could resist, and he would have her beneath him on the bed and—sober this time—kissing every inch of her body.

"I'll give you privacy in a moment. Take off your gown and everything else. Oh, let me get you a drying cloth, too. You'll need to dry yourself off before you put on my shirt. I have a comb on the bureau. Use it for your hair."

He fetched the cloth, handed it to her, and then grabbed a shirt and breeches for himself before starting out of the room.

"Where are you going?" she asked, finally managing to find her voice.

He cast her a wry smile. "Your old bedchamber. I'll change in there. I'll take your clothes once you have changed out of them and set them out to dry in the kitchen."

"Why there?"

"Because it is the warmest room in the house."

"Oh, that makes sense."

"We'll be using the stove and the hearth anyway to heat up the meal Mrs. Hawke no doubt prepared for me. Don't worry, there'll be plenty for the both of us."

"I can fend for myself with bread and cheese if there isn't."

"We'll share whatever there is. I am not going to leave you to nibble on scraps while I eat a hearty repast. I'll put on the kettle for tea."

"I can do it."

He arched an eyebrow. "Really?"

She sighed. "No. But I am willing to try. I've always wanted to learn how. If Mrs. Hawke was not around to do it for us when my sisters and I lived here, then Hen or Phoebe took care of the chore. They wouldn't let me near the stove or hearth because they thought I was too young and might burn myself."

"I'll teach you once you are done changing."

"Is that all you are going to say to me?"

He shook his head in confusion. "What else should I say?"

"I'm sure you are holding back an 'I told you so,' since you've accused me of being pampered and I have just proved you right. I don't even know how to boil water."

"I would never say that to you. I'm glad you have never had to endure hardship. I only wish I was in a position to provide for you in the same way your family has."

He strode out and shut the door behind him, ignoring the heat now roaring through his body because seeing Chloe with her wet gown slipping off her shoulders and barely covering her breasts had his organs in spasms.

He went into her old bedchamber and took off his clothes, then put on the dry ones. A moment later, he heard Chloe clambering about next door and wondered what she was doing.

Since when had removing clothes been so noisy? Was she searching through his belongings?

He left his discarded uniform spread neatly over one of the wooden chairs in her old room and knocked at his bedchamber door. "Are you decent? May I come in?"

She opened the door and peered up at him with big green eyes. "Yes, however, I am not really decent. I was looking for a robe, but you don't seem to have one."

"Because I don't use one. I don't sleep in nightclothes either." He was trying to appear unaffected, but she had combed back her long hair and tucked the strands behind her little ears. His shirt looked insanely alluring on her, and there was no mistaking she was naked underneath.

He cleared his throat. "My shirt fits you like a tent."

"It falls to my knees. You can see my legs."

"I've seen them before." And if he wanted to be accurate about it, he could see all of her body outlined beneath his shirt. The fabric was not quite as thick as he thought, and her pert breasts were visible if one looked closely, which he did.

Dear heaven, he did.

He gathered his clothes and hers, and then headed downstairs to set them on pegs beside the hearth, which he now took a moment to light.

The kindling was damp from the water-soaked air and took a little longer to start burning. But he soon had the fire going and tossed a few more logs on to keep it ablaze. He then filled the kettle, but set it aside on the table instead of putting it on the stove.

He was going to leave that for Chloe to do once he taught her how to light the stove. He would then have her tend to the kettle and set out cups for tea. Before doing that, however, he went to the larder, took out the pot of stew Mrs. Hawke had prepared for tonight's meal, and hung it over the hearth fire to warm.

Chloe had followed him down, but remained in the doorway just watching him move about the kitchen.

He glanced at her and saw her eyes tear up.

Blast.

Had he been too hard on her?

Now she felt awful because she regarded herself as a pampered princess. Well, she *had* been pampered, but it had not given her an ugly nature. She was not haughty or spoiled, as many of those of her rank were. In fact, she was kind and generous, and had made him feel welcomed from the moment they had met.

He did not think less of her because she did not know her way about a kitchen.

"This is why you loathe the idea of marrying me," she said in a ragged whisper.

"Chloe...never." She truly made him ache. "Come on, I'll teach you how to boil water. Are you still willing to learn?"

She nodded.

"Let me roll up your shirt sleeves first. They are too long on you and dangling. I don't want them to fall into the flames when you light the stove. You also want to keep your hair tied back so that the ends don't accidentally catch fire." She was such a pretty thing, with big eyes and long, silky hair. She had an earnest expression on her face, and he saw how much she wanted to gain his approval.

She had it, of course.

He thought she was wonderful and had so many fine qualities. That she had no experience in a kitchen did not diminish her in any way.

But he had made too much of it, he supposed.

Being so kind and good-natured, she had taken it all very much to heart.

He drew her up against him when he was done rolling up her sleeves, growling softly as he placed his arms around her and wrapped her in his embrace. This was where she belonged and had always belonged, only he had been too caught up in his dark past to allow her to shine her light on him.

He was still caught up in this dark void of his past, still haunted by all the unknowns of his life. But he always found solace in Chloe, in her sweetness and acceptance of him. He loved her beyond anything he had ever imagined possible.

Protecting her mattered more to him than his own life ever could.

Because of that love, he had wanted to give Chloe the opportunity to accept someone of more suitable rank and wealth, especially Lord Claymore, who was now returning to Moonstone Landing. He thought of it as making a noble sacrifice on his part. But in truth, he was just being cowardly and using his fears of disappointing her as a reason to push her away. He should have given her feelings more consideration.

But he had looked at the situation only through his eyes, his mind fixed on the fact he was not good enough for her. She had never felt this way, nor had she ever made him feel lesser. Quite the opposite—no one had ever made him feel more cherished.

And here he was, willing to pass her off to someone else.

Not only was he thinking to foist her on someone else, someone he deemed worthy while ignoring Chloe's wishes, but she must have been in agony thinking he would move on and find someone else for himself.

No wonder she had almost made herself ill when seeing him with Lady Dowling.

How could he have done this to Chloe, this sweet girl who loved him truly? Because of him, she had been in misery thinking she would lose him to the merry widow. Others thought the woman beautiful, but she could never compare to Chloe.

Chloe was far prettier in his eyes. Indeed, she was radiant.

She would never lose him to anyone else, because he loved her too much. But how was she to know this if he constantly pushed her away? He loved her to the depths of his soul, so why did he think she could not love him in this same, all-consuming way?

"Chloe..." She had never once belittled him or cared who sired him. She loved him for the man he was. For this reason, her family had come around to accepting him despite having expressed some initial concerns. This was no longer an issue. They understood what Chloe needed, what her heart yearned for, and were not going to stand in her way.

All along, he had been the obstruction.

He ran his thumb lightly along the line of her jaw. "There is something I have forgotten to do."

"You?" She looked up at him with so much misery, obviously believing he was about to comment on something *she* had neglected. "What is that?"

"Tell you that I love you."

She stiffened and held herself as straight as a board while still in his arms. She tried to pull away, but he would not let her. "What?"

"I love you, Chloe."

She seemed ready to burst into tears. "Do not say it if you do not mean it. You cannot lie to me because you think I am now ruined."

"I mean every word. I am desperate to have you. I cannot breathe for wanting you. You fill my dreams and my every waking thought. You soothe my empty heart. You *are* my very heart. It has only ever been yours."

Her smile was so hopeful and fragile, it broke his heart.

"It will only ever be yours. I love you, Chloe." He brought his mouth down on hers, allowing the tempest inside him to pour forth. This kiss could not be gentle, for he could no longer hide the truth of his feelings, the pain of all his empty years, and the joy in finding her.

She was surely his salvation. Surely this exquisite girl was all the missing pieces of his heart.

He kissed her with fervent longing, his desire raw and savage.

You are mine.

Mine.

He took no mercy, plundering her sweet, plump lips with a fury to match the storm raging outside.

No one but Chloe would ever possess him. With this kiss, he pledged his heart and soul to her.

And yet he'd made her doubt because of these obstacles he had thrown in her way. Part of it was fear that a woman like her could never really love a street urchin like him, for beneath the uniform this was all he was, a boy off the London streets.

She kissed him back with a fiery longing to match his own.

This was his Chloe and everything he loved about her. She cared passionately. She gave everything of herself and wanted him for who he was without demand for more.

He was the one throwing demands at himself when all she wanted to do was love him.

He lifted her up against him so that her soft, little body was pressed to his and not a scintilla of light shone between them.

He deepened the kiss.

Thunder rolled above them. Wind and rain surrounded their cozy nest.

"Chloe," he whispered.

His hands roamed up and down her body, for he needed to touch her, taste her, lose himself in her. Possess her. Memorize her every luscious curve. She was small and slender, but her breasts were full and womanly.

He adored her.

Revered her.

But also ached to bed her.

Was it not right that a man should burn with desire for the woman who was to be his wife? "I love you so much, Chloe."

Her eyes lit up like starlight. "I love you too. Please say it again, Fionn."

He grinned. "I love you, Chloe. Whether we are ever found out or not, I would like to marry you. So will you? Do me the honor of marrying me, that is."

She still had her arms around his neck, and he still had her soft curves pressed against the hard length of him. "Yes, you know I will. I love you so very much."

Something changed inside of him in that moment.

He could not quite explain what was happening to him, only that he was no longer that lonely boy who struggled each brutal day to survive.

He belonged to someone now. Someone who cared whether he lived or died.

He had Chloe with whom to share memories, to hold in his arms, to confide his concerns. To dance with him despite his limp, and worry if it pained him.

They would build a future together.

Having Chloe by his side would help him forget the pain of the past.

Well, one never forgot a past like his. But she would make it bearable.

"Fionn," she said, taking a hard swallow. "Does this mean we are betrothed?"

"I suppose it does." He cast her an affectionate smile. "Well, unofficially. We still need your guardian's consent."

"Cain will give it. He must."

He buried his face in the slender curve of her neck, suddenly struggling with the groundswell of feelings coursing through him.

How could someone as perfect as this lovely girl care so deeply for him? How could he possibly be right for her? Or she right for him?

And yet he knew it was the only way it could ever be. The two of them together, loving and supporting each other. Madly in love with each other.

"You are my everything," he said in a ragged whisper. "Never doubt it for a moment."

She was crying, and he was on the verge of it as well. But tears had left him long ago, for no amount of wailing or bemoaning his fate had ever helped against the freezing cold or pain of starvation.

"Look at us," he said with a surprisingly shaky voice. "Aren't we a pair?"

She laughed as she nodded, and then put her hands to her cheeks to brush them dry. "Yes, we are a pair. Matched in heart forever, I hope."

"Not a doubt of it, love."

She took a deep breath, and her face turned a deep red.

"What is it, Chloe?" It felt good to hold her in his arms and know they belonged to each other.

"Do you think we might sleep in the captain's bedchamber tonight?"

"Share a bed?"

She nodded.

With this luscious girl? They wouldn't get a lick of sleep. "Yes, love. Unless the roof caves in between then and now, I would say it was a certainty."

Her eyes widened. "Then you have no objections?"

"Only one. That I will not claim you until you are truly mine. That privilege is for a husband, and I shall heartily claim it once we are wed, but not before."

"Then we are only to sleep? I don't think I will close my eyes at all while that storm still rages. I think it is more than a passing squall, or it would have been through here over an hour ago."

"This is a tempest for certain, and there is no telling when it will pass." After they'd shared a light repast, he led her upstairs to his bedchamber, and then rubbed a hand across the back of his neck as he stared at the bed.

"We are going to share it," Chloe insisted, sensing his reluctance.

He grinned. "That isn't the reason for my hesitation."

She looked up at him in confusion. "Then what is?"

"Once I have you in my bed, how am I ever going to let you out of it?"

Chapter Fifteen

C HLOE COULD NOT help but smile at Fionn's statement, for she had never considered that she might be alluring to him, and this was a very heady feeling. "You find me appealing?"

"Very." He kissed her on the mouth, a hot, light kiss because this gorgeous man was a walking flame and she ignited at his every touch.

He glanced toward the window as another forceful gust rattled its shutters. "I hope that is not Captain Arundel marking his displeasure."

Chloe shook her head. "He never would because he understands what love is now that he has found it with my aunt. They are both quite pleased of our match."

"Oh, they told you that, did they?" He arched an eyebrow in amusement.

"Not in so many words, but I know they are."

"Perhaps they approve of my loving you, but not so heartily approve of having you in my bed before we are married."

"We are as much as betrothed, so you are permitted to take liberties." Chloe gasped as the realization suddenly struck her. "Oh, Fionn. Is this not the loveliest thing in the world?"

He emitted a soft, contented growl. "Yes, love."

She was afraid to blink, afraid to breathe and have this sinfully delicious man disappear before her very eyes.

Fionn, on the other hand, appeared ridiculously calm about their predicament. Did he not have a single qualm about their need to marry? Or the fact they were about to share a bed?

Well, this could not be the first time he was sharing a bed with a woman. She had never done anything like this before.

"Um…" She cleared her throat.

"What is it, Chloe?"

"Am I to keep your shirt on as my nightgown?"

"Yes." But he cast her a steamy look that warned it might not stay on her for very long.

Her heart raced and began to skip beats.

She had never been the object of anyone's desire, and even though she had no idea what to do once in bed, it all felt quite thrilling.

All the more thrilling because she suspected he loved her more than she loved him. Of course, she loved him completely and eternally. But she had never suffered as he had, and it was this suffering that made his love for her all the more poignant and enduring.

To bind himself to someone, share his heart and be willing to trust, was a far bigger step for him to take than it was for her.

In truth, she had been concerned especially about his ability to trust. Why should he ever trust when everyone who ought to have loved and protected him had betrayed and abandoned him? How was he to let down his guard when to do so on the streets of London might have led to him losing his life?

And yet he seemed ready to accept her into his heart when he had never known love from anyone before.

She threw her arms around him and drew his head down so she could plant kisses all over his face.

He laughed. "Chloe, what are you doing?"

"Trying to show you how much I love you."

He laughed and allowed several more kisses before he eased out of her grasp. "All right, now it's my turn to show you how much I love you."

She gulped and sank onto the bed as he removed his shirt and turned back to her with the most exquisitely hot look in his eyes. Even removing his shirt had been a beautiful thing to behold, the way his muscles strained and flexed as he drew it off him to reveal a lean, hard body that she was certain had been sculpted of stone.

"You've never done this before, Chloe. Just say the word and I'll stop."

She did not expect to be able to string a sentence together or even utter a word once he got started doing whatever he meant to do to her. She was not completely dense about what went on between a man and a woman, but she had never experienced so much as a kiss before Fionn had given her one.

She was not going to turn prim and urge him to stop. Whatever was going to happen would be splendid because it was with him.

Was this not the very bliss her Aunt Henleigh had found with her sea captain? A love that transcended time with a man who loved her without restraint and would protect her all the days of her life?

Chloe had not had serious conversations about intimacy with her sisters, never expecting to need instruction so soon. They would have explained things to her eventually had the need arisen. But finding herself trapped here with Fionn was unexpected, and she was caught unprepared.

However, not knowing what was to happen was also all right, because she trusted this wonderful man and knew he would never hurt her.

He seemed to be following her thoughts. "When I claim you truly as my wife, you might feel some discomfort. But not with anything we are going to do tonight, Chloe. You will only experience pleasure."

She cast him a smile in relief. "Well then, that's all right, isn't it? Let's get started. What must I do?"

He returned her smile with an achingly tender one of his own. "Just close your eyes and let me do the work. I will do my best to have you howling for me."

"Howling?" She laughed. "Wait, you're serious?"

His smile turned wicked.

"You are awfully sure of yourself." She grinned, finding the possibility quite extraordinary. He was so arrogant in his confidence.

But men like Fionn learned early about the art of survival, and if seduction was required to live another day, then he would have mastered it fast.

She held her breath when he gently nudged her onto her back. The mattress was soft, and she felt as though the two of them were wrapped together in their own cocoon under the canopied bed. She sank further into the mattress when he shifted his big, magnificent body over her slight frame and propped on his elbows.

She felt the weight of him atop her, and found it exquisite and divine.

He smiled down at her. "Ready, love?"

"All of my life," she whispered back, circling her arms around his neck.

He laughed and then kissed her as though she was the most precious thing in his life.

She felt a source of pride to have elicited such depth of feeling from a man who had spent his life suppressing all feeling.

He was hot as a torch, his skin emitting a sexual heat that had her pulse throbbing before he'd done anything more than look at her.

Dear heaven, that smoldering look. Flames tore through her. She wanted all of him. "Don't hold back, Fionn."

But she saw the determination in his eyes and knew he would not give her everything tonight, certainly not the physical pleasure of their bodies joined together. To take her innocence was a step too far for him. Of course, it was only out of concern for her.

Well, that intimacy would come later, when they were husband and wife.

As for her, simply being in bed with him and having him atop her was deliciously exciting and more than satisfying for this first time.

But there was still plenty for her to learn, and she worried about pleasing him. What if she was bumbling and awkward?

"You are not going to disappoint me, Chloe." He seemed to read her thoughts, which usually were too transparent for her liking. "Do not think too hard about this. In fact, close your eyes and do not think at all. Just take in each sensation. The touch of my hand. The taste of my mouth on yours. The lick of my tongue."

Tongues were involved?

She thought it was only because he had been falling down drunk the last time that his tongue had lolled out and he slobbered over her. Of course, it hadn't all been a slobber. Dear heaven, some of the things he'd done to her with that tongue of his had been quite nice.

"All right."

He lowered his beautifully shaped mouth to hers and sank his lips onto hers with a possessive hunger. Theirs was no gentle kiss, but a ravaging one filled with heat and meant to conquer her heart.

This man knew how to pierce her soul.

There was something quite magnificent in his barely leashed restraint, the perfect way his mouth pressed down on hers with aching need. He was not merely kissing her, but memorizing the touch and taste of her, etching her into his own soul, and taking her into his heart.

A heart that had never known love before.

She knew she was no mere bedmate for him, but the one person who could ease his painful past. Perhaps to forget it and try to move on.

Her heart beat faster than it had ever beat before.

Pulses began to throb that had never throbbed before.

A fiery heat coursed through her.

Her response was physical and intense, but more so because tonight involved more than mere physical pleasure. Tonight was all about trust...his trusting her and letting her in where others had betrayed and hurt him.

She melted at his every touch. Moaned softly with each sensation of his big, powerful body rhythmically sliding over hers. Since he had removed his shirt, she felt his smooth, hot skin beneath her palms, her greedy palms that wanted to touch all of him and know all of him.

She held on to his powerful shoulders and sighed as his rock-hard muscles flexed with tension.

She still wore his shirt, now an unwanted barrier between their bodies. She squirmed under him, trying to shed the garment so that nothing came between them.

He emitted a pained laugh. "Keep it on, love. My resolve is dangerously weak."

"But—"

He kissed her once more to silence her.

When she glanced down to work the buttons, she noticed her shirt was already unbuttoned and her breasts exposed.

Well, he had been a cutpurse in his younger days, his touch light and quick. She hadn't felt a thing as he'd eased the opening apart and now cupped one breast in his large, roughened hand. He began to run his thumb lightly over the soft peak until it became taut, and she felt the sensual heat of his touch coursing through her limbs.

She gasped when he lowered his head and put his mouth to her breast, gently suckling the sensitive tip. "Oh, dear heaven."

She almost expired when he moved to the other breast and took its taut tip into his mouth to tease it with his tongue in the same manner. "Chloe, you are the sweetest thing I've ever tasted."

She could not form the words to respond.

But he had to know what she was feeling, for he was not new

to this sort of pleasure.

Was there a storm raging outside? She felt as though the maelstrom was raging entirely within her body.

He kept his gaze on her as he ran his hand under her shirt and slid the fabric upward along her thighs in a slow, sensual arc. The sensation of his work-roughened hands upon her legs left her completely undone.

She began to wriggle beneath him, her body straining toward his as he continued to touch her and taste her, and tease responses out of her that made her feel wantonly delicious.

Something built up inside of her, and she moved against him to relieve this pressure.

"Slow down, love." He placed his hands on her hips to steady her. "This is not something you want to rush."

She had no idea what *this* was, but she was eager to find out and in fact *did* want him to rush it, and told him so. In this instance, patience was not a virtue.

He laughed, a soft, rumbling laugh filled with mirthful affection. "All right, you greedy thing. I was going to hold off and ease you into this new experience, but I see that I had better not."

He slipped the shirt off her completely so that she was now wearing nothing at all. She was usually quite modest, but felt no shame or embarrassment as Fionn's gaze raked over her body.

His gorgeous eyes were gray-hot embers. "You are so beautiful, Chloe. My sweet, lovely Chloe."

She was no siren by any means, but he made her feel as though she was the most alluring woman on earth, and all the raw pain of his past was forgotten merely by looking at her.

By loving her.

She saw everything in the steel glint of his eyes, that hot and dangerous glint. But she had not a moment's fear, for amid the turmoil was Fionn at his essence, a man who trusted her with his heart and would always be incredibly protective of her.

Which was why she did not leap off the bed and cry out in alarm when he used his broad shoulders to ease her legs apart and then, shockingly, lower his mouth to the intimate spot between her thighs.

"Dear heaven!"

He began to *lick* her there with his tongue.

She gasped, for it was the most wickedly wanton thing she had ever experienced, but she was going to do him bodily harm if he dared stop.

Thankfully, he did not.

He suckled and teased her until she begged for mercy and cried out in utter surrender, but he pressed on and would not relent even though there was nothing left of her but a molten core.

She gripped his hair with one hand and the coverlet with the other, tugging on both as her body turned to fire. "Dear heaven, don't stop."

Flames tore through her, the scorching heat relentless so that she simply turned to cinders. In the next moment, she cried out and shattered into a thousand fiery embers that floated toward the stars.

Moan after moan of pleasure escaped her lips while he now took her into his arms and held her possessively. He caressed her cheek and told her how much he loved her.

When she gazed at him, his eyes were the dark steel of a raging sky.

When she calmed, Fionn's gaze also softened, and he cast her a smug grin, for he was obviously quite pleased with himself.

"I suppose you are congratulating yourself on your prowess."

"You were beautifully responsive, love."

Because she had been howling just as he had predicted she would.

"Stop gloating, you evil man." But she laughed and snuggled against him, for mingled with his victorious joy of conquest was also his breathtaking love for her. She had never seen him so content or known his heart to be so light and carefree. "You are a beast," she said with another soft laugh. "You might have warned me this would happen."

His smile was as genuine and unrestrained as she had ever seen it, and for the first time, she realized he had dimples.

Sweet, youthful dimples.

"I love you, Fionn," she whispered with so much feeling, her voice shook.

He caressed her cheek. "I love you too, my beautiful Chloe."

She allowed him to revel in his moment of triumph, simply smiling as he studied her in fascination.

Was she also not victorious? What would it take to return the favor and pleasure him? Assuming he permitted such a thing.

She asked him.

He rolled onto his back and roared with laughter. "Blessed saints, you will turn me ravenous and uncontrollable. I love you, Chloe. But you are *not* returning the favor tonight."

She sighed. "All right."

He kissed her on the forehead. "How do you feel, love?"

She looked up at him and grinned. "Quite womanly."

He sank back beside her and drew her into the circle of his arms. "You were splendid."

"You did all the work. I merely responded."

She expected a glib retort, for he was quite pleased with himself. Instead, he became surprisingly serious. "I did not think it possible to love you more than I already do. But after this, I think there will be no boundaries to my love for you. It will simply continue to grow unfettered, too vast ever to be contained. I already love you beyond the moon and stars."

He kissed her on the forehead again and tucked her more securely within the circle of his arms. "I have never felt anything like this."

"I know, Fionn." She nestled against him and tossed an arm across his chest. "I may not know how to boil water, but I like to think I am good and capable in other ways."

"You are." He reached over and grabbed his shirt, the one he had so deftly removed from her body. "Put this on, or I'll be ravaging you all night. I'll probably do it anyway because you have the sweetest little body, and I did not have nearly enough of you. Also, it is a chill wind blowing outside. Wouldn't want you to catch cold."

"I'll just cuddle against you if I grow cold." She ran her hand along the expanse of his chest and then down his muscled arm. His skin was warm.

She looked forward to sleeping beside him for all the days of her life.

This was also her first night in this bedchamber. To be here with him was infinitely better than sleeping on her own.

More important, she truly felt Fionn belonged here beside her, that he belonged to this cottage…or perhaps the opposite-she and the cottage belonged to him, or were always meant to be his.

Perhaps his connection to the cottage was just fanciful thinking on her part.

She would continue to look into the captain's boxes of documents for answers, for this feeling was real. There had to be a link between Moonstone Cottage, the ghost sea captain, and Fionn.

If only ghosts could talk.

But she would figure out this puzzle eventually, assuming her family did not forbid her from ever setting foot in here again. Hen and Phoebe were not going to be happy to learn she had spent the entire night with Fionn.

Their husbands would be livid and might do something to him in anger. Not hurt him too badly, because they now needed him to marry her.

She only hoped they would remain calm long enough for her to explain how it all innocently came about. And she would not—even on pain of death—ever reveal what they had just done.

Dear heaven, her entire body was still tingling.

"Sweet dreams, Chloe," he whispered, kissing her softly on the mouth.

His arms were still around her, and she did not think he would release her at all throughout the night. She was right where she needed to be, close enough for him to touch and hold her, to know she loved him.

How tragic that she was the only person who had ever loved him.

Well, he'd known a fatherly love from Viscount Brennan, surely. And yet it wasn't quite that. A father's love was unconditional. Perhaps Viscount Brennan's kindness was more the generosity of a mentor. Still important, but not quite the same thing.

"I can hear your brain spinning. Go to sleep, Chloe."

She snuggled against him. "I love you unconditionally, Fionn."

He chuckled. "I know you do."

"We are going to make important discoveries tomorrow. I am sure of it."

"It doesn't matter. I'll be marrying you no matter what we find."

"But I feel we are very close to discovering important answers. There has to be a connection between you and Captain Arundel. There has to be. I could not be here in this bed with you if he did not approve of us as a match. And we are now betrothed."

"Unofficially. It is not a done thing without your guardian's consent."

"As you insist on reminding me. But Cain will never deny us. To do so would leave me ruined, and he will not allow that ever to happen. So, you see. We are betrothed. Aunt Hen and her sea captain will make certain no one interferes with our happiness. The storm did not throw us together. They did."

"How, Chloe? They are not all-powerful. Not even a ghost has the power to bring on a storm of this force. It is all coincidence, and our betrothal is the natural progression of the circumstances into which we have been thrown. Go to sleep, love. We'll be facing a bigger storm once this one passes."

"Do you mean the disapproval of my family?"

He nodded.

"Perhaps at first. But they'll get over it fast. I think Hen and Phoebe will be leaping for joy once they admonish me, as it is their sisterly duty. They know I love you and that you are perfect for me."

"Am I?"

"Yes, and we are going to find out something important about you tomorrow. Not that I care, for I already know your heart and nothing else matters."

"You're wrong, Chloe. Things change with each revelation."

She stared into his turbulent gaze. "Would it change your love for me?"

Chapter Sixteen

T HE STORM CONTINUED to rage as day blended into night and
back into day again. Fionn gave silent thanks the ghost
captain had built this house sturdy enough to withstand everything the elements could toss at it. However, there would be a lot
of damage in the village, and he desperately hoped the hospital,
with its structure not yet secure, survived this tempest.

It would be disastrous if the walls and roof collapsed. The
hospital plans might then be scrapped, and he could be trans-
ferred elsewhere. Where would that leave him and Chloe?

"You have been frowning all morning. Are you sure you love
me?" Chloe teased, casting him an impish grin as they finished
their breakfast and were now cleaning up. He was washing their
plates, and she stood beside him drying them. He'd never seen
anyone so happy to do chores, but Chloe did not think of these
duties as onerous. She saw them as an affirmation of their love for
each other.

What an odd girl.

But he loved this about her.

She smiled up at him, her face exquisitely radiant. "I don't
think you have given me a moment's thought throughout
breakfast."

He shook his head, for he knew she could not possibly doubt
his affection after what they had done last night.

Lord help him, that was fun. Exquisite fun. He'd brought her to pleasure twice, for the first time had not been nearly enough to satisfy his hunger for the beautiful girl. He was still greedy and aching for more of her.

For her part, she was deliciously responsive.

Nor had he been able to keep his hands off her while helping her dress this morning. That task had taken forever because he undid her lacings and buttons as fast as she was trying to do them up. For her part, she had been doing the same to him, tugging at his shirt and trying to pull it off him whenever he attempted to put it on.

Finally, they had managed to keep their hands off each other long enough to ready themselves for the day ahead, because they had a lot to accomplish and needed to get through as much of it as possible before the storm ended and they would no longer exist in their solitary cocoon.

He would have to return to the fort.

He stared at her while they finished their chores, unable to wipe that stupid, moonstruck grin off his face. "I've thought of nothing but you."

He kissed her long and hard to prove his point.

However, he soon turned serious. "The hospital construction worries me. If the damage is too great, the army might not move forward with the project. I could be given new orders and sent elsewhere."

She nodded. "Is this what has you so preoccupied? Would they allow you to bring me along?"

"Yes, quite likely. But it would depend on the location. I would never bring you to a battle site or anywhere I thought there might be danger. This is what concerns me most, Chloe. I never want to see you hurt. But look on the bright side—as a married lady, your family would allow you to reside here at Moonstone Cottage, which is where you've really wanted to be all along."

"I do want to be here, but not if it means being apart from

you."

"We are getting ahead of ourselves. The point is, you would be settled somewhere you love, and I would not worry for your safety so long as the Hawkes remained here with you." He finished washing the last of the plates and leaned over to kiss her again. "If anything were to happen to me, I would come back to you as a ghost and protect you forever."

"Three ghosts watching over me? Don't you dare think of dying for at least another fifty years. The light would burn out of me if I ever lost you, Fionn."

"Now we are *really* getting ahead of ourselves." He opened one of the kitchen shutters and peered out the window into the still-howling wind and pattering deluge of rain. "The storm shows no sign of stopping, but it cannot possibly go on much longer."

"We have plenty of food and kindling," she remarked. "It will easily last us the week."

"But everyone thinks you are here alone, and they must be worried about you. I hope the Hawkes do not attempt to return this morning."

"Cain might come, too. I'm sure Hen will send him over to find me and bring me to their home." She sighed. "Melrose will be worried as well. I think we'll have a crush of searchers here within a few hours. We ought to spend time on those boxes while we are still alone."

"All right, let's get to it before they find me here and all hell breaks loose."

They managed to work side by side without constantly distracting each other, each of them silent and concentrating, until Chloe suddenly gasped and leaped out of her chair. "Fionn, look at this!"

They had been working on opposite sides of the table, each of them taking a stack and going through it while making methodical notes. He set his papers aside and rose as she approached. "What is it, love?"

How easily he fell into these endearments when it came to

Chloe. She truly was his love.

"Fiona Arundel's marriage certificate," she said breathlessly. "And look who is named as the husband!" She was hopping about, too excited to wait for him to read it, so she blurted, "Joseph Brennan! *Brennan*. There's your connection. Fiona was married to a Brennan. You lived with the viscount for several years, do you know who this Joseph is? Was it the viscount himself? I cannot credit it. Surely he would have claimed you as his son and never abandoned you to an orphanage. Oh, I wish we had a *Debrett's* here. He would be listed if he were a peer."

"Chloe, stop." He put his hands on her shoulders to keep her from bouncing up and down. "I don't know who he is. Perhaps some wastrel relation of the viscount's, or no relation at all. It is not unusual for a common laborer to take on the name of his liege lord."

"Fiona Arundel would not have married a wastrel."

"How do you know? Why else would she have abandoned me? Of course, it requires a leap to assume she is my mother. Same for this Joseph. How could he possibly be my father? Perhaps they were the rogues who tossed me into that orphanage and went on their merry way."

Chloe caressed his cheek. "No mother would ever abandon you. She would not have let go of you while there was breath left in her. Sadly, I think we must look for her death certification. I would not be surprised if we found she had died when…"

"When I was born? Which would mean I killed my own mother, assuming she is mine. As I said, it is a stretch to believe we are any relation to each other."

"You must be. This is why you were led here and why you were the one to find the secret compartment filled with these boxes. And don't you dare blame yourself for Fiona's fate. We don't know what happened to her. But even if she did die in childbirth, it is not your fault. Children are born innocent. They are not killers, nor can they ever be held responsible for the difficulties a woman faces in delivering a babe into the world. So don't you dare cast blame upon yourself."

"What of Joseph Brennan, my supposedly loving father? Again, assuming I am in any way related to him."

"You must be. This is too much of a coincidence and sheds new light on Viscount Brennan taking you off the streets and providing you shelter and an education. Did he ever give you any hint of being something more to him than an urchin he happened to encounter?"

"No. Don't you think I would have grabbed at any possible connection, no matter how slim?"

"Yes, I suppose you would have." She shook her head. "But the viscount must have known there was a family connection between the two of you. How could he not? Viscounts don't simply decide to take in a child off the streets. And why you, of all the children running through the alleyways of London? Well, it is mere conjecture at this point. Let's dig through the rest of these documents and see what else we find. But we now have some solid leads to discuss with Cain and for his Bow Street Runner to investigate."

Fionn's mind was awhirl and his stomach was now tied in a painful Gordian knot. He could no longer concentrate.

Nor could he credit that Ducky had been right to sense something "squidgy" going on within the Brennan family.

It was not possible that Fionn Brennan had been his real name all along.

If it was, then what connection did he have to that family and this unknown Joseph? And why had Viscount Brennan never told him? The more he thought about it, the more questions were raised.

His heart ached for the mother he had never known. Could she have been Fiona Arundel, sister to their ghost captain?

He wanted it to be her, and yet it meant she had given him away, or died in childbirth—which would have been his fault—and then some dastardly fiend stole him away to dump him in that squalid London orphanage.

He rose and began to pace, for he felt his heart was going to explode if he sat and stared at those documents any longer.

Chloe watched him for a while but said nothing.

Finally, she sighed and returned to sorting through her stack of documents. He was still pacing, feeling like a caged tiger, and wishing the storm would pass.

He needed to get out of this house, which now felt oppressive, an airless tomb with its walls closing in around him.

He wanted to walk along the beach and think, or ride back to the fort and bury himself in work—anything but remain in Moonstone Cottage, where all the secrets of his miserable upbringing were potentially hidden.

Chloe had fixed her attention on the Brennans, but had Brioc Taran Arundel, the heroic ghost captain, known of his existence and done nothing to protect him? Had he been the one to deliver Fiona's babe to the orphanage?

Fionn raked a hand through his hair. How many people had known of his birth and done nothing to remove him from the nightmare of his surroundings?

He wanted to rage. He wanted to pound his fist through a wall. He wanted to howl and howl, and keep howling until his anger was spent, for he was so very angry at this moment.

Chloe was staring at him, her eyes wide and thoughts obvious. She was worried about what he might do.

Lord help him, he would never hurt a hair on her head.

He strode into the kitchen, sank onto one of the hard wooden chairs beside the long worktable, and buried his face in his hands.

He wanted to shed tears in the hope of easing his anguish, but none came.

They never did. They never would.

He'd cried them all as a boy.

Not a drop left in him.

After a while, he sensed Chloe watching him from the doorway. "Come here, love. I won't hurt you," he said, looking up and turning toward her.

She nodded and silently approached.

He put an arm about her waist and drew her onto his lap, circling both arms around her sweet, soft body and resting his head against her chest with a familiar intimacy.

She was his in heart, body, and soul. Just as he was in hers.

Her lovely, caring heart was beating in rapid, hitching beats. He knew he had scared her. "I love you, Chloe."

She wrapped her arms around his neck and hugged him. "I know, but you are so desperately unhappy."

"Not with you. Never with you, for you are my shining beacon in the darkness."

She kissed the top of his head. "And you are in a very dark place right now. I am so sorry, Fionn. I wish I could make it all better for you."

He nodded. "You do, love."

"You are only saying this to be kind to me. Do you want to know what I think?"

He looked up at her and cast her a mirthless smile. "Do I have a choice? By the stubborn look on your face, I think you are going to give me your opinion whether I wish it or not."

She nodded. "I think Captain Arundel died before he could find you. I think he never knew of your existence until he went through his sister's belongings shortly before his death and realized she'd had a child. He was always at sea and only returned for a brief time between sailings. He may have been holding these papers for years and never realized what was in them until it was too late."

"And what of their brother?"

"His name was Brendan Arundel, a younger brother who died shortly before Fiona died. It is all in the records contained in those boxes. I noted him in the family tree I created for this purpose. I did the same for Fiona's history. The poor girl, one brother dead and the other somewhere at sea…and she with child and left alone to fend for herself."

"You forget my father's responsibility in all this. Where was he?"

"I don't know, but it should not be too hard to find out. He may have died as well. A husband and brother dead, and her only other family sailing off to parts unknown. She would have come here and been safe had Moonstone Cottage existed back then, but it had not yet been built. So she must have gone to her husband's family, the Brennans, for help. This may have been her biggest mistake."

He frowned. "You suspect foul play?"

"It is a consideration. Perhaps she died naturally in childbirth, but with no one in her family around to protect her, and if her husband had also died, then who was left to protect a child who was the viscount's heir? Would it not be most convenient for the next in line to have this babe simply disappear?"

Fionn laughed in bitter disbelief. "Ah, you think I am the viscount's true heir? Wouldn't that be rich? Chloe, you have a vivid imagination."

"Why else would the viscount's family be so eager to toss you out of his home before his body had turned cold? They needed to get you out before you went through *his* private papers and discovered an incriminating truth. It is just as plausible as your having no connection to them at all." She kissed his cheek and then gave him a sweeter kiss on the lips. "I am going to heat us up some water for tea."

He laughed and held her tight. "You are quite proud of yourself now that you know how to boil water, aren't you? I don't need tea. I just need to hold on to your delicious body."

She cast him an impish grin. "Yours is quite delicious, too."

"Do not encourage me, or I shall carry you upstairs and have at you again."

"Do you think I would mind in the least?"

He groaned. "I am getting a special license and marrying you as soon as this storm abates. I don't think I can survive even a day without you in my bed."

He said no more, for there was suddenly a pounding at the

door. "Secure the papers, Chloe. I'll see who's there. Likely it is Mr. Hawke come to check on you."

She ran back to the dining room and placed weights on each neat stack. A candlestick atop one pile. A mantel clock upon another. A vase atop a third pile.

The wind howled through the hall as soon as Fionn opened the door.

Mr. Hawke and Cain, looking every bit the daunting Duke of Malvern, trudged in.

Cain scowled when he saw who had opened the door. "What are you doing here?"

"Good morning to you, too," Fionn shot back.

Mr. Hawke muttered a greeting and hurried to the stable to check on Sophocles, no doubt preferring to deal with a skittish horse than get caught between Fionn and the duke.

Fionn stepped aside to allow Cain in. "I was afraid for Chloe, worried she meant to cut across the beach to make it home before the storm hit. I rode over to give her a ride back to Westgate Hall, but the sky opened up while we had gone no further than the courtyard. I had to bring her back in here for her own safety."

Cain sighed. "So, you have been alone with her all night?"

Chloe approached them now that the door was shut and the documents secured. "It wasn't planned, for pity's sake. If you must know, Fionn was not in the least happy about it. But he has already done the honorable thing and insisted on marrying me. So we are betrothed, and you had better not lay a hand on him or I shall complain about you to Hen."

Cain emitted a deep, rumbling chuckle and held up his hands in mock surrender. "All right, truce. I expected no less of him. You'll have my consent as soon as Fionn signs the betrothal contract, which I shall have drawn up at once. And I do not need you riling Hen against me, or she'll chatter at me all night while I'm trying to sleep." He stared from one to the other before continuing. "Dare I ask for a full account?"

Chloe winced. "No, because I am sure you did worse with Hen before you were properly married. So don't you dare pass judgment. Besides, we actually got work done. We need you to write to your Bow Street man right away and ask him to dig up as much information as he can on a gentleman by the name of Joseph Brennan."

Cain arched an eyebrow. "You mean the former viscount?"

Chloe gasped and dragged her brother-in-law into the dining room. "You know of him? He was a viscount?"

"Yes, the elder brother of Fionn's benefactor," he said, taking the marriage certificate she now stuffed in his hands and perusing it. "When he died, Fionn's benefactor assumed the title. Blessed saints, do you mean to tell me that Joseph was married to Fiona Arundel? Who is she, exactly?"

"Our ghost sea captain's sister," Chloe said. "And I think it is no coincidence that Fionn's given name happens to be a masculine version of Fiona. I think Fionn is their son. Their *legitimate* son. Born in wedlock."

Cain raked a hand through his hair as he stared from one to the other. "You two have been busy. And you really think there is a connection between Fionn and this pair? Fiona and Joseph? Well, little Imogen noticed an Arundel family resemblance. But it is so far-fetched."

"Indeed, it is," Fionn agreed. "Chloe is letting her hopes lead her astray."

"I am not," she insisted. "Don't run from this information, Fionn. I understand what it means if all this turns out to be true. The current viscount was no kind benefactor but a usurper of—"

"Don't!" Fionn's heart was in his throat, and he truly could not handle any more of this discussion. It was inconceivable that these people might be his parents.

Nor did it escape his notice that there were significant consequences to this discovery, just as Chloe was attempting to point out. If Joseph was the eldest Brennan and viscount during his life…and if he had been lawfully wed to Fiona Arundel…and if she had given birth to a son, namely him…

No, that would mean he was the rightful viscount and his benefactor had actually cheated him out of his place in Society. Not that he cared a whit about Society, but that this man he had trusted and adored for his kindness had actually been lying to him all along and denying him the truth of his heritage?

It was not possible.

Why would his benefactor ever knowingly take him in, provide for him, and educate him if he were truly intent on stealing his birthright? A pang of guilt? It could not have been all that much of a guilty pang, since Viscount Brennan had effortlessly concealed the truth for all these years.

No, none of it made sense.

Why bring the heir into his home when he could have easily done away with the threat by having him killed in a squalid alley and no one would ever have investigated or cared about the death of yet another street urchin? Problem resolved. Threat disposed of.

Chloe seemed to be reading his thoughts and related them to Cain, her mind leaping to these same ridiculous conclusions. Now, both of them had their gazes fixed on him. "I am not a damned viscount," he growled.

"I don't care if you turn out to be the lost prince of Persia," Chloe muttered. "This exercise is for your sake, not mine. I don't care what titles you hold or whether you hold any at all. I am in love with the man you are. Cain, do you know what happened to Joseph Brennan?"

"Unfortunately, I don't. All I know is that he died and Fionn's benefactor became the new viscount." Cain tossed Fionn a pained glance. "I'm sorry you never knew your father."

"Assuming he is my father, which I doubt."

A candlestick fell off one of the stacks of documents at just that moment, toppling off the table and hitting the floor with a clatter that startled them all.

"See," Chloe said, "our ghost captain is getting irritated at your denial and telling you to stop being stubborn."

Cain cleared his throat. "Your friend Ducky sensed there was more to your benefactor's passing, and Mr. Barrow will get to the bottom of it now that we can offer him some guidance. It is little wonder the viscount's family wanted you out of the house as soon as he passed. I would not be surprised if he left you a letter confirming much of what Chloe has put together. Selfish man, he wanted the title for himself while he lived but intended to have you learn the truth after he passed."

"Leaving his other relatives to scramble for themselves," Chloe added, "since they had treated you abominably all of their lives and now realized you would not lift a finger to help them. So they needed to find that letter and destroy it before you learned of their secret treachery."

"Gad, Chloe. This is too absurd," Fionn said.

Cain did not agree with him. "Your friend Ducky and Mr. Barrow will get on it. I'll send word immediately."

Chloe put a hand on Fionn's arm to stop him when he began to pace again. "If it turns out you are Fiona's son, then there is something else that belongs to you...Moonstone Cottage. You, as Brioc's nephew, would have inherited it by rights. It did not belong to Brioc's cousins, who sold this property to my Aunt Hen. No wonder you were so drawn to this place. Brioc wanted you here to find those papers, to know all this belonged to you."

Fionn shook his head in a vehement denial. "Your aunt purchased it in good faith and paid fair value for the property. No court would overturn her acquisition of it, nor would I ever demand it."

"Well, there is no need to overturn anything now, since we are to be married. A one-third share already belongs to me, and I'll use my inheritance to acquire the other shares from my sisters."

"Nonsense, Chloe," Cain said. "Your sisters planned to give the cottage over to you as their wedding gift."

"Stop! Both of you." Fionn needed to get away from Moonstone Cottage right this instant. "I have to get back to the fort. Cain, please see Chloe safely home."

Chloe regarded him, distraught. "When will I see you again?"

"I don't know." He made some excuse about the hospital construction and turned to leave, but Cain stood in his way.

The duke was a giant of a man and did not look too pleased with him at the moment, likely fearing he was going to do something stupid that would hurt Chloe.

Fionn wasn't going to hurt her. He just needed to get out of here and take a breath before the walls fell in and crushed him.

"Come to see me once you are done inspecting the construction damage. We'll go together to obtain the license for your marriage," Cain said. "After all, I am Chloe's guardian."

"And you want to be sure I'll marry her."

Cain's expression turned fierce. "I like you, Fionn. But make no mistake, if you break Chloe's heart, I will come after you and kill you."

"Oh, do stop, both of you! I don't need either of you to behave like jungle animals fighting over a kill." Chloe turned to Fionn. "I don't need you to marry me out of duty. If you love me, then I'll marry you. If you are already regretting your proposal, then we can end it here and now."

She tipped her head up, too proud to admit he was breaking her heart by his behavior.

He was desperate to get away from the cottage, but not from her. "I do love you. Never a doubt."

"Good, because I love you too. And whatever distress you are feeling, we'll work through it together. I don't need you to go off angry and brooding on your own. You've been doing this all of your life. But you are no longer alone. You now have me."

She released a deep, shaky breath and continued. "I will stand by your side and love you through everything because we *belong* together. And if you dare deny it, I will toss punches and knock your teeth out. Don't you dare push me aside."

Fionn grinned. "Duly noted. Is there anything more you

would like to say to me?"

"No, that's about it."

He kissed her on the nose. "I have something to say to you."

"Besides that you love me?"

"I do love you, but I would like to make one point clear. Your sisters can give you their share of this cottage if they like, but it does not ever come to me. I want it stated in our betrothal contract that the cottage remains yours to do with as you wish."

She frowned at him. "But—"

"No argument, Chloe. This is to be your safe haven, a place where you shall always be protected and no one can hurt you as they did Fiona."

He turned to Cain. "Put whatever you want into that betrothal contract. I will sign it. All I ever wanted was Chloe. She can do whatever she wants with her assets."

He turned back to her, his hand shaking as he caressed her cheek. "And now I really must get out of here and inspect the hospital damage." He grabbed his hat and jacket and strode to the door. "I'll see you at the church."

"What church? When?" she called out after him.

But he'd already slammed the door shut behind him.

To his relief, Mr. Hawke had saddled Sophocles and was about to bring him into the courtyard.

Fionn thanked the man and rode off into town, his thoughts still angry and threatening to boil over in an uncontrollable rage.

If Chloe was right, then his entire life had been a lie.

A viscount?

Him?

Should he not have felt something? Seen his blood run blue instead of common red? How was a peer supposed to feel?

If any of it was true and he found the proof, then he had to give thought to what would come next. There would be a court challenge, of course. None of the viscount's relatives were going to allow him to claim the title without a bitter fight.

That did not scare him. He'd been fighting for survival all of his life.

In the meanwhile, those Brennans had been living in luxury and taking advantage of all that should have been his. Detesting and demeaning him when all along they knew of his stolen heritage.

Was there punishment severe enough for those loathsome leeches?

Chapter Seventeen

F OUR DAYS HAD passed since the storm, and Chloe had yet to hear from Fionn. She knew the damage to Moonstone Landing had been extensive and imagined the hospital construction also must have been set back. This explained his silence, for he had to be working day and night to repair the damage and salvage the entire project.

She did not want to interfere with his important work. Their marriage plans could wait.

Besides, she had more to do going through these boxes of documents on her own. Most of the cataloguing had been done, but she wanted to review every piece again to be certain she had not overlooked something important now that she understood the full history.

She had only a few hours a day to devote to this work now that Imogen and Ella were back from Falmouth. That town had been spared the brunt of the storm. In fact, Ella had told her they'd had nothing more than overcast skies with no rain at all. She was glad the girls were able to enjoy the fair, but it felt odd this storm had centered on their small patch of Cornwall and spared every other town around it.

She dismissed the thought, because this storm had brought her and Fionn closer together and she was not going to question the how or why of it. Instead, she remained on schedule, arriving each morning at the cottage and leaving by noontime to return to Westgate Hall and spend the rest of the day with the girls.

They had all kept mostly to Westgate Hall, since the town was still recovering from the storm's damage. Nor could they go down to the beach, because the water was too roiled and there were dangerous rip currents. One had only to look down from the heights to know the sea was quite gray and angry. She dared not even dip a toe into those turbulent waters.

"Lady Chloe, would you like a cup of tea?" Mrs. Hawke asked, bustling into the dining room as the noon hour approached.

"No, thank you. I'll be off soon."

The kindly woman cast her a pitying look. "You take your time and let me know if you need anything."

Chloe had learned from Mrs. Hawke that Fionn no longer returned to the cottage each evening and instead had taken to staying in the officers' quarters at the fort, his excuse being the mountain of work required to be done after the storm.

Chloe thought the real reason was her.

Perhaps she should not have been so strident in discussing these revelations about the Brennans and the Arundels, for she saw now that it hadn't helped him so much as brought more pain to his already burdened heart.

She sighed as she finished going through the stack of documents, and had just neatly packed them away when she heard Hen, Phoebe, and their cousin Prudence arrive at the front door.

Mrs. Hawke greeted them cheerfully and invited them in. "Good morning, Your Grace. Lady Burness. Mrs. Weston."

"We are here to call upon Lady Chloe," Hen said, craning her head to peer into the dining room. "There you are, Chloe. Don't bother to hide from us. We see you clearly. Oh, Mrs. Hawke, do not bother with refreshments—we won't be staying long."

Mrs. Hawke bobbed a curtsy and bustled into her kitchen domain.

Chloe said nothing as Hen headed straight toward her and

took a seat at the head of the dining table. Phoebe and Prudence walked in behind her but remained standing, as though serving as guards to prevent Chloe's escape.

None of them appeared pleased.

Chloe began to fidget with her quill pen. "To what do I owe the pleasure of your company?"

Hen pursed her lips and frowned. "He has not yet obtained the license."

"By *he*, I suppose you mean Fionn. I am well aware."

"He must do it, and soon," Phoebe said, her hands curling into fists in frustration over Fionn's unmistakable reluctance. "It isn't right, Chloe. People are starting to talk."

"Let them." Chloe was not going to force him to do anything he was not ready to do. He loved her, but he was a man in turmoil and not used to relying on anyone for help. Nor could he bear to be around Moonstone Cottage at the moment, this place where so many ugly secrets had been revealed. "He will come to me when he is ready."

"What if he doesn't?" Prudence asked. "Be practical, Chloe. He needs to marry you as soon as possible. Then he can go off and do whatever he likes. Let him sulk or rage or vent his spleen on those odious Brennans after you are married. He cannot leave things as they are, you with your reputation in ruins."

"I am not going to chase after him and beg him to marry me."

"You don't need to. Cain and Cormac will bring him to heel," Hen said. "Truly, Chloe. Something must be done, or Cain will go after him with cannons firing if he does not come around soon. I don't know how long I can hold him off. He takes his guardianship responsibilities quite seriously."

Phoebe nodded. "Cormac will be right beside him, pistol pointed straight at Fionn's heart."

"All right. I'll talk to him today." Chloe had planned on giving him the entire week to think things through, but four days would have to be enough. "Besides, I ought to let him know that Cain wrote again to Mr. Barrow providing him with more leads in his investigation."

Prudence glanced at her. "You found out something more?"

Chloe nodded. "Fionn does not know yet that I came upon Fiona's death certification as well as that of Joseph's. They passed away within months of each other, and the timing fits if Fionn is truly the child she was carrying. The only piece we are missing is an actual record of his birth. But we now know where Fiona died, and I am certain that will lead Mr. Barrow to witnesses who can tell us what happened to her child back then."

"Chloe," Prudence said gently, "why are you getting so caught up in this? Is this not his problem to solve? It seems to me he is running from this sad affair and wants to let it go."

"But he doesn't," Chloe said with a shake of her head. "He is holding back because he feels an uncontrollable rage and is worried what might happen if he confronts the Brennans now. How would you feel if everything you knew turned out to be lies? It is as though a gaping hole opened up under his feet and simply swallowed him up."

She rose and smoothed out her gown, a dull brown muslin that had no lace trim or frills other than a simple fichu to cover the swell of her breasts. It was not a very pretty gown, but would be suitable for making her way through the storm-damaged streets. "I'll have Mr. Hawke hitch up the wagon and drive me into Moonstone Landing. I don't need anyone following me. But do stay and enjoy a cup of tea with Mrs. Hawke."

She made certain the documents were securely sealed in their boxes, then started for the door.

Phoebe followed her out. "There is one more thing you ought to know before you talk to him… Oh, Chloe! Hen and I were at odds whether to tell you, but it is better to hear it from us than be shocked when you learn of it from strangers. I want to shoot him."

"Who?"

"Fionn. He was seen dining with Lady Dowling last night. How could he do this when he has promised to marry you?"

Chloe's heart sank into her toes.

No, it couldn't be. There had to be a logical explanation.

Even though Fionn had his rough edges, she could not believe he would invite another lady to dine with him, not after he had pledged his love to her and still owed her a marriage license. But what did she know of men? What did she really know of Fionn?

She did not want her sister to see how much the news upset her, so she held her head with pride and tried to shrug off her hurt. "Would you trust Cormac if he was the one seen dining with Lady Dowling?"

Phoebe gazed at her in surprise. "Of course I would. He would never... I trust him completely."

Chloe felt this same way about Fionn, for how could she ever fall in love with him or marry him if there was no trust between them? Nor had Fionn ever shown any inclination to flirt with other ladies. In all the years she had known him, he had always been reserved and kept to himself.

Of course, he was in turmoil now and not his usually composed self.

Still, she did not think he would so easily stray or ever do it so openly. It was a cruel thing to flaunt in her face, and he simply did not have it in him to ever be cruel to her. She held on to that thread to steady herself and stave off tears. "I trust Fionn as you trust Cormac. I'm sure there is an innocent explanation."

"But—"

"No, Phoebe." She walked toward the wagon, trying to remain calm. She was afraid to look at her sister, for she would see through her brittle façade and know her heart was breaking.

She did trust Fionn.

But why had he ignored her and chosen to dine with that woman?

She took a deep breath, not wanting to approach him blubbering like a baby and pathetically begging for answers. No, she would meet him head-on and not shed a tear.

In fact, she had worked herself into a state and was quite steaming mad by the time she reached the fort and asked to see him.

"Of course, Lady Chloe," said the guard at the gate. "He's at the construction site. I'll have him summoned right away. Let me escort you to his office first."

"Not necessary." She stormed toward the hospital construction.

The young soldier called out to her, obviously surprised by her response and uncertain what to do. He left his post to chase after her. "Please, Lady Chloe! That site is no place for a lady. They are hauling beams and striking hammers...and most of the men have their shirts off while toiling in the heat."

"Nonsense—take me there now or you shall have an angry reprimand from the Duke of Malvern." She hated to toss Cain's status around, especially since he would lock her in her bedchamber for a month if he ever found out she was traipsing across gigantic beams and ducking under scaffolds amid a group of shirtless men.

The worried soldier was now begging her to let him summon Fionn.

"Lieutenant Fletcher, what is going on?" Fionn growled, dropping down from one of the scaffolds. He was wearing his shirt, although it was pasted to his muscled torso and half undone. She noticed the sprinkle of dark hair across his chest and beads of sweat trickling down in a line from his neck into his magnificently broad chest.

He inhaled sharply when he noticed her standing behind the young lieutenant. "Blast, why did you not have her wait in my office?"

"I tried, sir. She wouldn't listen."

Fionn arched an eyebrow and cast her a wry smile. "All right, Fletcher. Go back to your post. I'll escort the lady to my office."

He picked up his jacket, but did not bother to don it before grabbing her by the elbow and towing her away from the site.

"Where are you taking me? Your office is in the opposite direction."

"I've changed my mind. I don't want us to be overheard by my men. Come with me." He led her toward the harbor walk, no doubt to give them privacy as he berated her for barging in unannounced. Or was he about to deliver heartbreaking news? Had he realized he loved Lady Dowling and not her?

She stopped in her tracks, suddenly overcome by doubt. What if her worst fears were realized? Could she hold herself together long enough to maintain a semblance of pride?

He emitted another soft growl, took her by the hand, and led her down toward the beach.

"Stop growling at me and dragging me along. I am the one with reason to growl at you. Four days and not a word from you."

He sighed and slowed his pace. "You know I've been busy trying to salvage the hospital."

"But still found time to have supper with the lovely Lady Dowling. I deserve an explanation for that, don't you think? Everyone is talking about it. Four days. No marriage license. And you being seen dining with the most beautiful woman in the village. Do you know how humiliating it is for me?"

His expression turned pained. "I didn't dine with her. And you are far prettier than she will ever be."

"Then you are the only man in Moonstone Landing who feels this way." Chloe felt ready to cry. "You were seen with her. Everyone knows she is the village beauty."

"Stop saying that. She is nothing compared to you." They were halfway along the scenic walk that led down to the fort's golden sand beach. He paused and turned to face her. "Yes, she was there at the Kestrel Inn when I stopped in for supper. But it wasn't... At least, I didn't count it as that."

"Then what did you think was happening when you sat to-gether for a cozy meal?" Chloe could not bear to look at him in this moment, so she shaded her eyes against the sun that now beat down upon the water and turned her gaze to the shimmering sea.

"I stopped by the Kestrel Inn to dine alone. *Alone*, Chloe. She came over to my table while I was ordering my meal, then sat and ordered her own supper brought over. I did not invite her, nor did I want her there. But she did not take the hint to go away, even though I was surly and very poor company. All right?"

"I don't know. Let me think about it."

He groaned softly. "Go ahead and kick my arse. You have the right, because I have been an oaf to you. I have every intention of getting that marriage license. I love you more than life itself, and that will never change."

"Are you sure? You have an odd way of showing it."

"Yes, I'm sure about my feelings for you. Lady Dowling does not tempt me in the least. Do you think I would ever trust a woman who betrayed your kindness toward her by going after the man you are going to marry? I know it looked bad, but I will never be unfaithful to you. I'm sorry about last night. I did not expect her company, but the point is, I should have been with you. That is on me, completely my fault. I'm not very good at groveling."

"You don't need to grovel."

"Yes, I do. Not for last night's supper, because nothing improper happened or was ever going to happen," he said. "You are the only woman who will ever claim my heart. The only one I would ever trust or desire to have as the mother of my children. But I've been avoiding you."

"I know. It is hard not to notice your disappearance after...after I gave you my heart and my body. Why, Fionn?"

"Because of what Moonstone Cottage represents. Because of what those documents found hidden there revealed. I had to stay away until my anger cooled. I am still in a blind rage, Chloe. I want to rip each and every Brennan apart. They are monsters."

"Indeed, but you are not like them."

"If we are interpreting these documents correctly, then their blood flows through me, doesn't it?" He drew her into his arms. "Their selfish, poisonous blood. I have it in me to kill them. Every last one of those heartless liars. I do, Chloe. Just thinking of them makes me ill. And I carry their name... I was so proud when I took it on."

"At your benefactor's urging, no doubt."

He nodded. "I thought it was an honor, and now I can only think of it as a curse. I dread putting it down on our marriage license. Bile rises in my throat at the thought of repeating it in our vows. *Brennan.* This is the name you will take as my wife, and it revolts me. This is why I haven't obtained the license yet."

He rubbed a hand across the nape of his neck and continued. "My concern has always been to bring something into our marriage. One thing that I could look upon with pride and bestow on you. I do not even have that anymore. All I bring is seething anger and a detestable name."

"Do you wish to postpone our wedding...perhaps forever?"

He regarded her aghast. "No, Chloe. Never. As much as I hate my circumstances, I love you and will not have you shamed. Last night, as innocent as it was, should never have happened. It is my fault I delayed acquiring the license. Lady Dowling mistook it as a sign things were not well between us and approached me."

"But are they well between us?"

"Yes. If anything, these days apart from you have made me understand how much I need you in my life. It is so empty without you, I cannot bear it. I'll speak to your brothers-in-law this evening and obtain the license first thing tomorrow." He turned her to face him. "I've also been giving our living arrangements some thought."

"Is that so? What have you decided?" She held her breath, worried he was going to require them to live apart.

"I know you love Moonstone Cottage, so this is where we shall reside if you wish. It is mine for the next year anyway under my lease."

Relief washed through her, for all she heard was "we shall

reside," and she did not care about anything else after that. All she wanted was for them to be together—it did not matter where.

"I am your landlord," she said with a wry grin. "You can end that lease whenever you like. My sisters and I will never hold you to it, especially if having to live there brings you pain."

"I'll get over it. Besides, I rather like the idea of sharing that big, canopied bed with you. I don't want to break the lease. I love the place, too. Truly. I just needed a little time away from it to absorb all these revelations."

She groaned lightly. "I have a few more for you to hear, if you are up to it."

"Lord help me, there's more? Yes, tell me everything. I would rather know the dreaded facts than be kept in the dark."

She told him about the record of Fiona's death and that of Joseph. "We now know where she was when she died, and it is very likely the same time and location where she gave birth. Cain has written to his Mr. Barrow to find witnesses who were there with your mother at the time."

"Don't call her that, Chloe. Whatever information we have is merely circumstantial. There's no hard proof that I am her son. Short of finding a written confession from my benefactor, I doubt we'll ever have sufficient proof to substantiate my claim. Even with proof, it may take years for me to be acknowledged as the rightful Viscount Brennan."

She noticed the glint of anger in his eyes and knew this news had done nothing but further enrage him toward the Brennan family. "Do as you wish in this matter. Pursue it or let it drop. But I think it is important for you to have the question of your parentage settled in your own mind. This is what counts most. Well, other than hoping you are serious about marrying me."

"I am."

"What do you think about holding a quiet ceremony at the parish church this coming Friday morning?"

"Three days from now?" he asked. "What about the wedding breakfast? Your family will expect us to have one. Can you organize it in this short a time?"

"I don't need to. Hen's annual village tea is on Saturday. We can marry quietly on Friday and announce our marriage at the tea."

He emitted a short bark of laughter. "Announce it at the tea? The entire village will know the moment we are seen walking to the church. Nothing stays quiet around here. Half the village will be peeking through the church windows as we recite our vows."

She smiled. "All right, it will not be a surprise to anyone. But Hen would be delighted if her tea did double duty as our wedding breakfast celebration."

"At no expense to me," he muttered.

"I can assure you, neither Cain nor Cormac will ever allow anyone to pay for something they consider their responsibility. Even had I married Lord Claymore—who is due back in town any day now, by the way—they would insist on all of the cost being theirs."

"Is that so?"

"It is. My brothers-in-law take their responsibilities seriously, and the wedding cost was always going to be theirs. But the expense of claiming your heritage, should you desire to pursue it, will be something you and I will need to work out."

"Chloe, I am not taking any of your inheritance for that purpose or any other. That offer is off the table."

"Well then, I shall simply have to put it back on the table," Chloe said.

"No, I am not going into further debt to you and your family over this."

"But how will you afford to pursue it without our help?"

"I may not move ahead with the claim."

"And spend the rest of your life eating your guts out? Can you stop being so pridefully stubborn for a moment? When you marry me, you will not only be acquiring a wife but an entire family. A very supportive, loving family. You are no longer alone, Fionn. You will be a part of us, and we will extend whatever help you need. You would do the same for us, so why should we deny you?"

"I'll have to think about it," he replied. "I am not marrying you to become your family's charity case. You know this is the thing I dreaded most. But since we are speaking of families, you'll soon be meeting my ragtag clan. Ducky, Muskrat, and Squirrel."

"Ah, your loyal band of brothers. They called you Guv and made you their leader even though you were the youngest of them. See, they knew your worth even back then. When do they arrive? Any chance it will be in time for the wedding?"

"Hell no," he said with a hearty chuckle. "I don't want them anywhere near Moonstone Landing until I am certain they will not be picking pockets. Those bad habits die hard."

"I look forward to meeting them, especially Ducky. We owe him a great debt of gratitude whether or not your claim to the title ever comes to fruition."

"Gad, it horrifies me to admit you are right. He is such a scoundrel. I had to save his stupid arse so many times over the years. And now..." He cleared his throat. "I've promised the three of them jobs here."

Chloe's eyes lit up with mirth. "You look downright pained. But we shall add them to our family and help them settle in. I would never break your little band apart."

"Squirrel is not a boy, by the way. Although she was as tough as any of us."

"Good for her."

"I suppose. I don't know what she's had to do to survive. She may be a little too coarse for your liking. The others as well. Muskrat is called that because he thinks his father was from the Americas, so he chose an American animal as his street name."

"Fionn, I am not going to pass judgment," Chloe said. "Nor will my sisters. We came close to having to face ugly choices ourselves. If not for Cain falling in love with Hen and coming to our rescue, our circumstances might have been quite different. If they want a chance at a respectable life, we will give them all the help they need."

He took her hand and put it to his lips. "Have I told you how much I love you?"

She smiled up at him. "It feels like forever ago, but it was probably no more than in the last five minutes."

"That is far too long." He drew her up against him and kissed her softly on the mouth.

They heard a distant cheer.

He glanced back toward the fort. "Bloody hell, is every blessed soldier under my command watching us?"

Chloe nodded. "Do you mind terribly?"

"No, love. Let's give them something to really cheer about." He swallowed her in his arms and crushed his mouth to hers, kissing her with a scorching heat that turned her body liquid.

The cheers became a deafening roar.

Or was it merely the roar of her elated heart?

Chapter Eighteen

O N Saturday morning, Fionn stood in Moonstone Cottage's garden beneath a brightly shining sun and surrounded by a gentle breeze off the shimmering sea. Chloe, looking more beautiful than ever, stood beside him under the rose arbor that had been fashioned into an altar for the purpose of their wedding ceremony.

With Cain's assistance, he had obtained a special license that allowed him and Chloe to marry anywhere and at any time. He had given it thought and realized the wedding had to take place right here, in sight of the cottage ghosts who had led them to each other.

He clasped Chloe's soft hands in his work-roughened ones as the vicar conducted the ceremony before her family, his soldiers, the Hawkes, and most of the villagers.

So much for a quiet wedding.

Not that he'd really expected this day to pass without fanfare, for the Killigrew sisters were beloved in the village and no one wanted to miss the joyful day. So the intended Friday ceremony had been pushed back to Saturday morning, after which everyone was to meander over to St. Austell Grange, where Hen and Cain were to host their annual tea.

This year, it would double as his and Chloe's wedding break-fast.

A breakfast for which Cain had not allowed him to contribute so much as a shilling. "I am incurring no additional expense," he'd growled, "since Hen and I were to host the annual tea anyway. If anything, you have saved us the entire expense of her sister's wedding."

Chloe's eyes sparkled as she now smiled up at him.

Ella and Imogen stood in their place of honor beside Chloe, their job to manage her wedding veil and keep it from getting caught on the roses. They looked like adorable cherubs in their pretty frocks and circlets of wild flowers in their curled hair. They were happy for reasons beyond serving as Chloe's maids of honor, for Cormac had received word last night from his brother that Lady Stockwell, whose influenza-type symptoms had then turned into an oddly presenting scarlet fever that fooled the local doctors, had finally been properly diagnosed by Dr. Farthingle, who promptly treated her with a salt cure and she was on the mend. In fact, she was responding so well, they would return soon to pick up their daughters.

Indeed, these last few days had brought nothing but good news.

Even the hospital structure he feared lost had suffered only modest damage upon closer inspection. After a solid week's repair work, it was now in as good a shape as before the storm. The oil cloths and heavy ropes had held their materials secure, allowing them to salvage most of the supplies and building materials, save for a beam or two. The construction would resume only a few days behind schedule.

"Do you, Major Fionn Brennan, take Lady Chloe Killigrew as your lawful wife, to love and to cherish…"

Fionn had listened as the vicar intoned the words, taking each vow to heart. To love her. Honor her. Protect her. "I do."

Chloe had done the same.

"I now pronounce you husband and wife."

Everyone in attendance began to cry tears of joy.

Not him, of course.

None would ever flow from him, no matter the reason.

But his smile was so broad, it actually started to hurt his face. He did not often smile except when he was around Chloe. He was not afraid to bare his soul to her, for she had such a sweet, compassionate nature wrapped inside her hot little body. She was beautiful inside and out, and he trusted her with all he held dear.

Her eyes were glistening with tears and her smile was soft and lovely.

The girls were sniffling and giggling as they hugged Chloe, who took a long moment to hug them back.

Chloe's sisters had their handkerchiefs out to dab at the tears streaming down their faces. Same for Mrs. Halsey, the Hawkes, and most of the villagers. Everyone was smiling and sobbing and slapping him on the back in hearty congratulations.

He strode past Lady Dowling, who was looking quite wistful and none too pleased. "Call on me if you ever feel the need," she whispered, drawing him down to kiss him on the cheek as other ladies in the crowd had done, only she kept her lips there a moment too long, and the little sigh she gave as she drew away was suggestive.

He moved on, ignoring the offer.

Lord Claymore had arrived two days ago with his retinue of friends, who were all in attendance. Claymore broke away from them to approach him. "Well, it seems the better man has won."

Fionn shook his hand in greeting. "Thank you, my lord. I know how fortunate I am and will never take this gem of a wife for granted."

"I wish you a happy life together. I can see how much she loves you. Too bad she never looked at me that way." He smiled wryly. "Perhaps I shall find this same happiness someday, a young lady who will look at me as though I am her world and love me for myself instead of my title and position in Society."

"I hope you do. I mean it sincerely. I speak for Chloe and myself when we wish you well in your search. There are good women out there. I am still amazed Chloe would have me, for she is far better than I deserve. I hope you will find your gem soon, perhaps even here in Moonstone Landing. Do you think you will stay on? Or have you had enough of us?"

Claymore laughed. "I have not changed my plans. I am determined to find a property here, and perhaps a wife along with it."

After a few more words exchanged, Fionn moved on and sought out Chloe, who had been pulled away from him as guests surrounded each of them.

He shouldered his way toward her, lifted her into his arms, and gave her a searing kiss that had the men cheering him on and the ladies tittering and fanning themselves.

Chloe laughed and nuzzled his neck. "Was that for my sake or Lady Dowling's sake?" she whispered in his ear. "What did she say to you?"

"Nothing that would ever tempt me. I promise you, Chloe."

"I know, my love."

When the tea ended, he and Chloe returned to Moonstone Cottage.

Her belongings had been brought into their bedchamber earlier in the morning before the wedding ceremony had commenced, and all was now neatly stowed away in the bureau and large wardrobe. "I'm afraid I've taken up most of the space with my gowns and undergarments. My reticules. Shoes. Parasols," Chloe said, kicking off her slippers and taking a seat on the big, canopied bed.

"Take all of it, if you like. I'll store my clothes in one of the empty bedchambers if you need more space in here. All I have is mostly my uniforms and little else."

"Does it feel odd to you, Fionn? Our being married."

"No, love." He removed the jacket of the military dress uniform he had worn for this day and set it aside on one of the plump chairs beside the hearth. "It feels very right."

He tugged off his boots and stretched out on the bed with a contented sigh, placing his hands behind his head as he relaxed.

"Our ghosts are happy. I can feel their contentment in the air. Do you think they haunted the cottage all the while just to bring us together?"

"My Aunt Hen and your Uncle Brioc? I never thought of it that way. But it is obvious they were determined to have us matched."

"Yes, they must have seen us together and immediately known we were meant to be together. All they had to do was give your stubborn, stupid husband a kick in the arse."

She turned to him in dismay. "Does this mean they are ready to leave us?"

"I don't know, love. Would you be terribly overset if they did?"

She nodded. "They are so much a part of our lives, but I would not hold them back if it is time for them to move on and find their peace. They deserve their own happiness, don't they?"

"They are happy," he assured her, for he truly felt it in the air, as though the wind played a melody and they were happily dancing to it.

"They might decide to stay around to see what happens with your heirship claim," Chloe suggested.

"Perhaps." He sat up and turned to her. "But that was never their true purpose. Whether I am ever recognized as viscount is merely a secondary concern. You did not marry me for a title. Dear heaven, we did not even know my true name until recently. You didn't care about any of it, so why should they?"

"Thank goodness you did not need to change your name. I know it irks you, but Fionn suits you to perfection. I cannot imagine you being called George or Ernest or William."

He grinned. "Then it is a good thing I am Fionn, or you might not have fallen in love with me."

She laughed, a soft, lilting trill. "Oh, I think I would have loved you no matter what your name turned out to be. Ambrose. Felix. Ranulf. Oh, I rather like Ranulf. One expects a big, muscled warrior with a name like that. Perhaps our daughter shall meet her Ranulf. As for me, I am quite content with you."

She rose and unpinned her veil, then set it aside while she removed the rest of the pins from her hair. He watched the mane of fiery silk cascade in a soft tumble down her back, knowing he would enjoy running his fingers through it tonight.

"Let me help you, love." He rolled off the bed and came to her side to assist her with the lacings of her gown. It was a particularly fine silk gown and trimmed in lacy ribbons.

But truly, she looked beautiful in everything she wore.

And even more beautiful wearing nothing at all.

He slipped the gown off her with ease, allowing his hands to graze over her breasts as he did so, for he would make her his tonight, and it would happen soon. The sun was only now setting over the water. The sky and sea were no longer blue but ablaze in shades of fiery golds, pinks, and lilacs.

"Is it not beautiful, Fionn?"

"Yes, love." He brushed her hair aside to kiss her neck before he removed the string of pearls at her throat.

Such a soft, lovely throat.

He quickly helped her out of her undergarments, then shed the last of his clothing before carrying her to the bed and settling her in the middle of it. The night of the storm had been for her pleasure, but tonight would be for both of theirs.

He was hard and throbbing by the time he readied her and felt his own wild need as he touched her intimately. She was ready for him, and her hips moved in a sinuous motion, eager to take him in. "Chloe, love. I will never have enough of you."

She arched against him, softly crying out in pleasure when he kissed her soft breasts.

He almost spent himself while easing into her hot, tight opening. She was a delicious ball of fire.

He loved everything about the way she felt, the silkiness of her skin and the scent of her arousal. She was a wildflower unfurling in the sun. Her breasts were full and responsive as he put his mouth to one lush mound and suckled the sweet tip.

He moved slowly, trying to be gentle, for this was her first time, and he did not want her to feel any discomfort. He had never taken a virgin before, had no idea what she could handle, although she did not seem to be complaining. "Chloe…"

It was hard to think straight or do more than grunt while he was now inside her and half mindless while thrusting into her delicious body. He tried to go slow, but that control left him when he realized she had taken all of him in and was not suffering for it. Quite the opposite—she seemed hungry for him.

He simply allowed his thoughts to disappear into the air and allowed the carnal part of him to take over. But it was not merely a matter of the flesh, for mixed in with his raw desire was also the wealth of feelings he had for Chloe.

Fire consumed him as he moved inside her, kissed and touched her. Wrapped his arms around her and held her with all the love in his heart.

He looked down at her, at her long lashes resting on porcelain cheeks as they lay closed, at her beautiful bow mouth slightly open and awaiting his kiss. Her body moved with his, following his lead, and she held tightly to his shoulders as pleasure built inside of her. He thrust harder, knowing he was close as well, and wanting them to reach their pleasure together.

Then it happened.

He felt her shudders and soft cries as she reached her climax and shattered.

He followed soon after, spilling himself into her until there was not a droplet left in him. He was wrung dry and collapsed atop her, growling in satisfaction.

After a moment to savor their lovemaking, he rolled off her and eased onto his back. "Blessed saints, that was good."

She chuckled.

He drew her up against him and circled his arms around her. "Did I hurt you, love?"

"No." She caressed his cheek. "It was wonderful. You were wonderful. This entire day has been everything I hoped it would be, even better than I'd hoped."

He lightly caressed her body. "For me too."

She reached up and kissed him on the cheek. "You sound wistful."

"Just thinking of my past and all the events that led me here to find you. I never thought I would marry, never believed I would have the capacity to trust or love. But it came so easily with you, Chloe. As though my heart had always left space for you to fill it. As though it had simply been waiting for you to appear in my life. Blessed saints, I am your husband. *Your* husband."

He shifted their positions and rolled her under him, loving the way her hair splayed like dark fire on their bed sheets. "I have a family," he said in amazement, burying his hands in her lush curls and gently sliding his fingers through the gloriously long strands. "I have *you*. You are my family, and I now belong to you. I *belong*, Chloe. If we are ever so blessed, I will one day be a father."

"Does it not feel a bit daunting? To be a parent." She cast him an impish grin. "And I am now realizing just how pampered I was as the youngest in the family. My parents and sisters doted on me. Good heavens, will I be an adequate mother?"

"You will be the best mother in all of England. I've seen you with Imogen and Ella. They adore you. More important, I adore you. I know our children will always be loved and protected whether or not I am around. They will know a mother's love as I never did."

"I am so sorry for all you were deprived. I will try my hardest never to fail you as a wife. You must tell me if ever you are unhappy over something I am doing. We must always be honest with each other."

"We'll be fine, love." He kissed her softly on the lips. "Well, the night is young. Do you not think we ought to work on creating these children for us to dote on?"

She laughed. "I think that is a wonderful plan."

He knew this was one task to which he would be most attentive.

LATER THAT NIGHT, while Chloe was asleep and beautifully lost in her dreams, he strode to the small balcony and stared out over the dark waters. The tide was out and the moon shone down upon the ebbing waters to illuminate the moonstones hidden beneath the sandy bottom.

The night was dazzlingly clear, the stars in their diamond colors shimmering overhead while the moonstones glowed beneath the surface of the waves.

This was what the sea captain must have seen when he looked out into the starry expanse whenever he was home from his travels.

Fionn would never tire of this view, or of knowing he had only to turn his head to find the woman who was his happiness, his sanctuary, asleep in his bed. Chloe made all his years of pain simply melt away. They would find happiness here, no matter what happened between him and the Brennans.

He was ready to build a life here at Moonstone Cottage, a life and a family with Chloe beside him.

He did not think he had ever been happier than in this moment.

A movement at the top of the stairs leading down to the beach caught his eyes. Could it be? He saw two wisps of white that resembled a man and a woman, holding hands with each other.

Brioc and Henleigh.

The Moonstone ghosts.

He could not take his eyes off them.

Was he asleep and still dreaming?

He knew he was not. "Blessed saints, you are real."

Indeed, Chloe had believed in them all along. They truly

existed.

Chloe noticed he was not sleeping beside her and came out of their bed to stand with him. "Lost in your thoughts, my husband?"

She looked adorably sleepy and irresistibly tempting in the night rail she'd hastily donned that was falling off her shoulders. He wanted to sweep her up in his arms and make love to her again.

Lord, he was pathetically besotted.

He shook his head and smiled. "Look toward the beach stairs. We have some visitors."

She followed his gaze, then grabbed his hand and gasped. "Fionn, it's them!"

"I know, love. I can see them."

"You can? How perfect!" She stared once more at their wispy forms. "They must be here to wish us well. Brioc looks happy...so happy. He has not only found the love of his life in my aunt, but has now rescued his nephew. This must give him the greatest joy."

She waved to them.

He thought it was ridiculous to wave to ghosts as though they were friendly neighbors. But this was a Chloe thing to do, and he loved this about her. She accepted everyone, his ragtag friends, the Moonstone ghosts, and most of all him.

A gust of wind blew across the expansive lawn toward the water, and the wisps disappeared.

Chloe looked up at him in utter disappointment. "Oh, Fionn. They've gone."

"It may only be for tonight."

"No, I think it is forever."

He wrapped his arms around her and kissed the top of her head. "But I am still here, and I fear we have not been nearly diligent enough in creating our offspring."

She laughed. "Dear heaven, you are a naughty fellow."

"Not at all, just trying to be a diligent husband," he said with a chuckle, undoing the ties of her night rail.

She smiled and took his hand to lead him back to bed.

He needed no further encouragement. "Chloe, have you ever seen those moonstones shining so brightly?"

"No, my love. Never as bright as tonight."

"Does it have a significance?"

She nodded. "Yes, it means we are going to have a very good marriage."

Chapter Nineteen

One year later
Moonstone Landing, Cornwall

FIONN RACED BACK to Moonstone Cottage, spurring Sophocles to eat up the ground beneath his hooves on this blustery afternoon. He dismounted as soon as he reached the courtyard and tossed the reins to Mr. Hawke. "Has the midwife been summoned?"

"Yes, m'lord. She is here already. So are Lady Chloe's sisters. I don't think they will let you into your bedchamber."

He frowned. "But it is mine, and Chloe is my wife."

"Aye, and a lovely wife she is, too. But that chamber is not yours today. It's a birthing room now, and you had better stay out if you know what's good for you. Those Killigrew sisters may be little things, but they will run you off quite handily. They don't care that you are now a viscount. They still outrank you, and are not going to let you interfere."

Perhaps this was how it was with other husbands, but Fionn had to let Chloe know he was here.

Lord, did all husbands go through this torment? His heart was in his throat. His lungs felt ready to burst.

Only Chloe could order him out of their bedchamber. If she wanted him to leave, then he would. It would devastate him, but he would do anything she asked. Anything to keep her safe and make her happy.

He heard her cry out.

He tore upstairs.

Blessed saints, he did not want her to suffer. "Keep her safe," he prayed, for nothing else mattered. He burst into their chamber and saw her doubled over on the bed, her sisters and the midwife beside her. "Chloe."

He could hardly speak her name, for his heart was tearing to pieces. She was in pain, and there was nothing he could do to relieve it other than pray harder than he had ever prayed in his life.

"Fionn…our babe is coming."

He knelt by her side and gently stroked her sweaty face. "I know, my love. What can I do for you?"

"Nothing, I'm afraid. This is one time I must be in complete charge and do this on my own. They'll chase you out in a moment, and I won't stop them. I…" She winced as another contraction overwhelmed her. "I am in good hands. I don't want you to see me like this."

"You are beautiful, Chloe. I will never see you as anything less than perfect."

She laughed through another contraction. "I love you, Fionn. I want you to know this no matter what happens."

His heart was in tatters, and even those tatters now shredded some more. "Nothing will happen to you. I won't let it."

"You know it is out of both of our hands, my love."

"Go downstairs, Fionn," Phoebe said, taking his arm and gently urging him away. "Stay close by, but you cannot remain in here. Chloe needs to be able to push her hardest and cry out in pain if she must. She won't do that while you are watching her."

"Our husbands have been through this before," Hen said. "They'll come over soon to keep you company. Just wait downstairs and grab yourself a stiff drink. It will be hours yet."

Fionn obeyed for Chloe's sake. He did not want her holding

back in any way. But the wait was unbearable.

Hours?

Pain tore through him every time Chloe cried out. More pain tore through him every time there was ominous silence.

When he could take no more, he strode out of the house and made his way to the beach stairs. He settled on the top stair and lost himself in worry while gazing at the fathomless sea. Nothing mattered but Chloe. Not the new hospital that had taken up these past few years of his life in the planning and construction. It would have its official opening next month, and he needed Chloe to be there with him, to see the hospital garden designed by her and her ladies' village beautification club in full bloom.

Nor did he care about his newly won claim against the Brennan family. He owed his brothers-in-law, Mr. Barrow, and Ducky for finding the evidence to prove his rightful place as heir. Mostly, he owed Chloe for her faith and persistence in putting all the pieces together. Without her, Ducky and Mr. Barrow might not have discovered the letter Viscount Brennan had written confessing what he had done.

Fionn still could not believe he held the true claim to the title. But that letter had been left with the viscount's solicitor, who "happened" to find it the moment pressure was applied on him. It was inconceivable to Fionn that the solicitor hadn't simply burned it at the urging of the Brennan clan, who would have given him a hefty fee for making that evidence disappear. But holding on to it and thinking to use it as blackmail leverage over the years had proven too great a temptation for the man.

Thank heaven for greedy men.

But right now, Fionn did not care about anything other than Chloe.

She would always come first in his heart, and he would give up anything and everything for her.

The wind stiffened and the sun began to slowly sink on the horizon. He wasn't certain how long he'd been outside, lost in his thoughts. Hours, certainly.

He had just decided to return to the cottage when he heard an infant's cries coming from his bedchamber.

The hearty sound carried across the garden and reached his ears.

He stared up to find Chloe's sisters standing on the balcony of the bedchamber, waving to him.

"Dear heaven," he muttered, breaking into a grin, for he could not overlook that Phoebe held a squawking bundle in her arms.

He raced to the cottage and was about to run upstairs when Hen scampered downstairs. She looked exhausted but glowingly happy. "Your wife and son will see you in a moment. The midwife is just finishing up now."

He heard men's laughter emanating from the parlor and realized Cain and Cormac had arrived to lend their support. "When did you get here?" he asked the pair, shaking their hands in greeting.

"About an hour ago. We saw you by the beach stairs but did not want to disturb you. We've been through this and know what you must have been feeling. Well done, Fionn," Cain said, giving him a congratulatory slap on the back.

Cormac did the same.

Fionn laughed. "Blessed saints! I have a son."

He ran upstairs the moment Hen gave him the nod, and then paused in the doorway of the bedchamber, afraid to approach until summoned by the midwife. "They are all yours," Phoebe said, then kissed him on the cheek before making her escape downstairs.

The midwife, Alice Hewitt, who happened to be the local doctor's eldest sister, cleared her throat. "I'll give you a few minutes alone with your family, my lord. There is more to do before I leave, but go ahead and enjoy them while I wash up."

He was never going to get used to being addressed as "my lord."

My lord.

Street urchin turned viscount.

And he had sired an heir.

That little heir had a tuft of dark hair on his head and was announcing his arrival with a hearty wail as he lay in his mother's arms.

Chloe was beaming, but obviously exhausted.

Fionn strode to the bed and knelt beside her to stare at the beautiful pair. "He's a noisy chap. Isn't he, love?"

She laughed and shook her head. "Well, he wants to make his presence known to us."

"He's beautiful. So are you."

"His face is red and squashed. He looks like a squashed red potato. But I think he will grow up to be as handsome as you. As for me, I am afraid to even look at myself in the mirror. I might crack it."

"No, love. I have never seen you look lovelier." He took her hand and kissed it. Then he carefully reached over and kissed her on the lips. "I love you so much, Chloe."

She caressed his cheek. "Likewise, my lord."

Their son had stopped fussing and was now resting quietly at her breast. "Chloe…" He had not cried in over twenty years, not since deciding to escape the orphanage and attempting to survive on his own on the London streets.

He had not cried through famine.

Or freezing winter nights.

He had not cried as others died around him.

But the tears came now.

He had gone from nothing…less than nothing, to this. Command of a fort. A beautiful home to call their own, for Chloe now owned all of Moonstone Cottage outright, and here was where they would raise their family.

A family of his own.

A wife he loved to distraction and who grew more beautiful every day.

And now a son who would know his parents and be loved

and protected by them every day. Every hour of every day.

This overwhelmed him. "Chloe…"

More tears came.

He hugged her and their son, careful not to squash him, for he was such a little thing and Chloe was quite fragile herself at the moment.

She was in tears now, too. "Fionn, I loved you the moment I set eyes on you. I was only fifteen, and back then you were that quiet, gentle young man who arrived in Moonstone Landing and knew no one. I lost my heart to you back then and never stopped loving you. I never will."

He laughed as he wiped his tears with the sleeve of his jacket. "I knew you would always be special to me, for your smile was magical and I was sure I would never forget you. Then seeing you again last year, a young lady soon to make her Society debut… I couldn't breathe. I thought you were stunning."

She laughed softly. "And now it has come to this."

He nodded. "Yes, this…your husband reduced to tears."

"But they are happy tears, are they not?" She caressed his cheek, her touch so soft upon the grizzled beginnings of his day's growth of beard.

"Yes, love. Happiness beyond measure." He kissed the palm of her hand. "We have to give our son a name. What shall it be?"

"I think there is no doubt what it must be…Brioc Joseph Brennan. How does that sound to you?"

"Sounds perfect, love. But what about honoring your father? His given name was Robert."

She shook her head and grinned. "Let's save that for our second son."

Fionn raked a hand through his hair. "Blessed saints, are you already thinking of another?"

"Not right away. Little Brioc was a demanding fellow and took quite a bit out of me."

Fionn kissed her on the lips again. "I know. I heard your cries, and my greatest fear was losing you, Chloe. It is a horrible, helpless feeling to be able to do nothing. But you've made it through, and now you must take all the time you need to recover. You are the most important thing to me. I would give up everything to keep you safe."

The door to their bedchamber opened and the midwife poked her head in. "My lord, your wife needs to rest, but first she needs to feed your son. I expect his appetite will be as hearty as his bellow."

Fionn winked at Chloe, and then glanced knowingly at her chest. "Lucky fellow." He rose and gave her another lingering kiss on the lips. "And so am I. Luckiest man in all of England."

Chloe smiled at him. "I love you, Fionn. Forever and ever."

"This Moonstone major loves you right back, Chloe. Forever and ever." He strode downstairs, his heart fuller than it had ever been in his entire life.

Those moonstones would be dazzlingly bright tonight.

The End

Also by Meara Platt

FARTHINGALE SERIES
My Fair Lily
The Duke I'm Going To Marry
Rules For Reforming A Rake
A Midsummer's Kiss
The Viscount's Rose
Earl Of Hearts
The Viscount and the Vicar's Daughter
A Duke For Adela
If You Wished For Me
Never Dare A Duke
Capturing The Heart Of A Cameron

BOOK OF LOVE SERIES
The Look of Love
The Touch of Love
The Taste of Love
The Song of Love
The Scent of Love
The Kiss of Love
The Chance of Love
The Gift of Love
The Heart of Love
The Hope of Love (novella)
The Promise of Love
The Wonder of Love
The Journey of Love
The Treasure of Love
The Dance of Love

The Miracle of Love
The Remembrance of Love (novella)
The Dream of Love (novella)
All I Want For Christmas (novella)

MOONSTONE LANDING
Moonstone Landing (novella)
Moonstone Angel (novella)
The Moonstone Duke
The Moonstone Marquess
The Moonstone Major

DARK GARDENS SERIES
Garden of Shadows
Garden of Light
Garden of Dragons
Garden of Destiny
Garden of Angels

LYON'S DEN
The Lyon's Surprise
Kiss of the Lyon
Lyon in the Rough

THE BRAYDENS
A Match Made In Duty
Earl of Westcliff
Fortune's Dragon
Earl of Kinross
Earl of Alnwick
Aislin
Gennalyn
Pearls of Fire
A Rescued Heart
Tempting Taffy

DeWOLFE PACK ANGELS SERIES
Nobody's Angel
Kiss An Angel
Bhrodi's Angel

About the Author

Meara Platt is a *USA Today* bestselling author and an award winning, Amazon UK All-star. Her favorite place in all the world is England's Lake District, which may not come as a surprise, since many of her stories are set in that idyllic landscape, including her award-winning fantasy-romance Dark Gardens series. If you'd like to learn more about the ancient Fae prophecy that is about to unfold in the Dark Gardens series, as well as Meara's lighthearted, international bestselling Regency romances in the Farthingale series and Book of Love series, or her more emotional Braydens series, please visit her website at www.mearaplatt.com.

Milton Keynes UK
Ingram Content Group UK Ltd.
UKHW022300170823
427026UK00015B/522